MILLENNIUM

A NEW WORLD, A NEW WAR

BOOK 1 OF THE MILLENNIUM SERIES
YEAR 000 ANNO REDITUS

CHRIS SMITHIES

For Jesus

The greatest hero who has ever lived.

And

For my mother

Ever a lighthouse guiding me through the fog.

Then I saw an angel coming down from heaven, holding in his hand the key to the bottomless pit and a great chain. And he seized the dragon, that ancient serpent, who is the devil and Satan, and bound him for a thousand years, and threw him into the pit, and shut it and sealed it over him, so that he might not deceive the nations any longer, until the thousand years were ended. After that he must be released for a little while.

Then I saw thrones, and seated on them were those to whom the authority to judge was committed. Also, I saw the souls of those who had been beheaded for the testimony of Jesus and for the word of God, and those who had not worshiped the beast or its image and had not received its mark on their foreheads or their hands. They came to life and reigned with Christ for a thousand years. The rest of the dead did not come to life until the thousand years were ended. This is the first resurrection. Blessed and holy is the one who shares in the first resurrection! Over such the second death has no power, but they will be priests of God and of Christ, and they will reign with him for a thousand years.

Revelation 20: 1-6

Prelude

The Earth was broken.

Where once had been green fields and rivers there were now massive, gaping canyons rimmed by towering volcanos spurting hot lava down their jagged slopes. Ash clouds and dust storms rolled across former farmland, tainted by radiation from the many nuclear weapons that had rained down on the world in droves during the seemingly endless conflicts that had ravaged the Earth in recent times. A one world government that had initially brought in an era of peace and prosperity had soon turned on the people that had hailed it as their salvation, revealing the true nature of its demonic leaders. Much of the fresh water on the surface of the planet had dried up in the heat of the many cataclysms that had rocked the world, including the impact of a giant asteroid the global press had ironically named Wormwood thinking they were clever to be using a fashionably biblical reference when they were in fact rendering themselves pawns of prophecy. The Earth was ruined and barely habitable, far from the paradise it had originally been at the time of its creation.

A number of calamitous historical events had led to the Earth being in its current state of chaos, beginning not on the planet itself, but in the spiritual realm millennia earlier. It started with the fall of a great many Heavenly beings, or elohim as they are called, from God's Kingdom. The main point of contention had been the planned creation of mankind and the great heights that GOD intended to raise them to in his Kingdom. It had been deemed offensive to the Heavenly host by some radical elements of the congregation. The first, and most outspoken rebel from Heaven had been the Son of the Morning, one of the cherubim and of the most exalted of Yahweh's servants. Being a charismatic and cunning individual, he had talked many of the malakim, or angels as they have come to be known, over to his cause by convincing them that his ideals were righteous. These unfortunate malakim then later became the shedim or fallen angels when the arrogant cherub's rebellion inevitably failed, and he was driven out of

Heaven with his followers by the archangel Micha'el and those of the Host that had remained loyal. Amongst the next to fall had been a group of Grigori, or Watchers led by one called Shemjaza. Like the cherubim, Grigori were highly ranked and powerful elohim and their betrayal came as a great blow indeed to those remaining loyal. Having turned their backs on GOD, some rebels set about trying to influence the new human creation in a way contrary to the ways of their Creator. If Yahweh was going to insist on creating these creatures, then the fallen elohim were going to twist them into a parody of GOD's original intention.

Grigori who had been originally intended to act as overseers over men and guide and protect them began to fancy themselves as gods and encourage men to worship them instead of Yahweh. They taught them metallurgy for the purposes of warfare, chemistry, mass farming techniques and perverted sexual practices amongst other forbidden forms of knowledge. They also performed sexual acts on humankind which resulted in offspring that GOD deemed to be abominations. Chief among these were the nephilim, giant human/elohim hybrids with dark souls who were cruel and treated their smaller cousins like cattle. When a nephil died, its spirit would not be drawn to the afterlife like a human soul would be and they would instead wander the spiritual realm as what are oft called demons, desperately seeking out other bodies to inhabit as their only remaining means of interaction with the physical world.

The fallen elohim twisted other aspects of creation as well, using their advanced knowledge to perform genetic experiments and breeding programs on animals to produce fierce creatures with vicious predispositions and voracious appetites for flesh. Elegant horns originally intended for decoration became deadly weapons and teeth made sharp for piercing the outer surface of fruit became fangs for rending flesh or inserting venom. The blood of GOD's good and gentle creations ran like rivers through the tainted earth. His intended children, created to live in peace and happiness were instead being sacrificed at brazen altars before they had a chance to live. All in worship of demented beings who had lost sight of their original glorious purpose and instead set their hearts after lust for flesh, wealth and power.

Yahweh grew weary of the multiple affronts borne out of the interactions between fallen elohim and godless man and decided to end the first phase of this behaviour with a worldwide flood. During this dreadful period, many of the rebel elohim chose to leave Earth and seek refuge in the stars, either under their own power or in star ships which utilised advanced Heavenly technology. Mars had been colonised by the rebels centuries before the flood, but now they explored much further afield. With no hospitable planets like Earth elsewhere in the galaxy it was a hard life for any mortal followers they took with them, but with the help of their masters' tech and knowledge they managed to eke out an existence for themselves. Eventually through a system of breeding programs, genetic experiments, and raids on Earth for breeding stock, fallen empires spreading over numerous star systems blossomed outside of the Sol system, all of them living in artificial environments as naturally hospitable ones could not be found.

Other incursions of rebel elohim took place back on Earth over the course of the next few centuries and mankind continued to endure chaos despite the erasure of the previous advanced fallen civilisation in the flood. GOD offered a permanent solution through the sacrifice of His own son, Jesus Christ, but not all men chose to accept this wondrous gift. Thus, it was that GOD gave the world over to the fallen for a period of two millennia which were destined to end in a time called the tribulation; a period lasting seven years during which the fallen ruled with an iron fist and GOD allowed the planet to be afflicted with natural disasters of every sort.

And so it is, that the Earth has become a corrupted ruin and rather than blaming their twisted fallen rulers as the culprits, mankind ironically blames their betrayed Creator. The seven-year tribulation is now drawing to a close and has reached its climax at the battle at Armageddon, the battle to end all battles.

*

The Jezreel Valley had known only drought for several years and not a thing could grow there in the last days of the Earth, but now its parched soil was being fed again, not with water however, but with blood.

The Malakim Royal Marines fought their way through the mass of humanity and fallen elohim that the twisted leaders of Earth were throwing at them. Unfortunately for the forces of evil, the elite soldiers of Christ's Royal Navy were nigh unstoppable. Malakim were on average 8ft tall and highly skilled warriors clad in technologically superior armour that, through the erection of directed energy shields, could stop most small to medium calibre weaponry, especially when the prayers of countless saints were behind them. The church of GOD was at the battle too, clad in white robes covered in silver plate and they fought primarily on their knees, keeping the malakim warriors charged with the power of the Holy Spirit through their prayers. The battle had lasted for hours, and it was only through the power of prayer that losses on the side of Heaven had been minimal.

The same could not be said for the forces of the Fallen. The dead lay everywhere, humans mostly, who had had their heads filled with the lies of the deceiver and fervently believed that their cause had been the just one. They had been tricked into believing they were fighting off a hostile alien invasion force. It had not been Satan's only deception in the last days, but it had probably been his most effective. Through a steady diet of alien invasion movies and false scientific reports the seeds of the deception had been spread by the media for years. Whilst humans formed the majority of the dead, there were other bodies laid amongst them as well. Shedim were the most numerous of the non-human dead, fallen malakim who had left their Heavenly place to serve the fallen gods of Earth following promises of power and freedom from GOD's rule. There were also the giant bodies of dead nephilim, the monstrous offspring of the forbidden mingling of human and elohim seed. They had been reintroduced to the Earth during the tribulation under the auspices of being a friendly alien force willing to join in the

Earth's defence. Foolishly, humans accepted them gratefully into society despite mounting evidence that they were vicious, cannibalistic, lustful, soulless beasts. Numerous organisations were set up defending the rights of nephilim and insisting that their 'culture' should be tolerated and that dissenters were engaging in discrimination. Drones were among the dead as well, small grey creatures that had been a fallen attempt to create an alternate human race, but one that had produced a frail mindless creature that was only fit for possession by demonic beings desperate for a way back into the physical realm. Finally, there were the corpses of Grigori, or Watchers, those who had been assigned roles of protector over human civilisations, intended to guide them in the ways of the Lord, but had instead fallen into the temptations of power, greed and lust and had dragged humanity in the opposite direction. Now the ones who hadn't had the foresight to flee the planet with their followers before Armageddon were lying dead on the dusty Plain of Jezreel.

The malakim warrior, Eret'el had been separated from his squad and was trying to link back in with them, but grinding its way towards him was a main battle tank of one of the human armies gathered against them. It fired its gun, but it had aimed directly at him instead of at the ground which might have been more effective if it had been firing a high explosive round. As it was, the discarding sabot shell narrowly missed him, leaving him entirely unscathed. The malak unclipped a pulse grenade from his belt and, activating its highest setting, tossed it under the approaching vehicle. As he did however a large dark-skinned creature appeared on top of the tank and, shouting a challenge, jumped down to spar with him.

"You are fighting for the wrong side brother, join us in the fight for freedom instead." the fallen angel hissed. It's voice, physical form and very mind had been twisted by millennia of living under deception, sown originally by the Father of Lies.

The pulse grenade exploded, neutralising the tank, and momentarily stunning the shedim.

"You poor fool." Eret'el chastised it harshly. With a side kick he sent the black skinned creature sprawling in the dust and strode over to it, his sword raised. He held the platinum-coloured alloy blade, the power of the Spirit swirling around it like a thick fog, against the creature's throat. "Surrender, and you may find mercy."

The shedim spat at him and attempted to bring its sword to bear but one thrust from Eret'el sent the blade on a coarse right through the fallen elohim's neck and out of the other side covered in the evil creature's dark coloured viscera. With its physical form terminated, the shedim's spirit would now be confined to the spiritual realm until it had enough strength to reconstitute itself or until it could be banished to the abyss. It was unlikely to be allowed to escape however, Eret'el knew that hundreds of loyal Grigori were waiting in the spiritual realm for slain fallen and would instantly banish any who appeared. He was about to resume his search for his squad when suddenly he felt a sharp pain in the back of his head, and everything went black.

As his eyes slowing reopened, blackness became a grey misty montage of blobs which eventually coalesced into recognisable objects as the world regained colour and slowly began to come back into focus. Eret'el staggered to his feet and looked about him, having little idea of how long he had been unconscious. Something had clearly stunned him from behind and knocked him off his feet but whatever it had been, it no longer seemed to be a threat. A headless nephil giant lay dead against a burning tank and he reckoned it was a prime candidate for having been his assailant, though how it had met its end he could only guess. A group of the saints, dressed in their white battle tunics were stood nearby, barely visible through the thick swirling smoke that seemed to be everywhere, and he wondered if they had contributed toward his rescue. Their eyes were focussed on something else in the distance though and he decided it had probably been one of his malak brothers who had saved him. What was he doing before he had been struck? His mind was muddled, and it was taking him forever to recollect what had occurred.malkim The elusive memory came to him at last, like a pigeon coming home to roast, he had been trying to find his squad and had been ambushed by this tank, a shedim, and then what?

"He lives! Get up here before you miss it." A booming voice shouted in exultation from above, interrupting his thought process.

Eret'el looked up to see the archangel Uri'el peering down on him from atop the ruined war machine. So here was his rescuer, which came as no surprise whatsoever as Uri'el was legendary in Heaven for his marshal skills. The powerful malak was dressed in his usual battered armour that he had favoured since at least the medieval age, his characteristic weapons of two Spirit axes were hung on his belt; no surer indication could there have been that the battle was over. The weary Eret'el clambered up onto the disabled tank next to his commanding officer and looked out over the battlefield. The plain of Megiddo was littered with smoking military equipment and the dead. All manner of fallen being had thrown themselves at the Lord's army this day and all had been vanquished. From the looks of things, without much loss on the Lord's side either. There was not a single saint amongst the bodies that he could see.

"You're looking the wrong way old friend." Uri'el prompted Eret'el, poking him in the side as he did.

"I'm sorry, I'm still a little dazed." The malak replied.

"No wonder, that nephil knocked you on the noggin so hard I thought for sure you'd need a good long sabbatical." Uri'el referred to the fact that when malakim bodies were critically injured they became confined to the spirit realm until they could recover enough strength to manifest physically again. Eret'el had been lucky this time, the strike had probably been a glancing one. Nephilim weren't generally known for giving love taps in battle.

A loud piercing cry of mixed agony and sorrow was what finally drew Eret'el's attention away from his contemplation of his near demise. Following Uri'el's pointing finger, he looked across the battlefield to the large Megiddo tell at one end of the valley where an ancient Canaanite settlement had once stood. A large oval hole had been torn in space above the tell, revealing only a deep enduring blackness beyond, darker than any night Eret'el had ever seen. In front of the hole on top of a crashed military cargo plane stood Micha'el, the general of the Lord's armies. He was clad in a highly advanced mechanical armoured battle suit which increased his normal 9ft physical size to a little over 12ft. His helmet was retracted, revealing his chiselled ageless face and his long dark flowing hair. One of the suit's metal robot-like fists was clamped around the neck of a battle-scarred cherub which was bleeding black blood that ran from a wound on its face and down the arm of Micha'el's suit where it dripped from his elbow onto the plane. The creature's normally elegant six wings were ragged and drooped pathetically from its back like flags in surrender. One of its arms was bent at an unnatural angle, indicating a severe breakage and the limb flopped about as if the cherub was trying to bring it up but couldn't. There was a brief flicker and a glimpse of a hideous scaled face as the cherub tried vainly to transform into the dragon aspect it had favoured at the beginning of the battle, but it now lacked the will, the strength or possibly both to do so, and the flickering faded as quickly as it had appeared. The two combatants were not the most impressive sight on the battlefield though, behind Micha'el on the plane's fuselage overseeing the event was the most powerful being that had ever existed. He stood at only 7ft tall and looked entirely humanoid but appeared to glow as if imbued with all the power of the universe, which was indeed the case. In one hand He held a sword with a blade burning so bright with fire that it hurt the eye to look directly at it. Eret'el gazed with admiration and adoration at the one the loyal elohim called the Beloved, the Creator of all things, the Lord of Hosts, the manifestation of GOD in human flesh, Christ Jesus.

"I will be back in a thousand years, stronger than ever." Eret'el's eyes were drawn reluctantly back to the injured cherub as he weakly challenged Micha'el, his cracking voice lacking the power to render the words any real impact.

Micha'el didn't acknowledge the fallen cherub's taunt, but moved closer to end of the plane and dropped his defeated foe in a crumpled heap onto the dented fuselage. The portal had been created around the crashed aircraft and so they had crossed its threshold and were now framed against the darkness inside, only visible due to the intense light emanating from the Lord. "I grant you the boon of entering Tartarus under your own strength. It is less humiliating than being tossed in." the archangel general offered his long-time nemesis.

The cherub stared at him; hatred etched deeply into its face like it had been carved there with a chisel. "Perhaps I shall make you throw me."

Jesus had witnessed enough, "GO." He instructed the Devil. The word hit the fallen elohim like a powerful physical blow and he reeled from it. It wasn't possible to refuse a direct order from GOD, rebel, or no. Satan appeared to resign himself to his fate, albeit with obvious reluctance. He stood as erect as he could, faced the crowd that had gathered and attempted to throw his arms out to his sides, intending a mockery of the sacrifice on the cross. His left arm hung limply at his side though and the vain effort did not have the desired effect. He dramatically allowed himself to topple backwards into the blackness and then suddenly he was gone. Micha'el walked dispassionately back down the crashed aircraft hull, showing no outward sign of satisfaction at having just defeated Earth's greatest foe. The portal to Tartarus closed after him, leaving its banished inhabitants cut off from the outside once more.

A white dragon soared past in front of Eret'el and Uri'el on their tank and then wheeled around to come at them. As it came near, it appeared to begin to dissolve and by the time it had landed on the tank next to Uri'el had transformed into its true form, a loyal Grigori.

"Well met Judicus." Uri'el greeted the tall elegant elohim with finely scaled skin.

"Well met Uri'el and greetings commander." he intoned, nodding at Eret'el who returned the gesture. "I wanted to make sure I have an unobstructed view of what is coming next. I hope you do not mind if I share your broken military vehicle." he explained.

"You'd have seen more from up there." Eret'el pointed towards the sky.

Judicus smiled wanly, "Not through this smoke, and I have little strength remaining to stay aloft. For some reason as soon as the last fallen enemy dropped, so did our prayer cover."

"I think the attention of the saints is elsewhere, as should ours be." Uri'el reflected, turning his eyes back to the Lord.

On top of the crashed aircraft, Jesus was looking about Him at the devastated Earth and was clearly deeply troubled by what he saw. Micha'el joined Him and they walked down the fuselage of the plane, coming to stand at the bottom, Jesus seemingly deep in thought. His armour was covered in blood and two of the nearby saints rushed forward, intending to clean it off but he raised His hand to stop them. This was not the Lamb of God standing on the Plain of Megiddo in the midst of the dead, this was the Lion of Judah. There would be no washing of feet, touching of hems or welcoming of little children on the battlefield of Armageddon. The Lord of Hosts reached a hand into the air and grabbed at the dust flying about, running some of the captured motes through His fingers as if to sample their texture. Then, as all the beings, men and elohim alike gathered on the plain watched, He began to grow. From 7ft tall he soon reached 20ft and then more. As He grew yet larger, more of those gathered on the battlefield could see him with their bare eyes. It occurred to Eret'el that this was most likely His intention. People began to fall upon their knees before the Lord and Eret'el did likewise in the same moment that Uri'el did. The Lord stopped growing when He reached what the malak reckoned to be about 100ft tall, towering over everything around Him. At His feet elohim and humans alike were shuffling around to avoid being stepped on, though Eret'el knew his God well enough to know that there would never be any danger of this. By this point every redeemed eye could see their Lord in His moment of triumph. Jesus looked about Him, His features softening, and His face shining, suddenly seeming transformed from Jehovah Nissi, God is my banner, to Jehovah Rapha, the God who heals. He reached His arms out, his palms upward and spoke one simple word, "NEW."

He had not shouted, but it hit the ears of all those around like a bomb going off and the word brought forth a wind that pushed the dust and radiation along in front of it like seaweed on an ocean breaker. A loud cracking sound came from deep underneath the feet of those gathered and the Earth shook, causing some of the wearier combatants to fall to their knees. Around the Lord's feet shoots began to break forth from the dry ground and spread outwards like ripples on a pond. The dust that had been in the atmosphere dissipated and was replaced with puffy white clouds of the kind that men hadn't seen in years and a soft, gentle rain began to fall. The much cratered and scarred plain of Megiddo was transformed within moments into a green pasture carpeted with luscious soft grass; but this was only the beginning. Eret'el felt the tank rock as a sapling sprang out of the ground near it and a giant cedar tree grew to full size within moments, tipping the vehicle slightly. The dead bodies around the tank appeared to sink into the soft earth and soon disappeared completely from sight. Butterflies seemed to materialise in droves as new leaves unfolded and seemingly from nowhere a young deer appeared and nuzzled one of the saints, causing her to laugh wonderingly. There were mutters of awe and wonder from the battle-weary combatants as they witnessed the recreation of planet Earth at its source.

Far up above, outside the Earth's atmosphere, the many space craft of the Lord's Royal Navy orbited the planet where they had formed a defensive perimeter. Now, malakim watched in wonder from these ships as the shrinking oceans' floors were raised and their waters were sucked into the Earth's crust. The Earth's deserts disappeared, ice caps vanished, and mountain ranges were levelled before their eyes.

Farther away, in a higher orbit than the ships lay the Holy City, New Jerusalem that had appeared as prophesied at the end of the tribulation. It was a stunningly beautiful 1400-mile-long golden cube comprising 700 levels, each offering nearly 2 million square miles of land for the saints to occupy once their work on Earth was finished. It was also dubbed Heaven as at the centre of it lay the Holy Temple of Yahweh Himself and any place He dwelt; Heaven was also. His light emanated from the temple, giving the immense structure an abundance of energy and life and the innate ability to be as close to the Earth as it was without exerting any gravitational pull. The caretakers of the enormous Holy City watched breathlessly as a wave of green swept over the globe, transforming the previously ruined orb into a verdant paradise. When it was complete, the entire planet was a giant garden criss-crossed with mighty rivers and dotted with small seas and great lakes. There was now no place on Earth that could not be comfortably inhabited by man.

Having finished His work of recreation, Christ shrank back to his habitual size and turned to Micha'el, "And now the next phase begins."

The archangel nodded, his mechanical suit folding in on itself and retracting into smaller and smaller pieces until eventually the malak general stood in his regular tunic and plate armour.

Eret'el heard a low baritone voice begin to sing a familiar tune, and when he looked over, he realised that it was coming from Uri'el."

Oh Lord my God, When I in awesome wonder consider all the worlds Thy hands have made.

Before long others joined the chorus and soon the garden of Megiddo, soon to be renamed Eden, rang with voices of the saints and malakim joined in praise of their GOD.

When the hymn finished, smaller groups broke into other songs of praise and Eret'el turned to Uri'el, "So that's it then? It's over for a thousand years?"

Uri'el laughed heartily but then his voice took on a serious tone, "No my brother, for us this is simply a pause for breath. Now we take the fight to the stars."

For we know that if our earthly house, this tent, is destroyed, we have a building from God, a house not made with hands, eternal in the heavens. For in this we groan, earnestly desiring to be clothed with our habitation which is from heaven, if indeed, having been clothed, we shall not be found naked. For we who are in this tent groan, being burdened, not because we want to be unclothed, but further clothed, that mortality may be swallowed up by life. Now He who has prepared us for this very thing is God, who also has given us the Spirit as a guarantee.

2 Corinthians 5: 1-10

One

Grasping the large unwieldy wrench with both hands, Cray tightened the bolt as hard as he could get it, tried it one more time until he was sure it couldn't easily be loosened and then pulled another along with a washer from a leather pocket in a belt around his waist and moved onto the next hole. The line of unfilled holes stretched away for metres ahead of him and he tried not to think about how many more he still had to do as he worked. He'd learnt the hard way that the only way to cope with the tedious work was to exist in the moment and not think too far ahead. He glanced off to his side briefly, where some distance across the shipyard another slab-sided frigate was being built identical to the ship he and his crew were working on. He found it mildly therapeutic to see the fruits of the other team's labours and picture in his mind his own team being at the same stage of completion. Of course, when this ship was finished, there'd only be another to follow, so it wasn't the most satisfying feeling to finish one but that feeling was all they had, and they had learnt to savour it regardless. Cray quickly turned back to his work when he saw the unmistakable shadow of an approaching nephil overseer out of the corner of his eye. Being caught slacking to any degree in the shipyard was always regrettable and he had no intention of winding up injured or perhaps even dead like so many before him had.

The overseers didn't know him as Cray, only as Unit 3768 and more often than that he was referred to simply as 'human', 'slave' or the hated 'food'. Names were not permitted on Frixar Station, at least not to humans, and any caught using them were severely punished, possibly even sacrificed to the nephilim if it was not a first offence. As such, no one knew that Cray had given himself a name, not even his fellow slaves. Very few humans on the station weren't slaves, a human had to prove themselves to be particularly loyal and capable before they could rise from the ranks of the slaves to be an overseer, administrator or similar. This often happened at the expense of one or more of their fellow slaves, one couldn't be loyal to the masters and your compatriots at the same time. Many of the humans who could be seen working in

17

higher positions were there because their bodies had been possessed by a demonic nephil soul and could therefore not really be considered to be human any longer, though their own souls were inside there somewhere, hiding a dark corner of their consciousness and probably completely insane. Life was harsh for humans on Frixar station with little hope for any bright future that Cray could see, not that the concept of a bright future even existed in his limited worldview.

Another slave was gradually working his way across to where Kray worked, welding his way along a seam that ran above the last line of bolts Cray had inserted. It was a man that Cray recognised well enough that he had felt the need to mentally assign him a name and had dubbed him Shorty due to his relatively diminutive height. He didn't dare call him that out loud of course or they might both be flayed within an inch of their lives. As Shorty drew closer, they nodded briefly in acknowledgement of each other but no more. All the workers on the shipyard floor were men, there was not a woman in sight. There were very few areas where men were allowed to make contact with women and Cray had very seldom seen one. He had been selected for breeding on two occasions, the first of which had been the first time he had ever seen a woman. He had been crudely informed of what he should be doing by an overseer and had not been allowed to speak to her. They had been allotted roughly five minutes for the exercise and then had been separated as soon as their task had been accomplished. The second time he had been anticipating the contact and knew what to expect which had made the experience less distressing for him, he had made eye contact with the woman, and he had felt like something had passed between them. He had tried to make the experience as tolerable for her as he could manage but couldn't know if he had spared her any distress or not. He thought of her sometimes, but it was with a confusing mixture of longing and guilt. Though why he should feel guilty for something he couldn't have refused to do, he didn't know. He imagined that his parents had met similarly when he had been conceived, but he could not ask them because he had no idea who they were. He had been raised in a huge nursery by multiple female carers like all the other humans on the station. He sometimes thought about the fact that his two children and their mothers were probably in that nursery now and he wondered if they were treated any better than the men were. He hoped so, even though he had never met his children and only their mothers briefly, he would want them safe and comfortable. That's if he even had children, for all he knew, there might not have been any conception at all. It seemed like everything on Frixar was designed to reduce humans to objects and Cray often wondered why that goal was so ardently pursued by their masters.

He wiped some beads of sweat from his brow with the back of an oily hand as he continued down the line of holes, inserting bolts and tightening them as he went on his laborious way. There was no natural light in the huge bay within which they worked and instead the men laboured by the light of large spotlights which were placed every 50 metres or so and tended to give off an uncomfortable level of heat when you were working close to them. Cray had never been exposed to natural light of any kind and had only known light generated by electricity in all of his approximate quarter century of life. It wasn't generally considered necessary for humans to know very much about their circumstances or place in the universe, but Cray had managed to ascertain that Frixar Station was built into a large, previously resource rich asteroid which had been mined out centuries earlier and turned into a factory. Their factory station was conveniently located relatively close to other facilities, mainly mining stations which were still operating on other rocks in the belt. Such facilities could only operate on the larger, slower moving rocks which were less prone to collision with other asteroids. The stations were protected by shields and were unlikely to suffer any large amount of damage from a collision, but shields required energy to operate and the less they were needed the better. Food and water weren't produced in the belt and was instead brought in via the portal generators. It was rare for goods to be brought in via ship, but occasionally an ice trawler would bring its load directly to the station and Cray and others might be pulled from their duties to assist in unloading its cumbersome cargo.

A loud clanging noise sounded across the shipyard, instantly dragging Cray out of his brief revery. The shift was changing and not a moment too soon, for Cray was utterly exhausted. He placed his wrench on the closest tool bench for the next worker to find and made his way toward the exit where large queues of dirty, sweaty men were already forming. Whilst it was good to be finishing work, Cray hated the queues because it meant extended exposure to the attention of the nephilim guards. The giants looked roughly humanoid in appearance but towered over their human charges and were horrifically fierce in appearance. The one Cray was currently approaching in his queue was roughly 11ft tall and heavily muscled. Its malevolently grinning maw contained a double row of misshapen teeth and its large flat nose hung like a squashed fruit beneath its small beady eyes. If Cray had ever seen a pig in his life, he would probably have drawn a comparison, but animals were not a feature on this station and Cray had no conception of one. Around the giant's head was a crown of variously shaped horns, one of which sported a brass ring from which hung a shrivelled human head on a short chain. A large sword hung in a scabbard on one side of its belt, and it cradled an oversized kinetic rifle in muscular arms that could easily tear a human in two without a great deal of effort. He nervously walked past the monster and could swear he heard it lick its lips as he did, but it could easily have been his paranoid imagination. He had long lived under the shadow of a pervasive fear that he would one day become a meal for one of the openly cannibalistic nephilim. He was not to be this day though, as he passed safely beyond the fearsome being and out through a pair of large metal doors into the packed corridor beyond. The part rock, part metal corridors of the station were high and wide in order to accommodate giants and so the ceiling ran high above Cray's head as he and his fellow workers made their weary way back to the accommodation section. They would make a brief stop at the showers before eventually reaching the busy canteen. Only one seventh of the men were directed down towards the showers by a brusque human overseer, and Cray happened to be one of those selected today. The showers were crude, and each man was made to quickly strip his overalls off and drop them down a chute before walking under a jet of tepid water followed by a powerful blast of cool air. They then picked up another set of clothes from a pile and hurriedly donned them before re-joining the queue for the canteen. This happened to each man roughly once a week, though the selection process was not particularly robust, and Cray had gone for weeks in the past without being selected.

The queue for the canteen ran past tables where other men were already eating and the smells tormented the hungry men still waiting for theirs. This was the only meal of the day and by the time it arrived there was rarely a man who was not more than ready for it. Despite the fact that the food was a wretched broth containing an unidentifiable mixture of suspect ingredients, Cray was half starved this day and was actually looking forward to it. He collected a simple metal dish from a pile and held it out to a server as the queue filed past them. A ladle deposited the broth unceremoniously in his dish and he tried to avoid seeing what was in it. He'd found a human toe in one of his meals once and this had put an end to any thoughts of him wanting to know what the various ingredients were. He found himself a place at one of the long tables and shovelled the foul fare down his throat before a larger slave could relieve him of it, as too often happened. He briefly wondered if Shorty would go hungry again today before reminding himself that Shorty's problems were not his own, he certainly had enough problems himself, without becoming concerned about other peoples'. It was his nature to think that way though, as if part of him had been designed to care about others. It perplexed him as he saw little outward evidence that anyone else thought this way and he often pondered over the possibility that he was different somehow. He had to admit that another distinct possibility was that everyone here was as repressed as he was.

He finished his food and got up from the table, depositing his dish and spoon into a receptacle on the way out. He made his way through the tables to an exit opposite the way he had entered and joined the huddles of tired men making their way to the bunk rooms. The crude bunks were the closest thing a man could get to experiencing pleasure on the station. Each room contained about ten pallets where men could sleep in order to recover for their gruelling 12 hour shift the next day. The pallets consisted of a leather sheet stretched across a metal frame. There were no coverings, the men simply slept in their clothes. Cray had never known any other life and so he did not have any comparison to make between this life and another. It was perhaps a blessing that it was so, because he would be likely to be even less content with his lot were he to possess knowledge of how others lived. He practically fell onto his cot and drifted off into a troubled sleep. Tomorrow would bring with it more tiresome bolts, more disgusting broth, and more hollowness of spirit.

*

Elsewhere on Frixar station, the sound of mewling babies was primarily forming the cacophony of 4478's day as usual. Though secretly she would have liked to have been called Becca, or Flora, she had never decided which she preferred. She walked down the lines of newborns checking temperatures and other physical observations and marked these down on a data pad she had with her. Like her, the babies had no names and each reading she took was marked under the child's assigned number. The babies in this batch were 5080-5110. It was all very clinical and although Becca might have wished it could be different, she had no concept of any other way of doing things to compare it to. Sometimes the babies had to be picked up and soothed and this was Becca's favourite part of her work. She enjoyed the brief connection she felt she made with a child as she calmed them down and often imagined what it would be like if she was allowed to form a bond with a baby over a longer period. She had always theorised that if a mother were to be left with her baby rather than separated that a more lasting bond might be formed that could have some purpose to serve other than calming a brief tantrum. She knew she would never be given the chance to test this theory on Frixar though. This thought led her to wondering where her own three children were as she had many times before. She berated herself as going down this line of thought often upset her and she didn't want another beating from a guard. Whilst she had given birth to three children there had also been a still birth and she tried particularly hard not to think about this. The stillborn were prized by the nephilim as delicacies and a guard had eaten one in front of her once, she could never forget the horrible sound it had made. Fortunately, she had managed to get the poor dead creature sufficiently far enough away from the mother first, to spare her the experience of hearing her own child consumed. She picked up the next baby and coddled it to put the dark thoughts out of her mind. The baby had bright blue eyes and held her gaze as she looked at it, she allowed it to grasp one of her fingers and her eyes began to fill when a deep coarse voice destroyed the moment:

"That one was not crying. Move on sister."

The nephil guard must have been paying closer attention than usual to pick up on something so trivial, or perhaps he just felt like harassing her. She didn't feel it was good for the babies to have one of the filthy unwashed monsters in the nursery, but she knew her voice would not be listened to if she spoke up. She lived in constant fear that it would suddenly reach across and grab one of the children, but it had never happened. She guessed the eating of a live baby would get a nephil into a lot of trouble, these children were after all the future workforce of the station. She knew that young men were made to work after they left the care of the women because a lot of focus was placed on them being fit enough to do so. What kind of work they did though, she did not know. Her own babies were not nearly old enough to be workers so she was spared from having to think about what work they might be doing yet. She didn't think about their fathers, she preferred not to think about how her babies were conceived, except for the one with the kind eyes. He had been more caring than the others and she felt sure that there was a goodness in him, though it was hard to imagine anything could be good on this station. She carefully put the cooing baby down and finished checking the others as quickly as she could. She knew she was going to cry herself to sleep again tonight, curse her inability to control her emotions. Perhaps if she could be angry enough with herself, she could avoid it, but then again that seemed to make it even worse sometimes. She'd had a panic attack once after a fit of anger and the response from the guards had been immediate and brutal, they had beaten her unconscious. It had taken her days to be well enough to work again. She desperately needed to keep her emotions bottled up and not let her anxiety reach that point again. She left the nursery and carried herself up the large corridor outside as quickly as she could without drawing attention. At the end of the next corridor was a strange room she sometimes visited to calm herself and she headed there now. Thankfully there was no one else in there and she settled herself down on a bench and focussed on the fascinating object in the centre of the room and the reason why she had chosen her second option for a name. The alien object they called the flora was the only thing of beauty in the entire station, the red of its blooms being the only bright colour Becca had ever seen. It grew out of a patch of brown material and up towards a skylight which allowed in a light source from outside the station different to the neon lights that lit every other room. Apparently, the station commander had brought it from a planet far outside this solar system. She had been told he had done it to cause the humans on the station pain by reminding them of what they could have had but they were so far removed from the flora's source that it failed to have the desired effect. You couldn't miss something you had never known. Becca instead found a sense of joy from looking at the flora and loved to imagine a place where they might be more than this one. She had extraordinarily little idea of what the universe might be like outside of the station. The human population was kept in ignorance about most things and only really allowed enough knowledge to perform their roles and little else. Humans learnt as much as they safely could outside of their assigned parameters as the thirst for knowledge could not be entirely tamed but opportunities for such learning were few. As such, Becca hadn't a clue of the true nature of their colony and the history behind its creation.

*

Frixar was just one facility in a star system that was part of an empire consisting of dozens of systems all controlled by a Grigori warlord called Kraan. He had fallen into the temptations of power, greed and lust millennia before whilst an administrator on Earth and had fled to the far reaches of the galaxy during the invasion of Canaan by the Israelites to avoid God's rule and judgement. Like his fallen kin, he had found the outer reaches of space to be inhospitable to life but had taken advantage of advanced technology to create artificial environments capable of supporting his small population of human followers. Through abduction from Earth and breeding programs, he built his population of worshippers up over the course of centuries until eventually he ruled a great empire spread across a vast tract of space. The populations of these systems consisted mainly of a handful of less powerful Grigori, shedim (fallen angels), nephilim, the genetically constructed drones and purebred Humans. The empire constantly had to be defended against incursion by followers of other fallen warlords and a fleet of warships was maintained for this purpose. The ships for this fleet were built at various factories across the empire and these were run by administrators, usually less powerful elohim than Grigori, and usually those not notably skilled enough for more challenging work.

In a section of the Frixar facility quite far removed from where the human slaves were uncomfortably slumbering, one of Kraan's administrators, a thoroughly malevolent entity named Livek scrolled through the production reports of the station on a datapad. He was a shedim, roughly humanoid but larger than a human and with dark ashen coloured skin, almost to the point of being black in places. His teeth were slightly sharpened, and his ears somewhat pointed. He was not solely a physical creature, but primarily a supernatural one. Of necessity he spent most of his time in physical form but felt just as comfortable slipping out of the physical and into the supernatural realm. He could even spend time halfway in-between if he so wished. It was easier to maintain this facility if he remained in the physical realm however, and he needed to maintain it well or he would have to answer to his master. Livek was a lowly ranked shedim and although this still placed him much higher up the pecking order than a human or nephil half breed, he only rated enough status to give him lordship of this wretched factory. Under him was a motley collection of nephilim, drones and a large population of human slaves. If the slaves ever became aware of just how few powerful beings there were on this station controlling matters, they might just decide to rebel. It was well that it was as easy as it was to keep them ignorant of such details. If such a rebellion were to happen, help was not far away, however. There were a number of portal generators on the facility which could instantly open a gateway to other stations or worlds, and he could have an army of shedim and nephilim pour through a portal in minutes if he sounded the alarm. Of course, his master would not be pleased if such an intervention were to be required and he was likely to be punished severely. Not destroyed, because shedim could not be replaced and he could not be killed anyway, only banished to the spiritual realm for a time to regain strength. The worst fate that could befall a shedim was banishment to the abyss, but no fallen could, or would inflict that on another. Only one of the loyalists could cast one of their fallen brethren to the abyss and Livek hadn't seen one of those in millennia. He wondered if the Tyrant had entirely forgotten about his errant children out here in the far corners of the galaxy to which they had fled millennia ago.

Livek shook himself out of his revery and got up from the comfortable leather armchair in which he'd been seated. The chair had been purloined for him during a raid on a remote farmhouse on Earth. He had only been assigned two raider craft, but they had proven sufficient to provide him with new slaves over the centuries to keep his gene pool fresh and also provide the odd luxury he requested of the crew. A light flashing on a console across the room had caught his attention and he strolled casually over to it, pushing a button on the console as he reached it.

"Yes, what is it?" He directed the question in the general direction of the console.

"Captain Rad is here sir, he is requesting to see you. He says it is urgent." a voice came from a hidden speaker.

Livek sighed and replied after taking a moment to contemplate how urgent it could possibly be, "Very well then, send him in." he replied. Rad had just been on one of the very raiding missions to Earth that the shedim had just been thinking on. If something had gone wrong, he needed to know.

A door on the opposite side of the room slid open with the low hiss of hydraulics in action and a human stepped through the open door. This particular human was possessed by a demon spirit named Rad and no one in fact remembered what his human designation had been.

"What is it Rad? I hope you have not come to inform me that you have returned empty handed."

"It has begun." The possessed man replied simply in the typically low guttural voice of a demon, without further explanation, presumably assuming that Livek would immediately know to what he referred.

The shedim administrator could not however fathom what the demon might mean. His reply showed his frustration at this, "What has begun you fool? Think you that I am a prophet who can read meaning into your babbling?"

Rad stumbled over his next words, clearly not expecting that the shedim would miss the import of the news he had to bring. "I'm sorry administrator, the Millennium has begun."

This limited added information did not help Livek to put the pieces together any better and his frustration with his underling only increased, "Which millennium? What are you on about?" The last millennium to pass on Earth had been the second anno domini and it would be some time before the third would arrive. He could not fathom what alternative millennium Rad could be referring to until suddenly it dawned on him, too late to prevent further humiliation, however.

"The so-called Millennial Reign of Christ." Rad informed his master anxiously, fearing that he had embarrassed Livek by having made too many assumptions in this conversation. He had indeed done so, and he would undoubtedly suffer for it, but not at this time, as Livek was currently too stunned to think on that.

The shedim turned from Rad and walked back across the room in a semi-trance, maintaining just enough of his faculties to try to hide his sudden consternation from his underling. What could this mean? He thought to himself wonderingly. How would this affect their plans, their operations? After a few seconds of contemplation, he turned back to the waiting captain. "Explain to me everything you have seen, spare no details."

The raider captain wasted no time, "When I arrived through spatial window to Earth it was as if I arrived in the middle of a great battle. A massive gold cubic space station was in orbit around Earth and was discharging space craft, shuttles and malakim warriors towards the planet. Even from space I could see some of the explosions on the surface below. I would have stayed to see more, but I was pursued by a Royal Navy cruiser, and I had to flee back here. As you know, my craft is not equipped for battle. We collected as much sensor data as we could before leaving, I have already had it uploaded to your console." Rad finished, realising that it was probably not as much information as his master had been hoping for.

Livek took in the information and after digesting it, had only one question, "Did you see Him?"

"Do you mean the Christ?" Rad responded nervously, knowing that mention of Him was scrupulously avoided by the fallen.

Livek did indeed flinch at the name, but needed as much information as he could, "Yes, of course I mean Him."

"I can't be sure," Rad responded, his voice wavering "but there was a bright light on the surface of the planet in the area of Old Jerusalem and many of my crew theorised that it could have been Him?"

"Old Jerusalem?" Livek queried.

"Well, yes." Rad paused briefly before continuing, "Surely the massive gold space station we saw is the long prophesied..."

"Do not say it!" the shedim interrupted with a shudder. "Do not say the words." He looked at Rad and then appeared to come to a decision. "Leave me, I must speak with Lord Kraan."

Rad nodded and practically fled from the room, grateful to be out of his master's presence and grateful that the fact that he had indeed returned empty handed from Earth had never entered the conversation. He wondered briefly what the future would hold for him as it was surely certain that Earth would no longer be a viable option for raiding.

Livek activated the holographic communicator in the office and waited impatiently for his call to be answered, it did not normally take this long. Eventually the image of a palace administrator appeared in front of him. It was a Grigori, and an important one judging by his elegant garb, but not the one Livek had been hoping to address. "I need to speak to Lord Kraan, it is urgent."

The Grigori's finely scaled lizard-like features took on an exasperated look and his reply was curt, "You and a thousand others, if it is about the happenings at Earth then we are already aware."

Livek sputtered incoherently for a moment, not knowing how to respond to this. He had thought to be the one to deliver important news and possibly increase his standing with his superiors but apparently, he had been beaten to the mark. "I see." He finally stammered, regaining his composure. "Well then, perhaps you can inform me what our response is going to be? Is the Lord Kraan concerned and..."

The Grigori cut him off abruptly, "I'm afraid you will have to wait for word once the Lord Kraan has made his decision, like all the others."

The transmission ended the moment the Watcher finished his sentence and Livek realised the insufferable attendant had cut the call off. Livek fumed but was also grateful that none of his underlings had been present to witness his humiliation.

He sat back down in his armchair and considered the situation. The prophecy of the New Jerusalem and Christ's millennium reign had been known for over 2000 years. Surely, someone in the upper ranks of the empire would have foreseen the difficulties this would cause and would have taken precautions against its advent causing too much disruption?

*

Lord Kraan fumed at the chaos that unfolded before him in his throne room. To think that none of his underlings had the ounce of competence it would have taken to foresee that the millennium reign was nigh and take some rudimentary action to prevent it from causing the mayhem that was now unfolding in front of him. One of his higher ranked shedim, Admiral Sulorth was raging at a Grigori administrator, flinging accusations of incompetence, treachery or both. Other Grigori were arguing heatedly with each other over what the likely outcome of the event would be. Some suggested Yahweh would cleanse the galaxy any second in one omnipotent stroke, others suggested He would continue to ignore them as he had for centuries, more prudent Watchers suggested the truth surely lay somewhere in between. Reaching the end of his patience, Kraan whispered in the ear of a nephil honour guard stood near the throne. The beast nodded and strode into the midst of the bawling crowd where it calmly unstrapped a huge war hammer from its back and then swung it into the floor at his feet, producing a deafening clang that brought instant silence to the throne room.

"That is better." Kraan intoned pompously into the newfound stillness. "It is clear to me, that there have been woefully insufficient preparations made for this day. It is doubly clear to me that this sad situation needs to be corrected imminently. I want my navy to be double its size within an Earth month. I want every mine and farm in this empire to double its production before the end of the week. I want a list of names of powerful Grigori warlords who would join me in an alliance before the end of today. Is that all understood?"

The response was a sea of faces looking at him in stunned silence.

"Go!" he shouted, a jet of plasma leaving his mouth as he did.

The attendants scattered in all directions as they rushed to do his bidding, leaving only his chief attendant standing at his shoulder.

"Giska." Kraan muttered, "How long must I tolerate these fools?"

Giska was a tall Grigori of 10.5ft with a longer than usual neck and an unusually long skull, even for a Watcher. The effect made him look ungainly and yet he managed to move with a smooth grace regardless. He pulled on the sleeves of his long red robes as if trying to stretch them to reach the ends of his long-clawed fingers as he replied dryly, "Possibly not much longer if the Tyrant decides to end us."

Kraan cast a searing gaze at Giska over his shoulder which would have terrified any other, but the chief attendant merely shrugged. "It remains to be seen what He will do about us, it is not written." Kraan growled.

"Just because it is not written does not mean we cannot surmise what the likeliest outcome is." Giska hissed in response through his finely scaled lips.

"Very well then, what do you think is the likeliest scenario to unfold here?"

Giska pulled himself little more erect as if he had been preparing for this moment and was about to give a grand performance, "It seems obvious to me my lord. The Tyrant loves His precious humans and takes every opportunity to train them and mould them into His image. It is my learned opinion that He will equip them and send them after us. Over the course of the next thousand years, they will attempt to whittle us down until no rebel remains free."

Kraan nodded his head slowly, his long scaly cranial ridges scraping the upholstery of his throne, leaving faint trails in the felt. "If that's going to be the case, then we will be ready for them. However well He equips his precious humans, they will still be no match for armoured nephil warriors. Let them try to grind us down, we will see which side emerges at the end of two thousand years."

"Indeed, my lord." The chief attendant's sibilant voice replied, his thoughts however were not in concordance with his words. The Grigori's brow furrowed as he pondered the probably that it would not be their side that would prevail in such a drawn-out conflict. He was already pondering the beginnings of a plan that could level the playing field somewhat though.

*

Charlie (Ward) Warden closed the ornate hand-carved front door of his home behind him and stood in the hallway for a moment in stunned disbelief. Had he really just taken part in the battle of Armageddon? With his own eyes he had seen the devil cast into Tartarus, and then he had watched the entire world remade anew. He looked down at his hands and saw that they were perfectly clean, as were his clothes which smelt vaguely like English lavender. Yet earlier in the day they had been covered in dust and blood and stank of smoke. In a daze, he walked into the kitchen and instructed the fabricator to make him a cup of herbal tea. Brandishing his fresh beverage, he walked through into the library where he settled into a comfortable armchair. Next to the chair was a teak side table upon which lay a leather-bound bible, the leather for which had come from a fabricator rather than an animal as there was no death in New Jerusalem. Heaven's fabricators were capable of making any known substance at an atomic level, or breaking unwanted objects down into their base elements. He took a sip from the cup and then placed it next to the bible on the table and closed his eyes to think, but was interrupted by a knock on the front door.

"Come in!" Ward shouted, unworried that anyone hostile could possibly be at his door in New Jerusalem.

"Charles?" a woman's voice sounded.

"In here angel." he called, recognising the voice of his wife immediately. Ex-wife, he mentally corrected himself since there was no marriage in New Jerusalem except to the Lord. He was still surprised to see each time he saw her, how beautifully Stella had been remade, even though he had known her this way for seven years now, since they had first been resurrected at the start of the tribulation. She had always had beautiful long blonde hair and dazzling blue eyes encased in a pleasing oval face, but now she was in peak physical fitness and even the tiniest flaws in her body had been removed. Despite his inability to feel physical arousal any longer, she took his breath away.

"There are parties all over New Jerusalem." she informed him as she came into the room, "I wanted to escape the excitement for a while, and I had a feeling you'd be doing the same."

He smiled, "I hadn't even known any of that was going on. I came straight here after the Earth was remade; I found the whole thing overwhelming to be honest."

"I'm not surprised, it's everything that we've been anticipating for so long. To have it finally be happening is a weird feeling. I feel almost disappointed, as if there's nothing to aim towards anymore." She sat down opposite him in a beautifully carved rocking chair that she had claimed for her own and started to slowly rock, as she always did.

He laughed, "As usual, it's like we share one heart. You did always have a habit of explain my own feelings better to me than I could myself. It's hard to admit the disappointment factor though. Surely, it's wrong to feel this way. Life will be so much better for everyone from now on."

"Oh yes, no-one's disputing that." she explained hastily. "I think that God gave us a yearn to work though, to accomplish things. Bringing God's Kingdom to Earth was our work for a very long time. What are we going to aim ourselves towards now Charles?"

"Well, about that." he said, leaning forward slightly from his chair, "Whilst the New Earth and the New Heaven are free of outside evil influence for now, there are other places that aren't."

She frowned, "You mean the fallen colonies? Aren't they just a bunch of rebel elohim? It doesn't seem like something we should get involved with, the malakim have been fighting that war for centuries."

"From what some of the malakim have told me, there are humans out there too. Slaves of the rebels, some of whom were abducted from Earth and others who were born out in space." Ward explained.

"Oh my, how dreadful." Stella exclaimed in shock, "I had no idea. I will pray for them."

"That's wonderful sweetheart, I'm sure they need it, I want to do more than pray for them though, surely there is missionary work of some kind to be done. Going out into the stars and telling the lost about the sacrifice of Jesus." he was full of fervour, just like when she had fallen in love with him over a century ago.

"I have a feeling that the fallen colonies will be a lot more dangerous than our mission trips to Nairobi, Charles." she cautioned him.

He scoffed dismissively, "So what? We have eternal life; we can't be harmed permanently."

"No, but you can be harmed." she pointed out. "I wouldn't want to see you hurt, even if it were for a short time. I'd be willing to bet the fallen out in space have some horrific practices."

Ward remained undeterred, "From what I've heard you're not wrong there, but surely, we must try anyway? Somewhere out there in the cosmos people are living and dying without the knowledge that they have a Saviour who bought their salvation. With everything that's just gone on here at home, I can't stand the thought that there are still people anywhere in creation who haven't heard the good news."

She sighed, he was clearly not going to be easily swayed from his new vision, "So what are you suggesting? That we buy a spaceship and point it in some random direction hoping to find a lost tribe of fallen eager to hear the good news?"

He could tell that she wasn't on board with his resurrected idealism, and he couldn't help but feel a little deflated, "I was going to talk to Men'el, and see if he could suggest anything."

Men'el had been Charlie and Stella's malak protector during their time on Earth, what some might call a guardian angel. The two had become closely acquainted with the elohim since reaching New Jerusalem and the three often spent time reminiscing on the past.

"That's a good idea. Maybe he can talk you out of this silliness." she chided with a smile that conveyed that she loved him despite his tendencies towards crazy ideas.

He decided to leave it there and just enjoy the rest of the evening in peace with his wife, or rather ex-wife. They stayed up late into the night talking about the many things they'd like to do during the millennium. When Charles woke up in the morning, still in his armchair, she had left, but there was a muffin on his side table with a kiss etched into it. Not a bad start to the second day of the millennium he thought to himself.

Then all the tax collectors and the sinners drew near to Him to hear Him. And the Pharisees and scribes complained, saying, "This Man receives sinners and eats with them." So, He spoke this parable to them, saying: "What man of you, having a hundred sheep, if he loses one of them, does not leave the ninety-nine in the wilderness, and go after the one which is lost until he finds it? And when he has found it, he lays it on his shoulders, rejoicing. And when he comes home, he calls together his friends and neighbours, saying to them, 'Rejoice with me, for I have found my sheep which was lost!' I say to you that likewise there will be more joy in heaven over one sinner who repents than over ninety-nine just persons who need no repentance.

Luke 15: 1-7

Two

Cray had thought that the shifts they were pulling previously were harsh. For the past week they had been made to work 14 hours instead of the usual 12 and the men were exhausted. The overseers showed no signs that this change was only temporary however and complaining was not an option anyone dared consider, the men laboured on in silence. Cray kept his head down and just turned bolt, after bolt, after bolt. He wondered if life would be better as a welder, or an electrician, but after a moment decided all of these were tedious. None of the faces of the men at work looked content with what they were doing. From one side of the giant shipyard hangar to the other, all he could see were bent backs and miserable faces as he cast his eyes across it.

Wait.

He looked back at a spot between two large capacitors waiting to be loaded into the neighbouring frigate. A man in spotlessly clean white clothes stood there smiling warmly at him. Something about the smile penetrated his soul and he stared until his eyes became dry and he had to blink. When he reopened them, the man was gone. He continued to stare at the spot for a few moments and when the man didn't return, he looked about the hangar hoping to catch sight of him again but to no avail. He wondered who it could possibly have been. No-one wore white on Frixar and if they did, they'd be filthy within minutes. No-one smiled on Frixar either, unless it was a callous smile, he'd seen plenty of those from guards over the years. This was decidedly different to that though; the smile had conveyed something unusual to Cray. Something that he was most unused to. The smile had made him feel cared for. The clomping of a giant overseer's boots interrupted his revery and Cray returned to work just as a large nephil walked past his work post.

"Work faster, food." The beast growled as it continued on its way, clearly bored out of its large but stupid mind, if its lack of enthusiasm was anything to go by.

Cray hated being called 'food' by the giants. It was a stark reminder that they would love to eat every human in the facility and the only reason they did not was that someone else was in charge and wanted the humans alive and working. Thus, it was the case that Cray's greatest fear would likely only happen if he stopped working and he had no intention of doing so. He placed another bolt in a hole and began to turn.

Much later than evening, Cray came into the bunk room from the corridor and fell into his cot exhausted. He had barely been able to eat, so tired had he been. He had intended to let his mind wander over the improbable sight of the white man he had seen earlier as he lay, but his weary mind would not focus, and it was only brief moments before he was fast asleep.

"Cray."

Cray stirred as his name was called, the name no-one but him was supposed to know.

"Cray." It came again.

Cray awoke with a start as he realised someone was using his forbidden name. He looked about and realised his cot was in the middle of the shipbuilding hangar near the large doors which would one day open to allow the ships into space. He sat up and swung his legs over the side of the metal bed frame, looking about him as he did so to find the source of the voice calling his name. It didn't take him long to identify the source as the man in the white tunic sitting on a parts crate near the large hangar doors. The man smiled at him as he caught Cray's eye and beckoned him over. Cray looked around, worried that this was a test and that as soon as he approached the man a pair of nephil guards would appear from behind one of the ships and tear him apart. It was so quiet in the shipyard that you could hear a pin drop though. Since you could hear a nephil breathing a hundred yards away, Cray figured it was safe. He wearily pulled himself to his feet and shuffled over to the man in white. As he got close, the man indicated towards another parts crate which Cray hadn't noticed before, presumably intending for him to sit on it, which Cray obediently did.

"Hello Cray." The man smiled again, causing Cray to once again get the feeling that this person cared for him in some way. It was an alien feeling and made him feel both welcome and uneasy at the same time.

"Hello." Cray replied awkwardly. He wasn't used to social interactions and wasn't sure what to follow 'hello' up with. He fell back upon asking the question which was plaguing his mind, "How do you know that name?"

"I have known that name since before you were born." The man replied paradoxically.

So, the man wasn't going to make sense then. Great, Cray thought to himself. Perhaps he was some overseer who had gone crazy, and the others let him wander around as some sort of joke. "Do you have a name?" Cray asked, deciding to humour the man for now and see what happened. This was the most interesting thing that had happened to him in years, and he thought he might as well see how it played out.

"I have many names." The man replied, "Some call me Emmanuel, some Christ, some Messiah and many others. Your masters call me the Tyrant, but you can call me Jesus."

Cray blinked. Was he really supposed to believe that this unremarkable looking man in a clean white suit was the terrible tyrant the masters were always warning them about? He laughed. "I'm sorry, what?"

"Stand with me." The man called Jesus said and held His hand out palm upwards by way of invitation. Cray noticed the man's wrists carried the faint marks of what had once probably been dreadful scars. So, this man had been tortured at some point in the past. It seemed unlikely to Cray that a tyrant would allow himself to be tortured so. Then he realised with a start that the massive hangar door had been opening while he had been lost in thought.

"Jesus! The door! There is no shield operating, we'll be sucked out into space!" he yelled.

Jesus just smiled, "Fear not, I will not allow that."

The door continued to open, revealing a stunning vista that Cray had only seen briefly a few times in his life when he had been lucky enough to witness a finished ship leaving the dockyard. Even on those occasions there had been a glowing shield masking the true beauty of the galaxy. Now it was laid out in front of him in all its glorious splendour; nebulas of varying colours melded with each other, and a distant galaxy swirled around its invisible axis. A green gas giant dominated one corner of the view whilst in the opposite corner a particularly bright star twinkled brightly enough that it managed to be obvious despite the thousands of other stars laid out in front of them. It was easily the most stunning sight that had ever crossed Cray's hitherto deprived eyes.

"It's so beautiful." Cray said breathlessly.

"Thank you." Jesus replied oddly, as if he had created it himself. And then, "I did."

"You did what?" Cray asked confusedly.

"I did create it myself." He smiled, "That is what you were thinking, no?"

"You want me to believe that you created all of this?" Cray stammered in disbelief.

"You must believe that someone did. Why not me?" Jesus replied.

"But you're just a man." Cray laughed.

"A man who is in your mind while you sleep." Jesus answered with a wry smile.

Cray blinked, if this was a dream, then it was more vivid than any he had previously had. "If you're the person who created this, then you must be a god." he mused aloud.

Jesus stared at Him as if prompting him to go on.

"...and if you're a god, then you should be able to show me something I've never seen before. That would prove that you're who you say you are don't you think?"

Without warning there was instantly no ground under Cray's feet, and he was surrounded by a white substance that felt moist to the touch, as if water but suspended in air somehow. He reached out to try and gather it to him, but it was somehow not as solid as it looked, and his hand just passed through it. Suddenly, he was out of the whiteness, and it was receding in front of him as if shrinking, now being replaced by blue from all sides, bluer than he had ever seen before. He also realised he was being blasted from behind by some force of air causing his clothes to billow around him. He tried to turn around and once he managed it found he was being blasted in the face by the wind causing his face to distort and his eyes to squint. He put an arm in front of him to try and block the air hitting his face and found he could now focus on a view of dazzling sparkling waterways wending their way through luscious green forests, though he could not have put any name to them as it was all completely alien to him. The details of what was spread out before him were blurry at first, but they slowly began to come into better focus as he got closer, and he could pick out little features in the landscape below like hills and particularly big green objects. It was then that it dawned on him that he was falling towards it all from an astonishing height that he couldn't have possibly comprehended before now and was almost certainly about to die.

He woke up screaming in his cot and scrambled out of it patting himself all over to check that he was in one piece. There were grumbled mutters from the other cots as angry men stirred in their disturbed sleep except for one other man across the room who was also stood next to his cot looking equally terrified.

That man was Shorty.

*

Becca could not concentrate on her work after the dream she had received the night before. She mentally used the word 'received' rather than 'had' as she felt certain the dream had come from outside of herself. It was so totally alien to her existence that her mind couldn't possibly have conceived of it without external prompting.

There had been a man first of all, and this already was a feature outside of her sphere. This man had possessed a kindly, peaceful disposition and that in and of itself was a second factor that she couldn't have imagined existing on Frixar. He had taken her by the hand and had walked her through a place he had called a field. He had explained that he was from somewhere where such things existed in abundance and where life was respected and cherished. He called the place Heaven and told her that she could join Him there if she so wished. He had even said that one day she could have a flora of her very own, which she couldn't possibly imagine having.

She robotically took another baby's pulse and noted the reading as she continued to think on the strange dream. One astonishing factor of the experience was that it had seemed so real. Even now if felt more like a memory of a real occurrence than a dream. She could still remember the feeling of the soft springiness of the field underneath her feet and the touch of the breeze on her skin. There had been no ceiling and an astonishingly rich blueness above their heads that she had no word to describe. Stella could not have known that such a thing as a sky existed.

She could not get the kindly man's face out of her mind, in a way he had been the most beautiful part of the dream, and she felt a longing to see him again. She suddenly remembered that he had called her Becca. That was the one part of the dream that suggested strongly to her that maybe a dream was all it was. No man could have known what her secret name was, so she must surely have imagined him and the dream in its entirety. Where had she gotten the name Jesus from though?

*

The asteroid belt around Frixar station twisted its way through space, massive rocks tumbling over and under each other in a seemingly chaotic fashion. They were in high orbit around a green gas giant the fallen called Crimmin IV, an unimaginative name for a planet in a solar system that was simply another dot on a map to its Grigori master, Kraan. The system was guarded by a single fallen frigate, the *Crimson Cleaver* which was currently orbiting Crimmin II, a toxic water planet which housed a number of chemical farms. As such, its crew were oblivious to the tiny starlike sparkle which suddenly appeared on the opposite side of Crimmin IV to which Frixar station currently sat. The sparkle became a tiny square which steadily became a larger square as its corners were gradually drawn apart by beams of energy emanating from the window emitters of a star ship on the other side.

Once the gap was large enough, The Royal Navy troop ship *Veneration* navigated its way steadily through the window, a view of the Sol system visible briefly through the portal before it snapped closed, leaving *Veneration* hundreds of light years from where it had been only moments before. On the bridge of the star ship, its malakim captain, Riga'el spoke briefly into his comm. "We have arrived commander, we'll take you to just beyond sensor range of the stations and then you're on your own."

In the large belly of the transporter, Commander Meto'el of the Lord's Royal Navy marines looked down at the five squads spread out before him, each of a hundred malakim marines. Each contingent was led by its own commander except the centre one, which was his own. The malakim marines were each fearsome humanoid beings, generally about 8 to 8.5 feet tall and clad in flexible black battle bodysuits overlaid with dark metal alloy armour. They were each armed with a pulse bow and a Spirit sword although towards the rear there were slightly larger malakim warriors armed with shock lances or long handled Spirit axes.

"Marines!" Meto'el called to them. "Remember your orders, each contingent to a station. This is not a battle mission; we are here to conduct a covert operation requiring stealth and patience. The humans on the stations are not to be harmed, we are here to protect and observe while the Lord does His work. You know your objectives, orb on my order."

From the outside of the ship, there was no evidence that a large number of troops was about to disembark. There was no opening of doors or disembarking of shuttles. Suddenly dozens of glowing orbs emerged directly through the alloy walls of the shuttle and out into open space where they shot towards the asteroid belt and began to weave around the rocks there, eventually losing themselves in the belt until they disappeared entirely. Once they were gone, beams once again sprang from the window emitters of *Veneration* and began to cut a hole in space back to the Sol system and the ship's home base of New Jerusalem. The ship moved through the window as soon as it was complete and then the window closed, leaving no evidence that either ship or window had ever been there at all.

*

Livek paced up and down muttering in his office. It had been a couple of days since the news of the arrival of New Jerusalem in the Sol system and the presumed ending of the tribulation period and the beginning of the millennium. No news had come in verifying these things as yet, the cowardly Captain Rad and his compatriot Captain Chimmon were refusing to risk their crews windowing to Earth. Livek didn't want to risk the crews if he was honest as he knew it would be an age before he was assigned replacements, so he let their reluctance slide for now. He would have thought that they'd have been contacted by the palace with news, but no such communique had come through.

He sat down and tried to concentrate on some production reports, but he couldn't focus, he was too agitated. It did occur to him that he could use the station's portal generators to travel to Earth himself, but he talked himself out of that with the excuse that he had to input specific coordinates, and he could feasibly end up inside a mountain or deep under the ocean if he wasn't careful. In truth, he most mostly afraid that he'd be seen by a Heavenly warrior and sent to the Abyss. No, it was far safer to be hundreds of light years away from Earth. He'd continue safely on in his role as administrator of this facility he decided, it was boring but at least it was safe. He got up from his armchair and turned to the computer console with the intention of continuing his tedious work but instead came face to face with a fearsome Heavenly warrior dressed in black. He didn't scream for help or look for a weapon, he was too dumbfounded. The warrior smiled and swept Livek's head clean from his shoulders with a swift backhand swing of his sword arm. The head rolled across the floor and under a computer console while his body slumped in a heap. Livek found himself cast to the spiritual realm where more malakim awaited him. They grasped hold of his writhing spirit form and shoved it through a black hole to Tartarus that had opened to receive it as he wailed in terror.

Meto'el wiped Livek's black blood from his sword as another malak materialised from the spiritual realm next to him.

"He appears to have been the only shedim on the station commander."

"Very good Toch'el. I'll remain here and assume the role of the late administrator so that the next phase of our mission can proceed as smoothly as possible." Meto'el's facial features twisted and withing a few seconds he was indistinguishable from the shedim he had just banished.

"An impressive likeness." Toch'el commented approvingly.

"Let's hope it suffices." The marine commander replied. "Please continue your observation of the nephilim and drones Toch'el."

Toch'el nodded and was about to return to the spiritual realm before a thought occurred to him, "What if we observe them planning harm to one or more of the humans?"

Meto'el thought for a moment. He would love to simply command his angels to kill anything that threatened the humans on this base without a second's thought, but he had a mission to achieve, and it required more finesse than that. "If you can effectively hide the bodies and take the form of the individuals responsible then do so, otherwise you must maintain your cover."

Toch'el nodded sombrely and returned to the spiritual realm. Meto'el settled himself to become familiar with the console and other items in Livek's office. If he was to become Livek then he'd need to look like he knew what he was doing.

*

Many hundreds of light years away a pair of men, one a tall, muscular man with long, black wavy hair and a regal posture and other slightly shorter but also possessed of a redeemed physique stood on one of New Jerusalem's observation decks staring down at the planet below. The taller man had never seen images of the earth from space before its recreation as no such thing had existed during his earthly lifetime. The second man was explaining to him what changes had occurred and just how different the world looked now.

"Over there are the Americas, and to their East that entire mass of land used to be what we called the Atlantic Ocean." The shorter man explained. The area to which he indicated was now forest and grassland crisscrossed by mighty rivers.

"And yet you say the Great Sea, which you call the Mediterranean, was contained in that relatively small area there. That is incredible, the Atlantic Ocean must have been immense. How ever did you traverse it?" the taller man wondered.

"With great difficulty your highness, even in my time." The other replied, "Whilst it was majestic and conquering it was exciting, the cons of its existence far outweighed the benefits. The Earth as it is now, is far more hospitable to mankind."

An orb came through one of the walls into the small observation lounge and materialised as the archangel Gabri'el. Both men bowed but the malak motioned them both to lift their heads, "Please your highness, Jack, let us not stand on ceremony."

The taller man who had been referred to as 'your highness' smiled, "It is good to see you, honoured Gabri'el. I was just telling Jack here how much I was enjoying one of his books, especially the lion character that is so much like our Lord, and he was describing to me how the globe looked before the great tribulation reshaped it."

Jack Lewis blushed and shrugged, "If I'd known it was going to be read by King David himself one day, I might have spent more time polishing it!"

Gabri'el laughed and walked to the windows where he gazed down at the planet, "It looks very much like it did before the flood now." The globe was nearly entirely green with some patches of brown and a few lakes dotted here and there, some of which were nearly large enough to have been considered small seas on the old Earth. There were no oceans, no snowscapes and no deserts any longer. Some higher areas that could be referred to as mountains were dotted here and there but the long mountain ranges were gone, replaced instead by plains or rolling hills.

"Whilst the old Earth was beautiful to look at, it never occurred to me just how much of it was dangerous and inhospitable until I saw it like this." Lewis commented.

"Whilst it may look beautiful from above, not everything taking place down there is as peaceful as it looks from up here." Gabri'el commented with some sadness.

David's face became serious, and his words confirmed those of the archmalak, "Already there have been some riots in Tel Aviv and in various other cities around the world. They have yet to occur in Old Jerusalem, but it is only a matter of time I imagine."

"Which is why I have come to discuss some finer details of the policing with you your highness. We will have to gather the other kings of course, but I wanted to have your input first." Gabri'el continued.

The king nodded, "Your malakim are doing fine work stopping many of the disturbances before they happen, it is more than a human police force could have accomplished."

"My thanks your highness, I think we could do more in terms of information outreach. There are elements of the population who are particularly outraged at how strenuous the laws are regarding subjects like sexual behaviour and mutual respect. I believe we should shift more focus onto why these rules exist in the first place and how beneficial acceptable behaviour is for both individuals and society as a whole." The archangel explained, "Your example and general leadership in this regard would be most helpful."

At this, Jack Lewis couldn't help but release a short laugh, for which he immediately apologised. The archangel looked at him quizzically.

"I think what my esteemed brother might be hinting at," David said with a wry smile, "is that my behaviour whilst on Earth regarding sexual morality was hardly exemplary."

"Which is what makes you the perfect candidate, as you can explain from the perspective of one who suffered temptation and tasted fully of its fruit but still ultimately decided to choose the Lord over it and come to the conclusion that His ways are the correct way." Gabri'el pointed out.

"He has you there, your highness." Jack grinned.

David laughed and reluctantly submitted to the logic, "Very well, I will prepare a speech, but you are going to help me write it Jack."

Lewis shrugged and smiled, "John can help, his sequel to the Lord of the Rings will have to wait."

*

Ward put his hand on a nearby tree while he caught his breath. He had just run 10 miles, virtually non-stop in an effort to test what his new body was capable of. He took the opportunity to admire his surroundings as he hadn't been to this part of the city before. His natural curiosity and yearn for adventure had led him off the gold paved streets and into a wooded area which he had followed into the wilderness he now found himself in. He had no idea where he was, but he was certainly glad to be here amongst the tall trees creaking in the wind with leaves crunching under his feet. He plucked an inviting looking piece of fruit from a nearby tree and bit into it, realising that it was an apple. Somehow, he'd managed to go seven years on New Jerusalem without having had one yet and the flavour surprised him. It was tastier and juicier, and he felt an instant burst of energy from the eating of it as he did with all the fruit in the New Heaven. He sat down on a rock to enjoy his find and meditated on the fact that this is what fruit was always supposed to have been like and felt a familiar sorrow that mankind's sin had prevented them from enjoying this level of pleasure for millennia before God's plan had finally reached fruition.

"I might have one of those myself, that looks good." came a deep sonorous voice from behind him. He turned to see a familiar and most welcome figure striding up the woodland path towards him. A tall, muscular humanoid in a white tunic with tan skin and dark brown hair. It was the malak warrior, Men'el. Ward had been the paster of a small church on the Old Earth and as such, he and his wife Stella had come under spiritual attack on a regular basis. Unbeknownst to him, Men'el had personally fought off a great many of those attacks, buoyed by the prayers of Ward's congregation. Since Ward's arrival in New Jerusalem, he and Men'el had become fast friends. The malak rooted through the branches and produced an apple of his own and then sat next to Ward to enjoy it. Though Ward was 7ft3, the malak still made him feel small at a well-built 8ft1.

"I thought malakim didn't need nutrition." Ward commented as the warrior bit into his apple, clearly savouring it.

"We don't" Men'el replied, apple juice running down his chin, "But that doesn't mean we can't enjoy it. The Lord has outdone himself with this one." He took another bite and groaned happily, his eyes rolling back into his head.

There was a break in the tree canopy ahead, affording a good view over the forest below their trail. As they watched, an eagle soared past in front of them, snatched a berry from a tree and alighted on a branch not far from where they were to eat its prize.

"Was Heaven always like this?" Ward asked his elohim friend.

Men'el shook his head, "No, Heaven has taken different forms through the ages, and this is but the most recent. The design of New Jerusalem is optimised towards the needs of humans, but make no mistake Ward, the elohim find it pleasing also." Most of Charlie's friends called him Ward rather than Charlie. It was short for Warden, the name he had been offered by Christ for being a good warden of his flock whilst on Earth. Ward nodded at the malak's reply and went quiet for a while, clearly deep in thought. Men'el allowed him to ruminate for a time before probing him, "Something is on your mind my friend."

Ward continued to think in silence for a time before responding, "I assume you're aware of the fallen empires spread across the galaxy and the existence of human slaves out there."

"Of course," the malak responded, "It is expected that the Lord will be addressing those now that the millennium has begun. Hopefully a great many humans will be brought out of slavery."

Ward looked at Men'el intently, "I want to be part of that."

Men'el looked his friend in the eye and considered him carefully before responding, "I'm sure people are needed to pastor the new redeemed. They will need schooling in what they have missed and how best to go forward in their new lives. I could make inquiries for you."

"Oh, I'm sure that will be a really rewarding line of work for some people." Ward replied.

"But not for you?" Men'el queried, confusion in his face, "It is after all where your experience lies."

"I got into pastoring because it put me on the front lines of the battle against Satan." Ward responded, "Now it seems that the front line has shifted, and I find myself watching from the side lines."

"But you don't want to be safely behind the front lines?" Men'el wondered, "You've more than earned the right to eternal rest, Ward."

Ward replied with great passion, "Not while people are out there suffering Men'el, I've been accessing Heaven's records to find out what conditions the human slaves live under. What they are going through out there in the cosmos is horrible and I can't enjoy paradise knowing that people are out there suffering like that."

Men'el studied his friend, whilst having been a short, balding, moderately overweight scholarly individual on Earth, Ward was far from that now. He was still very intelligent and curious, but he was also tall and strong with dark wavy hair. Such men could cause a great many problems for the fallen if they chose to take action. "So, what do you intend to do about it?" the malak finally asked.

"I want to go out there and witness to them, go out into the mission field." Ward announced, his voice full of determination.

The malak shook his head, "Ward, I don't think you understand just how dangerous it is out there. In the past the demonic entities and fallen malakim you encountered were confined to the spiritual realm. Out there in the cosmos they are unrestrained and can attack you with weapons of steel. You will be outnumbered and vulnerable."

"I can do all things through Christ who strengthens me." Ward countered. "Surely He will help me to do this."

Men'el smiled, he had always admired Charlie's reliance on Christ for everything, "Very well, I will make enquiries as to what can be made possible. Perhaps the Navy will give us a small fast craft we can use."

Ward started, "Us?"

Men'el chuckled, "You don't expect me to let you go galivanting around in the Watcher Empires on your own, do you? I didn't keep watch over you for all those years on Earth, just to let you die out there on some nephilim ridden dust ball. If you go anywhere, I will be coming with you."

"Are you sure you want to do that? I don't know how much of the millennium I'm going to spend on this." the human earnestly replied.

The malak laughed heartily, "Charlie Warden, I have served the Lord for millennia, I don't think one more millennium will be in any way onerous. Besides, whilst I have fought by your side many times before, you have never known I was there. I am looking forward to us facing the enemy side by side for once."

There was a loud rustling in the undergrowth near where they were sat, drawing the attention of the two away from their conversation. As they watched, the branches parted, and the large head of a brown bear poked out.

"It looks like we have a friend." Men'el chuckled as the bear padded over to the rock and started the sniff around them. "I think it's after your apple."

"I'll never get used to these predators all being vegetarians now." Ward commented, as he dangled the half-eaten apple over the bear's nose. It picked the fruit from his fingers and happily munched on it as he stroked its head.

"Bears have always been omnivores."   Men'el pointed out, unnecessarily as far as Ward was concerned.

"Well yes, I know that." the human replied a little sulkily, "But this one will never hunt deer or anything like that."

"No, although I'm sure he still enjoys a nice, tasty fish now and then." The angel grinned. Fish didn't possess a nephesh, or soul, as other animals did and so continued to be eaten in the millennium.

Once the bear had enjoyed its fruity treat, it sniffed the air and then padded off back into the woods, disappearing into a large patch of ferns. "Maybe I can train nephilim to eat out of my hand out there in space." Ward jested.

Men'el's faced turned serious, "Do not underestimate the Nephilim Charlie, you will encounter giants twice the size of that bear who would be more than happy to tear you in half with their bare hands and eat your heart raw.

There was silence for a while as the two continued to watch the ferns the bear had just disappeared into, thinking about the prospect of flying out into space to confront the many terrors that lay out there. Eventually Ward spoke, "Why does the Lord not just annihilate the fallen elohim and free the slaves?"

Men'el considered his answer carefully, "Because little would be learnt from that. Whilst the fallen remain out there, there remains an opportunity for both elohim and humankind to learn from their mistakes by observing the consequences. A day will come Ward, when all evil will be vanquished, and the Lord must be certain that those of us who remain would never choose to reintroduce it. The best way to do that is to allow us to watch evil play itself out and sear into all our hearts an eternally lasting determination to never let it rear its ugly head again once it is gone."

Ward stood up, "Well then, I say the sooner we get started with the lesson the better."

"Indeed Ward, indeed." replied the malak as he got to his feet. He planted a massive hand on the human's shoulder and the two set off back down the trail.

If you say, "The Lord is my refuge," and you make the Most High your dwelling, no harm will overtake you, no disaster will come near your tent. For he will command his angels concerning you to guard you in all your ways; they will lift you up in their hands, so that you will not strike your foot against a stone.

Psalm 91: 9-12

Three

The factory floor was a hive of activity and men were sweating and grunting as they went about their tasks. An atmosphere of misery permeated the place as ever, but Cray was happy; at least as happy as you could be in such an oppressive environment. He was no longer tightening bolts and had moved to fixing sheet metal. It was still hard work, but it was different, and different was good. At least it would be until he'd been doing it for weeks and it became as tedious as the bolts had been. His job was to hang a piece of metal by hooks which would hold it in place until someone could come and weld it down. He was busy hanging such a sheet of metal when he felt someone come up behind him.

"Look away." came Shorty's voice.

Cray obediently cast his head to one side as the man's welding torch blazed into life and Shorty began fixing the plate Cray had just been hanging. Cray was about to move on to the next plate, but something held him back. He knew that Shorty had experienced something similar to him a couple of nights ago and he was desperate to ask him about it. He looked about to see if there were any overseers or guards around. He had just about confirmed to his satisfaction that they were safe when Shorty pre-empted him.

"You saw him too, didn't you." the smaller man whispered conspiratorially.

Cray knew who he meant, but decided he didn't want to be the first to mention the name in case he was being tricked into betraying his use of a name, "Who?"

"Jesus." Shorty whispered in a tone Cray could barely hear above the crackling sound of the welder.

Cray nodded nervously, still keeping an eye out for anyone coming, "Yeah, I saw Him."

Shorty may have responded with a nod, smile or similar, but Cray couldn't tell because of Shorty's mask as well as his having to look away from the blinding light of the welder. A few awkward moments passed before one of them dared speak again. "Do you think He is who He says he is?" Shorty asked in a whisper between welds.

Cray thought for a long moment, it was something he'd thought about a lot. "Do you mean is he the Tyrant? He doesn't seem like one to me."

"I mean is He the Creator." Shorty hissed.

Cray thought furiously, it wasn't actually a facet of the experience that he'd dwelt on. He'd managed to forget that Jesus had made the claim and had rather focussed on the way He had made Cray feel. "I guess He could be, perhaps? I mean he can enter our dreams at will, both at the same time apparently. He must be very powerful."

This time Cray could see the nod of Shorty's mask, "Then why has He left us here to rot?"

Cray thought that comment was harsh at first, but as he carefully considered it, it did seem strange that a being so powerful wouldn't just snatch them away. Perhaps He was watching their torment and savouring it like the nephilim did. The thought of one of the giants made him realise he hadn't checked for them in a while, and he cast his eyes furtively across the hangar. To his horror there was a large guard stood not 50ft away staring right at the two of them.

Cray froze in dread; the creature met his eyes directly and the two stared at each other for an awful moment that seemed to draw on forever. It wasn't one of the larger Nephilim, but it was still 10ft tall and heavily muscled with jagged horns around its head and one tusk protruding haphazardly from a corner of its mouth. It was a dreadful sight indeed and Cray imagined what short work those strong arms would make of him tearing him apart. Any moment now it would walk up and seize him in those giant hands and rip him in two.

It did not however, the nephil simply turned and wandered off to another section of the hangar where it watched another man working for a time. Cray gulped the breath he had been holding down loudly and realised he had a wet stain spreading slowly across the front of his overalls. He would have to try and slip unnoticed into the shower queue later despite it not being his time. He realised that Shorty had moved on while he had been staring at the giant. Assuming their conversation was over, he tried to ignore the uncomfortable warm moist feeling in his overalls and go back to his work.

Later that evening, Cray lay in his cot grateful for the fact that he had managed to join the queue for the showers and get a clean set of overalls. He tried to get to sleep, his mind on the strange experience with the nephil earlier. He now realised that there had been no malevolence in the beast's stare which was possibly the oddest thing about the whole episode. It was obvious that the entire nephilim race despised humans, though Cray couldn't fathom why. The nephilim seemed to have it better than humans in every possible way, what could humans possibly possess that a nephil would envy? Cray was still pondering this mystery when he drifted off to sleep.

He was disappointed to wake up in his cot the next morning without having had another dream of the man who called himself Jesus. He quickly realised that the bunk room was empty and drew the immediate conclusion that he must be late for his shift. He stumbled out of bed, slipped his shoes on hastily and blundered out into the corridor which was strangely deserted. Starting to panic now, he ran along the passageway, his footsteps echoing eerily off the bare rock walls. The door to the hangar was locked, leaving him not knowing what to do, he had never been beyond that door, dare he now? Surely it would be better to inform someone that he was late and beg for mercy rather than just standing outside the door waiting to be let in? He ran on down the passageway encountering doors he had never seen before, all of which turned out to be firmly locked. Eventually he found one that was open and dived through it, finding himself in an office. Sat in a chair in front of the desk was the man from his dreams, the one who called himself Jesus. He smiled as Cray entered and indicated the chair opposite him. Cray looked nervously over his shoulder as if expecting to find an administrator of some kind glaring at him. When he saw no-one, he decided to take the invitation and sat nervously in the chair indicated. It was a padded chair and Cray wasn't used to such comfort. He couldn't help leaning back a little and settling into it with a sigh.

"You have been working very hard." Jesus began.

Cray nodded wearily at the kind faced man and shrugged his shoulders, "That's the nature of life here."

"It's not what I had intended for mankind when I made you. Here." With this last word, Jesus leaned forward and touched Cray's hand. Instantly every ache and pain disappeared, and a newfound energy replaced his exhaustion.

"How?" Cray uttered in disbelief.

"What's more important than how, is why." Jesus replied cryptically.

"Ok." Cray muttered, he could play this game if it led to feeling better than he did, "Why then?"

"Because my intention for men is for them to be full of joy and life, not be borne down by burdens of overwork and suffer torture at the hands of errant beings." The Lord smiled again, and Cray felt like a light was entering his soul each time He did.

"If that's the case, why don't you end it all right now? You could maybe take me somewhere better than this?" Cray was looking for answers to the question Shorty had raised which had been troubling him since.

"Indeed, I could, but I'm less interested in your temporal comfort and more interested in life eternal." Jesus leaned forward in his chair and looked Cray straight in the eye. I serve my Father, Yahweh who is the Lord of Lord and King of Kings. No other can compare to Him. He is a holy being though and those who are contaminated by evil thoughts and deeds cannot enter his presence. I cannot therefore take someone like yourself, with an impure soul, into paradise where He resides."

Cray's face fell, as he was sure Jesus was right about the state of his soul, "Well if you can do nothing for me, why are we having this conversation?"

With a reassuring smile, Jesus shared the gospel with Cray, "Because I can make you clean. There was a price to be paid for the cleansing of souls and I paid it. I can stand in your place when the Father stands in judgement of your life. I need something from you though."

Oh great, Cray thought, there had to be a catch. It would probably be a pretty onerous one too if it was required to pay for a place in a paradise. "Tell me what it is." Cray muttered.

Jesus explained, "Firstly, you need to admit any wrongs you have done. You need to have a heart that truly desires to be different and live as purely as you can. As once long ago I died for you, so your old self must die for Me, and you should live as a new man."

Cray nodded slowly, it sounded hard but not impossible, "You said firstly, what comes next?"

Jesus caught his eye and held it, as if to fully convey the import of what He was about to reveal, "You need to take the decision to break from the path you have been on, stop chasing any other gods or desires and devote yourself to following Me only. Do that, and you shall have life eternal and live it in a state of joy."

Cray sat back and thought for a second, it was an incredible offer on one side, but was he truly prepared to live for someone other than himself? True, he wasn't living for himself right now, but if he could somehow break free from the factory, perhaps he could forge a life where he didn't have to answer to anyone but himself. He looked up at Christ, "How long do I have to decide?"

*

Becca had hoped beyond all hope to dream of the field again, and now that she was here, she felt nothing but anxiety. The green plant matter underneath her feet felt just as luxuriously soft as it had the night before and the ceiling above, or lack of it rather, was the same incredible hue of blue that it had been before, only now it was dotted with puffy white patches which only made it seem all the more beautiful to her. There was no one here yet and perhaps that was where her anxiety stemmed from. She was certain she was not afraid of the kindly man, but waiting for the possibly of him arriving was making her heartbeat as fast as a newborn's. Eventually she sat down to try and calm herself down and it was after she had been mediating like that for a few moments that she felt the presence behind her.

"Hello again, Becca."

She spun around to find him just like she remembered, dressed in a spotless white linen tunic with a face that seemed to shine like love itself. "Jesus?" she whispered.

"You remembered my name." He smiled as he sat down next to her. "I brought you a gift." He reached from around his back and produced a young rose plant in a pot.

She was stunned, "It's like the flora. How did you…?"

Jesus smiled, "I created it, like I created all things."

"You created all things? Like the world I live in? Like the flora? Like the…like the nephilim?" The questions poured out of her like she'd sprung a leak, and she instantly regretted them as she saw what appeared to be pain on His face.

"Sadly yes. In truth I did create a universe in which there was the possibility for the nephilim to be born, though it was not my intention for it to be so. I also created the rock you call your world, though it was never my intention for humans to dwell on it. And yes, I created the flora, though it was never my intention for it to be taken from Earth and transported hundreds of light years across the galaxy." Jesus finished with a sombre tone to His voice.

Much of what He had said was too far outside of Becca's world for her to fully understand, but it was all knowledge and she stored it eagerly for future reference. "So, did you create me? And if you did, why did you create me to live here?"

Jesus sighed, "I did create you in your mother's womb as I provide the spark for all life when it is first conceived. It was not my intention for you to be born as a slave however, and that is why I am here Becca. I wish to set you free." He smiled at this, and she saw from His face that He really meant what He was saying.

"How is that possible?" she asked eagerly.

"I have servants on the station right now who will deliver you all from the hands of your evil masters. I need you to get the women prepared to bring the children out." He explained.

"I can do that, is that all you require of me?" she asked nervously, knowing somehow that it would not be.

"No. Because if I only rescue you from Frixar then I will only be saving you from physical pain and I wish to save you from so much more." He took her by the hand, "You see Becca, all humans are born to die because their hearts are corrupted. The limited lifespan you live is a consequence of a rebellion against me many millennia ago. I wish to restore mankind, and indeed I have restored many of them already, but many of you still remain scattered amongst the stars, like yourself Becca."

She nodded. It was hard for her to comprehend what he was saying, but it made the pain she had suffered all of her life make sense. She had always felt that something was very wrong with the lot men had been given. "I want to be saved Jesus, tell me what to do."

He smiled radiantly, "Trust in Me Becca. Promise to follow me and leave your old life behind and I will restore you to perfection and my servants will bring you to Paradise."

"Oh Jesus. I will promise that; I will follow you all of my days."

"Take this and hold it Becca." He handed her the rose plant, and everything went black.

From the coarse feel of the cloth under her knew that she was back in her bunk. She didn't want to open her eyes because she was afraid that it had been just a dream, but something was clearly wrong in the room. There were voices close to her cot that sounded excited, upset or both. She opened her eyes to find that her bed was suddenly the focal point of the room, and all of the women were gathered around it.

"What's wrong?" she asked one of them as she checked herself to see if she had grown an extra arm or something.

The woman closest to her pointed down towards the end of the bed and Becca gasped in wonderment. At the foot of her bed stood a pot containing a rose plant with a striking red flower.

*

Cray woke up in his cot to the sounds of other men stirring from their sleep. He went over the conversation he had just had in his dream and his heart stopped from fear, had he just squandered the only opportunity he might get to reach paradise? Jesus had just offered him salvation and rather than accept the offer immediately, he had procrastinated. What had he been thinking? He glanced over at Shorty's cot and saw that the small man was practically beaming. Had he just surrendered his life to Jesus?

As Cray went through that day, he started to take note of every thought he had and imagine it was being judged by the Father that Jesus had spoken of. He quickly realised that whatever the standards were, he was probably not meeting them. A lot of his thoughts involved violence, both towards his captors and towards the other workers at times. He realised he was a very angry man, and that anger was unlikely to be considered a virtue in this paradise Jesus had spoken of. Jesus had said that He would be standing in place of Cray though, but only if Cray had taken the decision to follow Him. I wish I had chosen to follow you Jesus, he thought to himself, if you gave me another chance, I would choose You without hesitation.

*

The atmosphere in Kraan's palace was even more tense than usual. Slaves were keeping their heads down in an attempt to not be noticed and even Grigori attendants were more subdued than usual. The change in atmosphere was most notable to Giska, who had been required to fill the role of the bearer of bad news on more than one occasion. It was not a role he savoured, especially not since his lord possessed that most frustrating combination of arrogance and incompetence. He strode through the ranks of demonic courtiers and came to stand before the throne, he coughed and waited for the self-styled emperor to pull his attention away from the half-naked demon possessed woman who was sat in his lap. Eventually the warlord reluctantly turned his attention to his waiting chief attendant with an exaggerated sigh, "What is it now Giska? Not more bad news I trust?"

Giska had to exercise a great deal of self-control to keep his voice calm when every part of him wanted to launch a tirade at his emperor for his unreasonable childish behaviour. "I am afraid it is more bad news my lord." Rather than explain, which would have required more patience than he currently possessed, he handed his emperor a datapad.

Lord Kraan found himself looking at reports from his various holdings. As some of his minions had warned him, the forces of Heaven had started moving on his positions. A number of outlying colonies had been infiltrated, all the fallen entities slain, and the human occupants liberated. It was infuriating. He flung the datapad back at the chief attendant, causing the woman to tumble from his lap, and scowled at him. "This is totally unacceptable. How have you allowed this to happen?"

Giska was dangerously close to losing his temper, "We have taken every action you have requested my lord."

"And why do I have to request everything? Are you incapable of acting on your own?" Kraan yelled.

Giska would have loved to have pointed out that every time he did so, he was berated for not having gotten the emperor's permission first, but he still maintained enough of his faculties to realise that to do so would be suicide, he chose to moderate his response accordingly, "I would not want to overstep my boundaries my lord."

Lord Kraan changed tack, "Is it too late to protect our other holdings?"

Giska sighed and answered, "I suggest we not wait to find out. If you act now, perhaps we might salvage something of your empire."

"By the fires of Hades, you are right." Kraan bellowed and Giska winced at the unfortunate choice of words. "Send as many ships as we can afford to the remaining colonies, but make sure we have enough left to defend this system if there is a concerted attack."

"As you wish my Lord." Giska hissed, attempting to ooze as much deference as he could manage towards the master he was rapidly holding less and less respect for. "You have made a most wise decision."

*

So it was that a window opened in the Crimmin system some hours later, permitting the entry of a fallen destroyer and two frigates. The captain of the destroyer was leading the protective detail and immediately opened communications to the *Crimson Cleaver* which was patrolling the belt.

"This is captain Gorsk of the *Savage Attack*," the nephil captain of the destroyer began. It was unusual for nephilim to rise to the rank of captain, but he was a particularly capable one. "I have been sent to make sure this system is clear of loyalist infiltrators."

The captain of the frigate was a shedim who had scant respect for nephilim in general and refused to acknowledge the giant's rank. "I am Captain Sek of the *Crimson Cleaver* charged with guarding this system and I can assure you Gorsk, that if the forces of Heaven had been here, I would have known about it."

"Nevertheless, we must conduct a thorough search, starting with the largest station." the nephil stared hard at the shedim on the screen, making it clear there would be no compromise on this.

"If you insist. The largest station is Frixar, I suggest we start there." the shedim ended the communication and muttered to his second in command, "Idiot, if we find any malakim in this sector I will eat my own head."

The *Crimson Cleaver* would be first at the station since it was already in the belt. It was currently heading on a bearing directly away from the station and the pilot carefully turned the vessel to go back the way they had come.

*

On Frixar station, Meto'el had just been informed by a drone inferior that the fallen ships had entered the system. He summoned Toch'el and the marine lieutenant arrived almost immediately, he was disguised as a nephil and had to squeeze through the door to the office. It was a particularly ugly nephil with a tusk protruding awkwardly from one corner of its mouth and Meto'el didn't envy his comrade for having to maintain such an ugly facade. As soon as he got inside the office and closed the door behind him, Toch'el shrank to his normal size and breathed a sigh of relief.

"We have incoming." Meto'el informed him simply.

The implications of this were not lost on his experienced lieutenant, "How long do we have?" he asked his commander.

"Not long. Probably not enough time to rid ourselves of the remaining nephilim. We could end up fighting a battle on two fronts." Meto'el sighed, perhaps I should have just let you finish them all before now.

"Ah, about that." Toch'el began, his face showing some trepidation.

"What have you done Toch'el?" Meto'el responded, his face showing concern that their crucial enterprise could have become compromised.

"Well, you did say we could replace any that threatened humans when it could be done in an efficient way. It just turned out that that meant all of them." Toch'el explained.

Meto'el stood in disbelief, "All of them?"

Toch'el shrugged, "Well, there is still one guard left in the nursery, but he's being taken care of as we speak."

Meto'el shook his head in disbelief, "How did you get rid of that many giant bodies?"

"The erm, the food processors." Toch'el admitted reluctantly.

"Are you trying to tell me that for the past few days the station's inhabitants have been eating the remains of cannibalistic giants?" Meto'el asked incredulously. In reply he got another shrug, confirming that this was indeed the case. To Toch'el's surprise his commander suddenly laughed, "Well I'm not sure if this breaks any codes, in fact I'm fairly sure it will break at least one, but the irony of it doesn't fail to escape me. Please keep it from the population, I can imagine they'd be traumatised if they found out."

"So how should we proceed?" Toch'el wondered.

Meto'el did not hesitate, "With the military arm of the station all gone, we have full control. Get all the marines to the main hangar, if there will be a landing, that's where it will be."

Toch'el turned towards the door but then had a final thought and turned back to his commander, "What about the Lord's work? Did he finish what he planned here?"

Meto'el laughed, "I wouldn't worry about His side of things, nothing will stop Him from achieving what He wants to do."

*

Becca looked up at the nephil guard nervously. He seemed even more attentive than usual, and she was wondering if the beast knew what she was planning to do this day. As she fussed over the babies another nephil came in with one of the other women. The horrible looking creature stalked straight up to her, and she flinched as it came close, thinking that this was surely the moment in which she would pay for her treachery against the Masters, even if she hadn't actually acted yet. The nephil turned its head to the woman it had brought with and said to her, "You must do everything this woman tells you today, no matter how strange it might seem. Do you understand?"

The other woman nodded nervously and gave Becca a suspicious look. "I will do whatever she tells me."

"Good." the nephil then turned to Becca and whispered to her in a voice which sounded most unlike a nephilim, "It's okay Becca, you know what to do."

Becca nodded with her heart in her throat, how could a nephil know her secret name? And then to know it and not punish her for it!

He looked towards the other guard in the room and strode over to him, "I must talk to you outside. I have instructions from Commander Livek."

The guard grunted, "I'm not supposed to leave my post."

The new nephil smiled, "Are you worried that these two puny human women will find weapons and kill everyone in the base because you were not here to watch them for a few moments?"

The guard scowled, "No I... I will talk to you for a moment, but then I must return."

The second giant nodded and the two left the room. Becca listened in horror as there came the unmistakable sounds of a scuffle outside, and then quiet. The two women stared at each other terrified until Becca finally remembered what Jesus had told her, "We need to get these babies out of here."

The woman nodded nervously and the two went to work.

*

It was oddly quiet in the hangar today with fewer guards than normal, but Cray still dared not ease off his pace too much in his work. He felt sure someone would find out somehow if he did. It did give him some leeway to let his mind wander occasionally though, and he could contemplate the situation with his night visitor. He was still regretful that he hadn't immediately taken Jesus up on His offer when He had presented it, and he was plagued by worry that the offer would never come again. He was contemplating this when the steel doors providing entry into the hangar from the inner station opened and a line of fierce looking nephilim began to file through with a smaller but nasty looking creature with black skin at their head. This cannot be good, Cray thought to himself, they must know about the dreams. He thought about running, but where would he go? He would eventually be found and then whatever punishment he faced would be even more severe. He settled for trying to make himself seem small by hunching over and shuffling closer to the unfinished frigate. The long line of fearsome figures filed straight past the workers and took position facing the hangar doors, just beyond the ends of the incomplete ships. The shorter dark figure took position in the centre with twenty nephilim to either side of him, it made for an impressive but terrifying sight. Cray decided the shorter black figure must be their leader, but how a single smaller being could control so many giants was a mystery to him. Come to think of it, he hadn't thought there were even so many guards on the station. As he continued to watch, the massive hangar doors began to open, much as they had in his first dream. Fortunately, this time the shields were up, and he breathed a sigh of relief until he saw what lay just beyond the shield. A frigate held station just beyond the shield, very much like the ones they were currently constructing. The line of guards seemed unmoved by the sight and Cray imagined they must be expecting the ship. Perhaps it was an important visitor of some kind? As he watched a smaller ship detached itself from the frigate and came towards the shield. The shield moulded itself around it as it came through and alighted on the hangar floor into front of the line of guards. A ramp dropped at the opposite end of the shuttle and men began to march out carrying rifles. A pair of nephilim also joined them stomping forward on either side of a being very similar in appearance to the dark skinned one. As they did, an even larger ship appeared behind the frigate and also began to disgorge smaller vessels. The two dark skinned creatures met, and Cray could just about pick up what they were saying.

The newcomer was the first to speak, "I am sorry for the intrusion commander Livek, it would appear that the captain of that destroyer is under the mistaken impression that there are malakim in the system."

"It's okay Captain Sek," Meto'el was grateful that he had informed himself of the details of the system's only combat vessel and its crew. "As you can see, we are prepared to welcome our visitors."

Sek looked down the length of the assembled nephilim warriors, "I wasn't aware that we had so many nephilim stationed here on the station, it is most erm, impressive."

Meto'el grinned in response, "We want to give our honoured guest the best reception possible, do we not?"

As he spoke more shuttles pushed their way through the shield and landed next to the first. Captain Sek and his small force turned and took places amongst the disguised malakim, unaware of who they were allying themselves with. The men seemed uncomfortable with being in such close proximity to giants, but Sek was keen to stand alongside his shedim comrade and present a united front to the foolish nephil captain who had intruded into his domain. Humans and giants descended down the loading ramps of the newly landed shuttles as soon as they opened. They approached the two shedim with one out front, looking rather oddly dressed in the uniform of a star ship captain.

"Commander Livek, I presume." the giant captain stated in a more formal tone than the still listening Cray had ever heard from one of the creatures.

"Correct, and you are?" the disguised Meto'el answered.

"I am Captain Gorsk of the destroyer *Savage Attack*." he proudly indicated with one arm the large ship holding station outside the hang shield, just beyond the *Crimson Cleaver*. He did not look back however, and if he had, he might have noticed the 80 glowing orbs leaving the station for the two ships.

"And to what do I owe the honour of your presence here? Apparently, you believe we have malakim here?" Meto'el continued.

The giant captain grimaced and glared at the smaller frigate captain, "I do not presume that there are, but I have been ordered to make sure. As you may or may not be aware, there have been some incidents on other bases. We merely want to take precautions."

There was something very different about this nephil that struck Meto'el. He was outwardly different in that he possessed less pronounced physical qualities of nephilim, he still had six fingered hands, but he only had small horny protuberances on his head rather than actual horns and less brutish facial features. His manner was most striking though, he spoke with an eloquence the malak had never encountered in a nephil, and it intrigued him. "Most wise of you captain. I believe that precautions should always be taken wherever possible." Meto'el replied, and he was rewarded with a glare from Captain Sek who had thought that Livek would be far less receptive of this invasion of their little kingdom. The nephil captain grinned at his shedim equivalent as if knowing exactly what he was thinking.

"I am pleased that you chose to honour me with such a display of nephilim power commander. It is most gratifying." he again grinned with a mouth full of double rows of jagged teeth.

"I am pleased that you like my display captain, but they aren't nephilim." Meto'el said with a smile full of perfect white teeth. He gave a sharp order and the line of nephilim to either side of him dissolved into the forms of black clad heavenly warriors.

Captain Sek recoiled in horror as the giants around him shrank to his size and revealed themselves to be his hated enemy. Suddenly he decided his allegiance lay with Captain Gorsk after all and he slunk over to stand in the group of fallen. His two nephilim guards stood growling at the group of malakim whilst the fallen human soldiers were rooted to the ground in fear. The two groups were more or less even in number, but the fallen had seven nephilim amongst their ranks. It would be hard going for the angels if a fight broke out.

"You fool malak." Gorsk rumbled, I only need to call my ship for reinforcements, and you will be overwhelmed in moments.

"Try it." Meto'el challenged him.

Cray watched in fascination as the nephil captain thumbed a communicator on his wrist, "*Savage Attack*, this is Gorsk. Send reinforcements."

There was a brief pause before a voice Meto'el recognised as Toch'el came back over the line, "I'm sorry, all of our operatives are currently busy on other calls. Please try again later." The malak commander sighed under his breath at his comrade's attempted insertion of humour into this most serious of moments. Gorsk glared at him, and he simply shrugged, "Your crew is clearly not as savage as you would have liked."

Gorsk's determined expression wavered, but he remained resolute, "We can still send a great many of you to the spirit realm loyalist."

It was at this moment that Cray realised he had an opportunity to show where his allegiances lay. He steeled himself, grabbed a large wrench and jumped down from the platform he had been working on. He began walking towards the front of the hangar where the two opposed groups stood facing each other. Some other men saw what he was doing and began to fall in step with him, brandishing whatever tools they could put hand to, whilst many more men shrank still further into the hiding places, they had found for themselves. Cray came to a stop behind the malakim and planted his feet, another fifty or so men assembled behind him.

Well, thought Gorsk to himself, the malakim would now be surrounded if these men were loyal to the fallen. They would have a good chance of winning this fight, and then perhaps they could retake the ships somehow. "Human," he growled at Cray, "With whom do you stand?"

Cray glanced at Shorty who had come to stand next to him with a long steel pole in his hands and the little man simply nodded.

"We stand with Jesus." Cray announced to rumbles of agreement from the others stood with him.

Gorsk knew in that moment that they were defeated but at the hated name of the Lord the other nephilim could contain themselves no longer.

"Hold!" Gorsk shouted, but to no avail. The giants roared and began to flail their huge melee weapons at the closest malakim to them. Nephilim knew that surrender was not an option as there was no place in Heaven for half human / half elohim abominations. The fallen human troops had no intention of throwing their lives away though and dropped their guns. Without their aid, the giants did not stand a chance.

Each nephil was roughly 10ft tall, but malakim averaged 8ft tall themselves, had the better numbers, millennia of experience and vastly better training. The shock lances and spirit swords of the Royal Navy marines made short work of the giants. Through it all, Gorsk and Meto'el continued to face each other in a standoff. Captain Sek had not drawn his sword; he was the only fallen present who had seen malakim in battle before and he knew the rebels had never stood a chance. The malakim gathered their defeated foes together in a huddle and Meto'el posted a guard over them.

"What will become of us now malak?" Gorsk grumbled.

Meto'el wasn't sure to be honest, he had never captured a nephilim alive before. "Judgement." He stated simply. "It's up to the Lord of Hosts what to do with you. All I can guarantee is that you'll be judged fairly." Sek began looking around him furtively as the certainty of banishment to the Abyss loomed large in his mind, "Keep a close eye on this one, if he moves, banish him." Meto'el ordered his troops. He had no doubt that the shedim would slip away into the spirt realm and disappear if given half the chance.

The marine commander walked over to where Cray stood chatting nervously with the other men. The import of what had just happened had shaken their senses and their lack of a concept of freedom made it impossible for them to fully grasp their new circumstances. "What is your name, human?" Meto'el asked as he came to tower over the barely 6ft tall man.

Cray started, he almost feared to admit he had given himself a name and he glanced around him looking for reassurance from the others but received none. Years of conditioning had forced them into silence.

"It's okay, Heaven does not forbid the use of names, you may tell me." Meto'el encouraged him.

"Cray." The man said reluctantly in a quiet voice.

The Holy Spirit whispered to Meto'el and he smiled at the revelation, "Well, Cray Ironheart. I am thankful for your intervention, there would have been greater casualties here today if not for it. I lost not a single malak thanks to you."

Cray beamed and Shorty slapped him on the back. Behind him there were murmurings and while he had the malak's ear he decided to address their concerns, "Sir, what will happen to us now?"

Meto'el replied with the typical attitude of one who had much on his mind but understood that he had to give some consideration to others who had concerns of their own, "We have some cleaning up to do here which will take some time. We also have to make sure that the other stations in this sector have been liberated by my other detachments. Not to mention that we have to assist them as well." With these last words, the malak pointed towards the back of the hangar where the doors had opened to admit the entry of a pair of malakim leading a long line of haggard looking women, many of whom were leading young children or carrying babies.

Cray's mouth dropped, he had rarely seen such young children or women and the sight of so many at once was astonishing to him. He would never have believed there were so many in residence on the station. To him they suddenly represented the embodiment of human life and resilience and he found it incredibly uplifting. And then he realised he recognised the woman in front, could it really be her?

Becca swallowed hard as she saw the heavily armed and intimidating looking malakim marines standing around the hangar and held the baby tightly to her chest. She kept repeating to herself to have faith that Jesus would do as he had promised. Then she saw one of the workers staring at her and realised instantly that it was the man with the kind eyes. It made her think of the fact that their child was one of the babies the women had rescued, and she had no idea which. All of the stress of the past few hours suddenly rose up in her and she broke into tears and stumbled.

Cray did not hesitate upon seeing the woman's distress and immediately ran over to her, "It's okay. We're here to help you, these beings may look fearsome, but they are good and are going to take us all to safety."

She looked up at him as she felt his strong arms supporting her to stand and her heart leapt as she saw that it was him who had come to her aid. She hadn't been wrong about his kind eyes.

Rescue me, LORD, from evildoers; protect me from the violent, who devise evil plans in their hearts and stir up war every day. They make their tongues as sharp as a serpent's; the poison of vipers is on their lips.

Psalm 140: 1-3

Four

In a prisoner processing facility deep inside New Jerusalem, Gorsk paced up and down in the cell, pondering his new circumstances. Thus far his treatment had not been what he would have expected from the forces of the Tyrant. He had been led to believe by his Grigori masters that their foe was an unforgiving monster who delighted in crushing the spirits of his people under the weight of strict rules and restrictions. Everyone he had encountered thus far had been firm with him, but also light in spirit, exuding only peace and contentment and they had all treated him with a modicum of kindness. The humans that is, the malakim were clearly not lovers of nephilim and whilst not being abused, he had received only stoic silence from them. Unbeknownst to him, he was being watched through a panel of one-way glass. On the other side a small group of fascinated elohim had gathered to observe their intriguing new captive.

"Note how smooth his skin is compared to most of his kind." A Grigori dressed in a long flowing white robe noted. Like most loyal Watchers, his finely scaled skin almost glowed as it reflected the light, and he was tall and graceful.

"What do you suppose the Beloved will make of him?" another Grigori pondered aloud.

A rugged looking dark skinned malak with a topknot dressed in battle scarred armour grunted as he stood with his arms crossed and feet planted at the glass, "Destroy him of course. He's a nephilim."

A Grigori tutted behind him, "Come now Uri'el, I think the situation requires a little more nuance than that?"

"Nuance...pfft." the archangel grunted. He pulled an axe from his belt and held it towards the jailed nephil. "Let me in there and I'll give you a demonstration of nuanced axe work."

One of the gathered Grigori leaned over to whisper conspiratorially in the ear of a colleague next to him, "Which virtue do the humans consider him the angel of again?"

"Hmm," the other watcher pondered with a wry smile, "wisdom I believe?"

"Hmm, and which school of wisdom do you suppose this behaviour falls into?" the first responded meaningfully.

"The school of wisdom that suggests a dead enemy can't stab you in the back," Uri'el growled menacingly and then ominously added, "and also that an unconscious Grigori can't talk behind it." He continued to glare at the captive giant and the two Grigori went conspicuously silent.

"While you do have a point brother, about the enemies and not about the Grigori, I look at this creature and see potential. There is much human in him." This speaker was the archangel Micha'el, leader of the malakim. He was often clad in bright polished armour but on this day was wearing white flowing robes with a smart blue tunic over the top. He towered over the most malakim at nearly 9ft, but the tall thin Grigori averaged 10ft and thus it was his broad shoulders rather than his height that rendered him an imposing presence in present company. When Micha'el spoke, all listened.

"The Lord is here." A Grigori intoned. He needn't have, because all elohim could sense the closeness of Christ, who they fondly referred to as the Beloved.

A door opened into the nephil's room, permitting the entry of the Lord. He was dressed as he often did in a simple white linen suit. At nearly 11ft tall the giant should have towered over Jesus at slightly over 7ft, but it shrank from Him, seeming somehow small in the Lord's presence. Jesus emanated power in waves, and it washed over anyone who came close to Him. Those not redeemed became quickly overwhelmed when He drew close.

"You are Gorsk." The Lord began.

The giant nodded nervously; all semblance of his former brutish arrogance utterly gone in the presence of the Creator of the universe.

"Son of the fallen Grigori Kraan and of the former human slave Suriah." Jesus continued.

Gorsk's face registered clear shock. He hadn't expected that revelation, nephilim were never told who their parents were in fallen culture. He knew who Lord Kraan was of course and had never imagined that he was the emperor's son, he had never really cared whose son he was. He had never heard of a woman named Suriah, but that was not unusual, she would likely have been known only by her designated number as a slave. A great many slaves died in childbirth when birthing a nephil, even though steps were often taken to try and preserve their viability for future breeding. "My mother..." he muttered confused.

"...is here with Me in Paradise." Jesus continued. "She is very content."

Gorsk didn't know what to make of this information. He hadn't given much thought to her before, there was a pain there he had always tried to avoid.

"Giska's seed was not as strong as Suriah's. You look much like her father, despite the elohim side of your being." Jesus continued.

The giant simply nodded, he wasn't sure where the Lord was going with this, it hadn't been the painful judgement and retribution he had feared though and so he kept quiet to see what would happen next.

"You have never tasted human flesh like your kin. Why is that?" Jesus asked him.

Gorsk shrugged, he wasn't sure why he was being asked the question. Surely the Creator knew the answer anyway. He waited to see if Christ would move on, but He simply looked at the nephil waiting for an answer, so Gorsk rumbled, "It seemed distasteful to me, eating a sentient being."

Jesus nodded and continued, "And you spared many of your human crewmembers when they made mistakes. They would have been brutally punished, possibly even executed by many other captains, why would you do this?"

Again, the giant shrugged, "To kill them would have been a waste of a valuable resource."

"A valuable resource, or a valuable person?" Jesus pressed.

Gorsk hated this digging into his character. He had always been deeply ashamed of the compassion he had held for others; it was not a characteristic nephilim valued. Instead, it was a source of shame.

This time Christ did not push for an answer and instead spoke again, "Would you like to be free of the dark, Gorsk?"

"Free? In what sense? I don't understand." The nephil stammered.

"The nephilim genetic makeup is an abomination Gorsk. It was never intended for elohim and humans to mix their seed and the combination results in a twisted soul that is irredeemable. Your soul is largely human however, with your elohim genetics mainly manifesting in your physical appearance. I can cleanse you of the elohim side of your being and leave you fully human."

Gorsk was stunned that such a thing could be possible. He looked at his massive six fingered hands and imagined them missing a finger, they were just hands though. It was his spirit that concerned him more, and the constant battle he fought within himself to try and be as much a nephil as his kin, whilst always knowing that he was something else. He had always felt more affinity to the humans in his charge, and now he knew why. The decision was not a difficult one for him. "I would like that."

Jesus raised a hand to Gorsk's bowed head and the giant recoiled slightly, expecting that what was about to transpire in his body would be excruciatingly painful, but instead he felt like a knot untying and with each loosening a sense of peace and release. He hadn't realised to what extent his being was twisted and malformed. It was over sooner than expected and Gorsk looked down to see the flesh on his hands was softer and he indeed now only had five fingers on each. He raised a hand to his head and ran it through thick, soft hair which covered a smooth cranium, free of the horny nodules he had previously had. He ran his tongue around his mouth and over a single row of smooth teeth. He felt softer, but also strong. He arms, legs and chest were still a mass of muscle but now he felt like he had reserves of energy he couldn't access before. He felt a sudden urge to run. He also realised that he had only diminished in size slightly, for a human he was gigantic. He recognised that his Creator was standing in front of him still, and he dropped to his knees in front of Christ.

"You are free now Gorsk, to choose who you will serve, whether yourself or a new master." Jesus offered him.

"I will serve and follow you all the days of my life Lord, whether I live for a year or for all eternity my GOD, I will follow you."

Jesus smiled, "Then you are Gorsk no longer. I name you Titus Strong, both strong in arm and strong in spirit." He looked at the blank wall where the one-way glass was and grinned meaningfully, "Uri'el will show you around your new home."

Titus looked at the wall confused, and then looked back at Jesus, but He had left the room, leaving the door wide open behind him.

*

Cray Ironheart soaked in a warm bath, the first he had ever experienced. On the side of the large bath was an empty bowl which had been full of fruit but now contained only a grape shoot that had been completely stripped of its bounty. Cray couldn't stop examining himself, when he had woken up after his first morning in New Jerusalem, he had woken up a new man, literally. He was a good foot taller than his previous 5ft11 and he was well muscled. All of the scars he had collected from working on the treacherous factory floor were gone and even the callouses on his hands had disappeared. He felt energised like someone had plugged him into a battery and there was no sign of the little aches and pains that had seemed to riddle his abused body before. He got out of the bath and stood under a large skylight, brushing the larger droplets of water from himself and allowing the warm light emanating from the throne of GOD at the centre of New Jerusalem to dry his skin. Once dry he padded out of the bathroom into the bedroom where he had spent the night before in the most comfortable soft bed imaginable. He could never before have conceived of such comforts existing before his arrival here. He quickly dressed himself in some cotton garments he found in a cupboard and went through to a sumptuous living area containing seating for himself and possible guests and a modest but well-equipped kitchen. It wasn't the mansion that many residents of New Jerusalem enjoyed but it was more than Cray could ever have wished for. He walked out of his apartment onto a wide balcony and looked out onto a magnificent vista. The apartment he had been given was in the centre of a beautiful bustling city and from where he stood, he could see more people than he ever thought could exist waving to each other, holding conversations and going about their business. Hover cars zipped here and there and below him a pair of people were being carried through a garden on the backs of large brown animals which appeared so totally alien to Cray that he was a little frightened at the sight.

The door of the apartment next door opened and a blonde man with short, cropped hair came out and stood at the balcony. He was slightly shorter than Cray but still nearly 7ft, he was also slenderer and didn't have Cray's broad shoulders, though he still possessed a strong athletic frame. The man noticed Cray and nodded in acknowledgment of his presence and then turned to enjoy the view, but moments later turned back and examined Cray more closely. Cray studied him back, there was something oddly familiar about him.

"Bolts?" the man asked.

"Shorty?" Cray replied.

Both men laughed, "So that's what you've labelled me in your mind all these years, I did wonder." Shorty said with a grin, "I suppose it was appropriate, at the time."

"It certainly isn't now." Cray grinned. "I suppose 'Bolts' describes my old life pretty well. My actual name, now that we can give them, is Cray Ironheart."

"I know, I heard the malak on the station give it to you." The other man grinned, "My name is Lance Keen."

"Lance Keen, I like that, short and to the point, excuse the pun." Cray jested. He realised he hadn't had reason to make a jest in, well, ever really.

"So, here we are in Paradise." Lance observed, looking out over the bustling city. The city was busy, but not with people going to 9-5 jobs, but with people meeting for drinks, talking in the gold paved streets or working at jobs they loved. The paving stones weren't actually solid gold, that would have been deadly in the rain, but rather they were of stone with gold seams running through which glittered in the light emanating from the Temple. Much of what was going on below was beyond the experience of the two ex-slaves and it was fascinating but hard to take in.

"What do we do now?" Cray wondered aloud.

"Well, I was told we can have just about any job we choose, or we can just enjoy ourselves for a time. The malak who dropped me at the apartment said balance is important for true fullness of joy, whatever that is." Lance explained.

"Fullness of joy sure sounds good." Cray responded, "I know which job I'd like to do already."

"Oh?" Lance was surprised Cray could have seen something so quickly, "What's that then?"

Cray's voice was full of excitement, "You know that malak from the station, the one who saved us?"

"Do you mean Meto'el?"

"Yeah." Cray continued, his face displaying a fierce determination, "I want his job. I want to save people."

"We'd better go looking for him." Lance suggested.

Cray thought briefly, "We should, but there's someone else I need to find first."

*

A being that had no interest whatsoever in saving anyone but himself was Emperor Kraan. He paced up and down his throne room, his attendants watching his every move nervously.

"Three colonies in one day, three!" he kept repeating.

Even Giska shrivelled at his ferocity, "We will stop the loyalists my Lord, one advantage of having less ground to cover is that we can concentrate our forces in the remaining systems and discourage more attacks."

Kraan stared at him in disbelief, "You dare to try and paint my losses as gains?" He looked about exasperated as if trying to decide what to do, "You!" he pointed at his shedim admiral, "What is their largest ship?"

The shedim had been placed on the spot and took a moment to respond, "The *Judah* class battleships my lord."

"Then build ships that are bigger!" Kraan roared, causing his attendants to share nervous knowing looks with each other.

A Grigori coughed to gain Kraan's attention and when he made eye contact, he nervously added, "We already have bigger ships my lord, it's not the size…"

"Then what is it?" Kraan interrupted.

"If I may," Giska interjected, "it is not the size of the ships but rather the poorer quality of the materials, inferior skill employed in the design of them, poorer quality human stock for the crews and much more. We can simply not realistically be expected to field better ships and crew than Heaven itself."

Kraan was about to go into another rant but managed to stop himself as he realised his chief attendant was entirely correct and no amount of motivating his minions through violence could change that. Instead, he changed tack, "Then we will bury them in bodies. Build cheap disposable ships and fill them with the workers, guards and administrators. Throw everything at Heaven that we can muster until blood runs down the walls of the Holy City in rivers!"

Giska sighed, this was not at all what he had in mind. "Perhaps something a little more subtle is called for my lord. I have an idea that would require substantial resources but would only require technology we already have and if it succeeds, would decimate New Jerusalem."

Lord Kraan was about to dismiss the idea out of hand, because it was not his own and he suspected Giska of ambition beyond his station, but his hatred for Heaven overwhelmed his dislike for his chief attendant and he forced himself to listen to his odious advisor. At the end of Giska's explanation, he was glad that he did.

*

Becca couldn't stop tapping her foot. She had washed herself and had taken ages to get dressed due to spending far too much time marvelling over her new body, which was larger, fitter and stronger than her old. Now though, her thoughts had gone back to her main concern, the babies. Three of them were hers and she was desperate to know that they were all safe. She knew she'd never know which were hers, but if all the babies were safe then she knew that hers would be as well. She had been placed in a comfortable lodge a little way outside a large city. It was part of a complex that contained many other similar dwellings in a beautiful, wooded environment. The plants had of course held her attention for some time as well. Paradise was indeed well named, but like her physical transformation, their importance paled in comparison to her worry over the children. Then there was a knock on the door, and she ran over to see who it was, hoping it was someone with news regarding the children. She opened the door to find that it was none other than Christ Himself. She immediately fell to her knees.

"Please, stand up Becca." He pleaded with her and reached down, placing his hands gently on her shoulders. "I have brought you something."

"Is it another flora?" she asked.

He laughed, "I think you will enjoy this gift far more than the rose plant I gave you." He stepped to one side and three redeemed women walked past Him into the home, each of them bringing with them a young child, one of whom was only about six months old.

"Becca, I'd like you to meet your children." Jesus smiled.

The newly redeemed woman stared in disbelief at a young boy who clearly had her eyes, a feisty looking little girl who had the same kind eyes as Cray and a little bald head poking out from a blanket to look around the room. Once she had recovered her senses, she reached for the baby, "May I?" she requested eagerly.

"Of course, he's your son." the woman responded with a kindly smile.

The next couple of hours were the most joyful of Becca's life as she began the first few tentative steps towards forming a bond with her children. She was provided with everything she would need in order to make a home for the children, everything except a father figure, although her Lord promised He would be visiting regularly.

Later that evening long after Jesus and the women had left there was another knock on the door and Becca opened it to find a handsome redeemed man stood there. She didn't recognise him at first and was about to ask who he was when she looked into his eyes and realised.

Cray had knocked on three doors before this one but although the woman in front of him was now in redeemed form, he knew he'd finally found the right house immediately. He couldn't believe how stunningly beautiful her transformation had been, although in all honesty he had thought her quite pleasing to look upon before, "May I come in?" he asked. She stood to one side in implicit welcome and he stepped across the threshold. "I wanted to introduce myself to you. My name is Cray, Cray Ironheart."

She smiled at him, "I am pleased to finally make your acquaintance Cray, I am Becca Gentle." He was beautiful for a man she thought as she led him towards the sofa.

"That's a lovely name." he complemented her awkwardly. He suddenly could not remember any of the many things that he had carefully planned to say to her and instead sat in silence like a fool looking anywhere except at her. He was frightened if he looked at her, he would see something in her eyes he didn't want to see. He carried a deep hope in his heart that this beautiful woman would grant him access to a life he could hitherto had not even have imagined and he was terrified of being rejected and denied that access.

In Cray, Becca saw a good, strong, handsome man who might provide a good role model for her growing children. Also, she had liked the feeling of his strong arms around her and wanted him in her life but couldn't think of any reason why he would want to stay and be involved in her new little family rather than embracing the excitement that New Jerusalem might have to offer a free spirit. They sat in silence for a few awkward moments until suddenly the obvious occurred to her, "Would you like to meet our daughter?"

*

The following day, Cray and Lance set out on their mission to find Meto'el, though Cray was somewhat distracted thinking on the events of the night before. The hand had been waving in front of his face for a few moments before he realised it was there and looked up.

"You disappeared again." Lance laughed, "That must have been some night you had last night."

Cray smiled, "It was, I can't tell you how it feels to meet your child. The other children are wonderful too, and Becca is…well." He tapered off as he became lost for words.

"Are you thinking you might not have time for the marines?" Lance asked anxiously.

Cray looked surprised and then shook his head, "No, nothing like that. I'm determined to join the marines if they will permit it. I do feel a responsibility towards Becca and the children though and I'm going to have to make room for both somehow."

Lance shook his head wonderingly, "I don't know how you're going to do it. I wouldn't even begin to know how to be a father. It wasn't a skill anyone bothered to teach us on Frixar."

Cray laughed, "Do you think I have any clue? I'm going to learn though, one way or the other."

"Perhaps there's something to be learnt from GOD about fatherhood. We're told He's our Father after all." Lance suggested.

Cray grinned widely, "That's a great idea, I'll get hold of one of these manuals that we've been told about. I bet there's something in there about it."

"Manual?" Lance queried, "Oh, you mean a bible?"

"Yes, one of those, a bible!" Cray seized upon the word like he'd just won it in a competition.

"I have a couple at home that I was given yesterday." Lance assured him, "Now that we have that settled, can we focus on finding Meto'el?" Lance grinned.

"Sorry." Cray offered, "I will try to get my head back on track."

They looked about the plaza they had found themselves in trying to discern if anyone about them looked like the type of person who might know where they would find a malakim commander. Most of the people walking past looked like they were simply enjoying themselves and those that weren't were employed in activities far removed from combat. A man had handed them each a food stuff he had called a 'hot dog'. He had taken lengths to explain it wasn't like the hot dogs they had on Earth and the two had attempted to explain that they weren't from Earth but that they were grateful for the food anyway. The man had looked at them blankly in disbelief, unable to imagine where else they could be from. New Jerusalem had only been in place over Earth for a couple of weeks at this point and everyone was still adjusting to their new circumstances. Very few people were aware that there was life beyond the Sol system, that although there was no alien life, that humans had been born and had died without ever setting foot on the beautiful planet created for them, all thanks to the treachery of fallen elohim.

"We need to find somewhere to sit and think about this." Cray commented after they had been walking in circles for a while.

"How about there?" Lance pointed to a collection of tables in a small, paved area surrounded by trees covered in blossoms. Some people were already sat at some of the tables eating food and having drinks. It was an idyllic scene that the two men couldn't have possibly imagined a few days earlier.

Cray nodded keenly, their mission could wait till later he supposed, and the area looked so inviting. The two found a table next to that of a man who was engrossed in something on a large data pad in front of him. He was drinking a dark beverage from a ceramic cup which looked quite intriguing to the two ex-slaves. After looking about for a few minutes and seeing no obvious way for them to acquire drinks for themselves, Cray decided to ask the busy man. "I'm sorry, I hate to interrupt you, but we were wondering what that drink is, and how we could get some for ourselves."

The man looked up from what he was doing and smiled, he was good looking even by redeemed standards, with dark wavy hair and strong cheekbones. "It's just a black coffee." He said, as if they should immediately know what a black coffee was, "You can ask that fabricator over there to make you one each." He pointed at a plinth amongst the trees that contained a device of some kind, totally foreign to Cray.

"Er, thanks." Cray responded and the man smiled again and nodded, immediately turning his attention back to whatever it was he was busy doing on his data pad.

Cray and Lance walked over to the fabricator and looked for buttons but saw none.

"What do we do now?" Lance pondered.

Cray tried to think, "He said to ask it to make us black coffee."

As he said the words 'black coffee' a compartment in the machine began to glow and a cup exactly like the one the man had been using shimmered into being. An instant later the dark beverage appeared inside it. The two men stared at the drink as if it was going to jump out of the machine and attack them. Eventually Lance reached forward and put his hand on the cup but upon touching it immediately pulled it back, "It's hot." He commented.

"Perhaps you're supposed to drink it hot?" Cray wondered. The only thing either of them had ever drank before was room temperature water. The idea of a hot beverage was totally foreign to them. Cray reached out and poked the cup, it was warm but not to such a degree that he wouldn't be able to hold it he thought. He grabbed the handle tentatively and pulled the cup out of the machine.

Lance looked at him and Cray shrugged so he leaned close to the machine and carefully phrased the words, "Black coffee." He was rewarded by another cup of coffee rapidly formed in the compartment. He reached over and took the drink, carefully cradling it in his hands as if it were incredibly fragile.

A thought occurred to Cray and he approached the fabricator again, "Spanner." He instructed it.

A voice emanated from somewhere inside the machine causing the men to jump, Lance spilled hot coffee on the back his hand and glared at Cray, "What size spanner would you like?" the fabricator asked him.

Cray didn't require a particular size spanner, he had just wanted to test the machine's capabilities, but still the answer was obvious to him.

"10mm?" he asked tentatively.

The shimmering appeared again and a basic 10mm spanner materialised in the compartment.

"What did you do that for?" Lance asked his friend. "Have you seen anything at all around here that needs fixing?"

Cray shrugged and grinned, "I just wanted to test it. Besides, if there's one thing I learnt from ship building, it's that you can never have too many 10mm spanners." He shoved the spanner in his trouser pocket, quite pleased with himself.

Lance shook his head at his friend's dubious logic and laughed. They made their way back to the table near the wavy-haired man who was looking over at them interestedly, "Did I hear you say you were ship builders?"

Lance looked at Cray and they both shrugged at each other, "I guess so, I wouldn't say it was a profession exactly. We were forced to it as slaves."

"Slaves? That explains a lot then. Did you two come in with the refugees we've all been hearing about from the outer systems?" the man guessed. "People haven't stopped talking about it."

"I would think that's us. I couldn't say for sure if we're who you're referring to? We were rescued by a group of powerful beings called malakim who were in what they called the Royal Navy, do you know of it?" Cray inquired hopefully.

"Know of it? I work for it. I'm going to be designing ships for the Royal Navy, here's something I was messing around on last night." The man turned his data pad around and showed Cray and Lance a picture of a sleek vessel, far more elegant than anything the two men had worked on.

"This is you just messing around? That's incredible, far better looking than the blocky frigates we used to build." Lance commented.

"Well thanks." The man blushed a little, "My intention is for it to be a stealth ship, for carrying the marines on covert missions. I imagine it having the ability to bend light around itself, giving it the ability to hide to some extent."

"And Heaven has the technology to do that?" Cray asked him.

The man shrugged in reply, "I don't know for sure yet, but have you seen this place? It doesn't seem like anything is impossible here."

It seemed more than coincidence that they had met this particular person when they had been looking for the navy and Cray wondered if God was somehow involved. He'd been quickly learning about his God and about someone called the Holy Spirit who seemed to be able to facilitate this kind of thing.

"Sorry, I'm forgetting my manners. I haven't gotten your names." their new acquaintance smiled.

"Oh, we're still getting used to the name thing." Cray replied, "I'm Cray Ironheart and this is Lance Keen."

"Those are good names. Pleased to meet you Cray and Lance, my name is Jonathan Sharp, but you can call me Jonny."

"Sharp, that's an interesting name." Cray commented, "Everyone here seems to have been given their name by the Lord because of some aspect of their character."

"And I'm no different." Jonny grinned, "the Lord said He gave me this name because of my sharp mind."

"Well, that stands to reason, given that you design star ships that appear to be far beyond what our side came up with despite thousands of years of development." Lance pointed out.

Jonny blushed again, "I'm sure you've realised by now that when the Lord created our new bodies, it also included far more acute cognitive abilities. Just about anyone in New Jerusalem could do what I do if they set their mind to it, I'm doing it because it's what I'm passionate about."

Cray had indeed noticed he was far quicker of mind than he had been in the past, but he hadn't had the opportunity to test his enhanced cognitive function to any great extent.

"We're looking for someone in the navy called Meto'el." Lance interjected. "I don't suppose you know him?"

Jonny looked thoughtful for a moment, "The name doesn't sound familiar, but there are millions of malakim and its impossible to remember each one. We can go to the navy yard where I signed on and start asking around. If he's high ranking, someone will know of him."

Cray and Lance grinned at each other. Their mission to become marines had taken a step forward.

*

Meto'el meanwhile, was conferring with Micha'el and a number of other high ranking malakim on the subject of the marines that very moment.

"I am in favour of admitting humans to the ranks, it has always been the Lord's way to have humans involved in everything so that they can learn and grow. The navy provides a plethora of growth opportunities." a veteran marine named Tedra'el offered the conversation.

The archangel Gabri'el provided a counter, "I am not so sure the Lord wants mankind placed in mortal danger at this point in their journey. Does the word not say there is no death, no pain in Heaven?"

"There will still be no permanent death, any marine killed in duty would have their soul translated back to New Jerusalem and instantly resurrected in a new body." Uri'el reminded them.

A lower ranked but highly respected malak named Orgo'el presented a question to the group, "Why has the Lord not made this decision Himself and simply instructed us what to do?"

"Because He doesn't want to impose this on us against our will for one thing, it is too big a change to the way we have been doing things for millennia to simply push it on us." Micha'el explained, "For another thing, He believes that in the deciding we will learn and grow, much like He is intending for the humans."

There were mutters of assent to this from around the room, those gathered were well acquainted with God's abiding emphasis on personal growth by now.

An orb flitted into the room and manifested as an angel, "I apologise for the interruption, but there are two humans here to see Meto'el. They say they know him."

All faces turned to Meto'el as if he would have an explanation, but he did not, "Did they say what they wanted?"

"They want to join the marines apparently." the messenger informed them.

There was a chuckle from Uri'el and smiles from most of the malakim who had been in favour of humans joining the ranks.

Gabri'el sighed, "I can see where this is going."

*

Cray and Lance sat in a beautifully decorated foyer area waiting to see if their request to see Meto'el would bear any fruit. There was no part of New Jerusalem where care had not been taken to create a peaceful and pleasant atmosphere, even in the military installations. There was no attitude of rationing resources and limiting expenditure as resources were unlimited.

Meto'el recognised the two men immediately when he came in, despite the physical changes they had undergone upon becoming redeemed. He had seen the results of humans receiving their new bodies enough times to recognise the remnants shining through. The two men stood as he entered, and he was about to motion them to sit down when he realised that standing to a superior officer was probably a good start for what he had in mind. He addressed the two men, "Cray Ironheart, and…"

"Lance Keen." Cray said in introduction of his friend, "He was with me on Frixar, the closest thing to a friend it was possible to have."

"And you have come because…" Meto'el continued. He knew of course, but he wanted to hear how they expressed their goal themselves. Their motives were a crucial factor.

"We want to do what you do. What you were doing when you freed our people." Lance blurted out excitedly.

Cray's response was slightly more considered, "There must be many more like us out there who haven't had the opportunity we were granted to find a way to Paradise. We want to play a part in them having that opportunity."

Meto'el nodded and stared down at the for a moment that seemed like an eternity to the two men, then abruptly announced, "Welcome to the marines, gentlemen, your training begins now."

And the eleven disciples went into Galilee, to the mountain where Jesus had appointed them. And when they saw Him, they worshiped Him. But some doubted. And Jesus came and spoke to them, saying, "All authority is given to Me in Heaven and in earth. Therefore, go and teach all nations, baptizing them in the name of the Father and of the Son and of the Holy Spirit, teaching them to observe all things, whatever I commanded you. And behold, I am with you all the days until the end of the world. Amen."

Matthew 28: 16-20

Five

The Pillabis system was about as far away from Sol as could be achieved within the expanse of Kraan's empire. Because of its dying star it had never been colonised by the fallen but Kraan laid claim to it due to all surrounding systems being under his sway.

An elegantly designed space yacht came out of a window within 1000 clicks of the system's sun. Following the smaller ship through the window came a massive slab-sided craft festooned with huge cranes, outsize tools on the ends of robot arms and various other construction devices designed for the swift building of space stations.

On board the smaller ship, Giska gazed upon the roiling mass of hot gas and plasma that constituted the system's sun. He opened a communication channel to the captain of the larger vessel. "You may start here captain; this is where our work begins and where the interference of the Tyrant will be brought to an end."

"We will begin immediately my lord." The construction ship's captain replied and the larger vessel began unloading canisters of building materials which were immediately set upon by the ship's robot arms. As it worked, more windows began to open, and cargo vessels arrived to deposit their loads of metal sheeting, piping and huge coils of thick electrical wire. The materials were corralled into a storage area close enough to the construction area to be easily accessible but not so close as to be in the path of the work. A projector was placed near the construction ship which, when activated, created a holographic image of a huge steel ring which would act as a template for the first stage of construction.

Giska watched the process in fascination and filled with an obscene sense of pride at the thought that his project might be pivotal in the final breaking away of the rebel elohim from the will of their Creator. He looked again at the sun and smiled at the irony that it could prove to be instrumental in their war against the very Person who had placed it there. Eventually he tired of watching and ordered the yacht's captain to set course to Obelis, Kraan's homeworld. He would return regularly to check on progress, but for now he had to secure access to more slaves, there was much to be done still aside from the actual construction to ensure that this project reached completion.

*

Many light years away, a window opened into a system called Hobar and a sleek 100ft vessel came through the portal. It had no obvious offensive capability and bore the name *Hope* along the side.

"That's the outpost." Men'el stated, pointing out a shining dot in the distance through the cockpit canopy.

Ward was stood behind the pilot chair looking over his malak friend's shoulder, "And you say they're not part of a fallen elohim faction?" he asked.

"They're a small group of independents, operating from an abandoned fallen space station. I can't guarantee they'll be friendly, but they are at least all human." Men'el confirmed.

Stella came up behind them, "How is it that they haven't been pulled back into an empire by a Watcher? The elohim must have expended substantial resources either bringing them out here or breeding them."

Men'el explained, "Their original warlord is gone, his empire wiped out by a competing warlord. The new warlord doesn't even know these humans are here. They've been surviving by scavenging wrecks and other abandoned outposts."

"There's a ship incoming." Ward pointed to a blip on the scanner screen."

"Take over Ward." Men'el instructed and orbed from view.

The screen flickered and the face of a ragged looking human appeared, sat on the bridge of what appeared to be an old freighter. "You're trespassing." he challenged Ward brusquely.

"We don't mean you any harm, we brought you some supplies." Ward explained.

"What supplies? From where?" the man countered. "We aren't expecting any supplies. Who are you?"

Ward tried to keep any tone of challenge from his voice, "We've come on a mission of mercy from New Jerusalem. We bring good food and water. Also, some medical supplies."

The man appeared to be caught off guard and took a moment to think, "Give me a minute." he finally replied, and the communication was terminated.

"He's probably gone to ask someone what he should do." Stella suggested.

"You're probably right, I doubt they've ever had to deal with anything like us out here before. Ah, here we go..." Ward said as the man's face came back on the screen.

"You can follow me in." he instructed the redeemed pair.

"My thanks." Ward replied and ended the transmission, "Well, here goes nothing." he commented to Stella as he settled into the pilot chair and turned the ship after the now retreating old freighter.

"You do realise they're going to try and take our ship. I assume that old hulk is the best one they have." Stella pointed out.

Ward nodded his agreement, "We've thought of that, this ship requires a redeemed genetic code to operate. Also, I'm sure Men'el is more than capable of fending off any hijack attempts."

Stella nodded, "Oh, I'm sure he is, I'm just as impressed with him as you are, but he's only one malak."

"Well, if the worst comes to the worst, we'll lose the ship and our lives and get reborn back in New Jerusalem into new bodies. At least we'll be able to say we tried." Ward offered. Stella simply looked at him without comment with a glare that said she thought he was mad. He knew that look well and decided to focus his attention back on his flight controls.

As the space station drew closer Ward wondered how it could possibly support life. There were gaping holes in the structure and pieces of it were only held to the station by trailing wires. The freighter docked in a hangar bay in one of the larger intact sections and Ward followed it in, landing the craft carefully in a bay next to the fallen craft.

He and Stella descended the landing ramp to find a ragtag group of around ten fallen men and women stood pointing weapons or various kinds in their direction.

"I believe you have some food and water on that ship?" a man who appeared to be their leader asked abruptly.

"We do indeed." Ward answered, "And medical supplies."

The man turned to a gaunt woman next to him and they grinned at each other, "Well you see, here's the thing." he continued with a nasty grin, "We have nothing to give you in trade for your cargo, but we're going to have to take it anyway."

"That's okay." Ward answered, "We weren't asking anything for them, they are a gift."

The fallen leader had obviously been caught off guard by this and stumbled over a reply, "No-one gives anything away for free in this galaxy. What do you want?"

Ward smiled, "We want you to listen to what we have to tell you, and then we'll leave."

"And what if we take your ship? How are you going to leave then?" the man laughed, obviously glad to be back in his comfort zone of being a threatening presence.

Stella was quick to reply, "Well, then we won't be able to come back with more supplies at a later date."

The man looked at the redeemed woman who, even wearing a flight suit, was the most beautiful he had ever laid eyes on, "And what if I decide to take you, good looking?"

Stella laughed, "Well, for one thing, I'm fitter than you are, so I'd like to see you try." She was correct in this, as a redeemed woman she was a little over 6ft tall and possessed the physical abilities that came with a perfect physique. She would likely be more than a match for the man if it came to a fight.

"And for another thing," Ward interjected, "he's much bigger than you are." Ward pointed behind the group of fallen. They turned around to find the massive 8ft1 figure of Men'el standing behind them brandishing a large pulse cannon. He took one hand off the weapon to wave and smiled at them meaningfully.

The leader of the group coughed, "I was joking of course, I have no intention of harming the woman."

"You fool, Moss." a woman from the group with short cropped red hair and a scar across her cheek growled. Lowering her weapon, she stepped forward, "Can we talk about the food? We'll let you tell us what you came to say, if we can just have a meal."

Ward smiled at her warmly, "We have enough aboard to last a group your size for at least a month, and you are more than welcome to it." He stepped aside and indicated up the ramp with one arm, "The stores are in a loading area just at the top of that ramp."

A couple of the fallen men looked at each other and then ran past Ward and Stella up the ramp. Moments later a call came down, "Moss, you've got to see this!"

The man called Moss walked cautiously past the two missionaries, scowling as he did, and up the ramp as one of the men came running down with a crate full of apples," Have you ever seen anything like these before?"

Moss reached into the crate and pulled out an apple, he looked dubiously at it and then took a tentative bite. Ward couldn't stifle the laugh that came at the look of pleasant surprise that appeared on the man's face and he turned back to the other fallen with a wide smile, "Please, go and help yourselves."

Soon, the weapons had all been put down as the fallen people started filing in and out of the ship with wares of every kind.

"Hey! There's a power generator!" a man cried.

The woman who had chided Moss looked at Ward questioningly, "That's for you as well." he confirmed.

She smiled and nodded, "Bring it down Loff, they said it's ours!" she called out. "My name is Bree by the way."

"Pleased to meet you Bree, I am Ward, and this is Stella. The big guy over there is Men'el." Ward answered.

They were in a loading bay which had mostly been filled with empty crates when they had arrived, but now piles of food, water canisters and other supplies were being piled high. The fallen began to sit down and avail themselves of food that they couldn't have imagined existed. Men'el, who had been watching with his gun trained from a distance, let his guard drop a little and walked up to where Ward and Stella were observing the proceedings.

"So far I'd say it's a success." Ward suggested.

"Hmm." the malak grumbled, "Back on Earth I saw many a missionary attacked and killed after achieving almost exactly what you just have. Don't be overconfident."

"We'll be careful." Stella assured him.

Bree called to them, "You said you wanted to tell us something." She looked meaningfully around at the other fallen who were happily taking their fill of the food, "I think you've earned that much."

Ward stood up and a number of the fallen turned their eyes to him as he stepped forward, he coughed to hide his nervousness and tried to remember the sermon he had spent the last week preparing. His mind was blank though and he decided to 'wing it'. "For years, centuries even, you've all been lied to. You've been told that the warlords, your gods, were heroes, rescuing their loyal populations of humans from the clutches of a mean violent tyrant. This so called tyrant, who calls Himself Yahweh, is no tyrant at all, but a loving benevolent Creator who wants nothing more than to have a relationship with you."

And so, Ward continued, telling his now enraptured audience about the love of GOD, the price of sin, and the wonderful redemptive power of Christ Jesus.

When he had done, Bree was the first to speak, "So what do you expect us to do now? How do we know you're telling us the truth?"

Ward had expected this response and had a plan, "I suggest I take one of you back to New Jerusalem with us, you can see for yourself what it is like and then come back with us and tell the others. Then you can each decide for yourselves if it's something you want to be a part of."

The fallen all looked dubiously at each other and from their body language it was clear who was going to be the guinea pig, "I'll come." Bree offered.

*

Back on New Jerusalem, Cray and Lance were in a training room with seven others learning how to do an inventory check. Most marine squads had ten marines, but thus far theirs only had nine for a reason that had yet to be revealed to them. They had been trainee marines for a month now, and it had been hard but satisfying. Their new bodies had been pushed to the limit and they were thrilled to find out just how much they were now capable of. The two men were checking the E6 suits which was the armour that had been created for human marines, activating each one to make sure it was operating withing acceptable parameters. They each consisted of a skin-tight black mesh which had pieces of moulded armour attached to it. Whilst being resilient, the materials constituting the suit itself were not the main protection though. The suit would detect incoming fire or a melee attack and raise an energy shield directed towards the threat. The E6 designation was a reference to Ephesians 6 in which the apostle Paul compares the Christian walk to wearing a suit of armour.

Meto'el came in followed by a hulking giant of a man even taller than the malak. He looked oddly familiar to Lance and Cray but neither of them could place him. "Razor Squad!" the malak called, instantly getting all of their attention, "It is my pleasure to finally introduce you to your 10th member. This is Titus Strong. Titus, meet Razor Squad."

Lance and Cray got up from where they were working to go over and greet their new colleague, but another marine named Rudi Fire who had paid close attention to recent events stood up and pointed at Titus, his hand shaking, "Nephil! He is that fallen captain Gorsk!"

The two men stopped in their tracks and took a second look at Titus, the sheer size of the man was an obvious major hint as to his origin but nothing else stood out as being instantly recognisable, it took some inspection but eventually, by mentally adding a few no longer present features, they could see the resemblance. Cray was still reluctant to condemn him however, the behaviour of the captain on Frixar had been reasonably honourable, for a nephilim.

"Marines, take heart." Meto'el declared, the words were of reassurance, but from the big malak commander they came out sounding like an order. "It is true that Titus was once Gorsk, a half-breed abomination, but he has been cleansed by the Lord Himself and he stands before you as human as any one of you."

"May I speak?" Titus asked in a deep rumbling voice that betrayed a little of his nephil past. Meto'el nodded, and the giant continued, "I was indeed the nephil, Gorsk, but I am no longer, and I have repented of that life just as you have all repented of your previous lives. I now live for the Lord and would die for Him if I must. If you are to be my brothers in arms then I would give my life to protect you also, this I swear."

There was a moment of silence which was finally broken by Cray who had decided he was willing to take a chance on the newly redeemed man, "Good enough for me. Welcome to Razor Squad Titus." He went up to Titus and offered out his hand, the 7ft marine had big hands but it still disappeared into Titus' as if Cray were a child. Cray noted that the man possessed only five fingers which he found somewhat reassuring as nephilim all possessed six.

"Thank you Cray Ironheart." the giant growled.

The smaller man reacted with shock, "You remember me?"

"How could I not? the huge man explained, "If it were not for your actions that day, I may have attacked Meto'el and his fine malakim marines and died in my sins. Instead, the intervention of you and your brave workers caused me pause and I was handed the opportunity to meet my Saviour. I owe you a great debt Ironheart."

Cray beamed at the thought that he had made a difference in someone's life so early in his walk with the Lord. That it had happened even before he knew his prayers had been answered made it all the more impactful.

"It is our hope," Meto'el interjected, his comments directed at the entire room, "That Titus will be a valuable addition to your squad and open possibilities that may otherwise have been unavailable."

"You mean like wrestling elephants?" a marine called Sarah Stead teased with a laugh. Some of the other marines broke into laughter at that point and the icy spell that had held sway over the room until that point seemed to be broken.

"I will leave you to become better acquainted," Meto'el said as he turned to leave, "tomorrow, you have weapons training."

*

Whilst Cray and Lance were getting to know the largest man on New Jerusalem, Becca was getting to know one of these smallest. She had named her youngest Joshua and was getting to grips with something called a 'nappy'. Such things had not existed on Frixar and babies simply slept on wipe clean mats. Becca's new velvet sofa was hardly wipe clean though and she had no intention of letting Joshua have his messy way with it. "Hold still." she instructed the flailing youngster as she struggled to figure out how to fold the corners in such a way that it could be pinned closed without coming loose or slipping off.

"Mummy?" came a small voice from behind her, and there was a pulling on her dress.

She looked down to see her middle child, who she had named Esther, looking up at her with those big eyes that reminded her so much of Cray. "What is it, Esther?" she asked as kindly as she could manage, given her current flustered state.

"Game?" the girl continued, her small voice tugging on Becca's heart strings relentlessly. She had played with Esther earlier and had inadvertently created an addict. There were no games on Frixar and playing was a new thing to both of them.

Becca knelt down to her, "I will come and play with you as soon as I'm done with Joshua's nappy, okay?"

"Now mummy." Esther complained.

Becca was tempted to be angry at the insistence, but she had been struggling with the nappy for nearly an hour at this point. She could understand how the patience of a two-year-old would have been stretched to breaking point. "Where is Matthew?" she asked of the little girl, referring to the older of the two brothers who was a little over three. "Couldn't you play with him until I'm finished?"

Becca shrugged, "He go out."

Oh no, what if he went and did something dangerous, Becca thought. Motherhood was a lot more complicated here than it was on Frixar where everything was strictly controlled. She couldn't leave Joshua and Esther to go looking for Matthew. What was she going to do? She was beginning to be jealous of Cray having gone to try and join the marines today; fighting nephilim warriors in the far corners of the galaxy would have to be easier than this.

Then there was a knock on the door. What now? Becca thought to herself, I can't take much more of this. She ran to the door and opened it to find a striking olive skinned, redeemed woman with extremely long dark hair stood there with Matthew perched on her hip.

"I think this might be yours." she smiled.

"Oh, thank you so much." Becca replied, taking her errant son from the woman's arms.

Matthew's rescuer took a quick look over Becca's shoulder, "You look like you could use a hand." Becca sighed and her slumped shoulders told the newcomer all she need to know, "Here, let me help." The woman declared confidently and went over to the table where Joshua was laid and started to inspect the nappy.

"Have you had many children?" Becca asked her.

"I think at last count it was about 110 billion." The woman laughed with an enigmatic wink, "Most of those are grandchildren, great grandchildren, great-great grandchildren and so on though." She lifted one corner of the nappy dubiously, "It's been a long time since I had my last though, I'm probably not going to do much better at this than you."

"Well, right now, any help I can get is better than no help at all. My name is Becca by the way." the relieved new mother declared.

The woman smiled warmly, "Well, I'm pleased to meet you Becca, my name is Eve."

*

The riots on Earth continued to escalate as preparations were made for King David to give his speech. Eventually, not only had Lewis and Tolkien joined his speech writing team, but also Billy Graham, John and Charles Wesley and the Apostle Paul. Although all the men made some contribution, for the most part they watched on in awe as Paul went to work. The man was clearly a genius on a level that was rarely encountered. Eventually they produced a document that they felt would be as convincing as could be realistically expected. It was generally felt by those in the room that the protests against GOD's rule would likely never completely end as it had ever been man's will to self-rule and to cater to his inherently sinful nature. Whilst the redeemed who had given their lives to the Lord had been given new bodies purged of any sinful nature, the denizens of Earth continued in bodies prone to temptation, albeit healthier and longer-lived than prior to the millennium. Paul argued that this was necessary as mankind had always been able to justify any action and was ever prone to blame anything but themselves. This was therefore the purpose of the millennium, to prove to mankind finally, with the Devil locked away in Tartarus and disease and poverty ended, that each person primarily had only themselves to blame for being separated from God and nothing else. As such, he deemed it likely that push-back against the will of God would continue to the end of the age and possibly even get worse as the millennium went on.

Paul, as in so many other things, was to be proven correct in this matter.

So it came to pass, that whilst King David's speech was heralded a masterpiece in the media and generally considered a success, only a small dent was made in the number of protests being held and in the days that followed, Gabri'el's malakim police forces were required to incarcerate an inordinate number of perpetrators for challenging the will of God.

Exacerbating the problem was a poisonous belief spreading amongst the world's population that dated back to the time of the tribulation when fallen elohim had actively attempted to introduce a great deception. There were secretive murmurings that Christ had not returned at all, but that the Earth was in fact being deceived into being ruled by an advanced race of malevolent aliens masquerading as Christ and his angels. In some circles, the Anti-Christ who had bodily perished in the tribulation and had been banished to Tartarus was in fact considered to be Earth's last hero who had died in a desperate last-ditch attempt to save the planet from captivity. When challenged about how comfortable life was under the rule of Christ, proponents of this worldview would simply explain that it was customary practice for conquerors throughout history to bring populations into submission by making them as comfortable as possible to encourage compliance.

And so, despite the advent of a paradise on Earth and long life because of Christ's return and direct intervention, there was active rebellion against His rule.

Therefore do not be ashamed of the testimony of our Lord, nor of me His prisoner, but share with me in the sufferings for the gospel according to the power of God, who has saved us and called us with a holy calling, not according to our works, but according to His own purpose and grace which was given to us in Christ Jesus before time began, but has now been revealed by the appearing of our Savior Jesus Christ, who has abolished death and brought life and immortality to light through the gospel, to which I was appointed a preacher, an apostle, and a teacher of the Gentiles.

2 Timothy 1: 8-11

Six

A few months after the mission to Hobar, Ward was feeling pleased with himself. There had been numerous mission trips since, and all of them had met with some success. Of the 10 fallen souls he had evangelised to on Hobar, six had chosen to follow Christ and that was a pattern that had repeated itself on other stations. Even when fallen didn't choose to follow Christ, they nearly always chose to live out their lives on Earth and so there was always a chance they could repent and choose to follow Christ before their souls were lost forever. Today he had been called to the navy yard where *Hope* was docked, and he wondered if it might be to discuss the successes of the last few months. When he arrived at the docks, he was approached by one of the higher ranking malakim, named Yara'el, who he had had limited dealings with when it had come to the acquisition of their ship. The malak was in the company of a beautiful, redeemed woman with long red hair.

"Greetings Charlie Warden, I am pleased to see you again." Yara'el greeted him warmly.

"I am honoured Yara'el, was it you who summoned me here?" Ward asked.

"It was, I believe you are already acquainted with my companion." the admiral stepped aside and motioned towards the red-haired woman with one arm.

"We have met." the woman confirmed in a slightly husky voice which Ward did think sounded vaguely familiar. He couldn't place her though.

"I'm sorry, I'm afraid you have me at a disadvantage." He stammered, embarrassed by his inability to remember this rather striking woman.

"It's me, Bree from Hobar, Ward. Bree Hopebringer now, as our Lord has suggested. You might remember me with somewhat shorter hair." she prompted him.

Ward couldn't believe his eyes, the woman from their first mission, "Oh my, how wonderful to see you here. I'm sorry, I just didn't recognise you now that you look so... different."

She laughed at his awkwardness, "It's okay, I look nothing like I did when you met me. For one thing, the scar down my cheek is gone."

Ward hadn't even noticed the scar the first time he had met her, but that was far from the only thing that had changed. "So, as happy as I am to make Bree's reacquaintance, I'm guessing that isn't the only reason you asked me to come here admiral?"

"It is in fact the very reason why I wanted you to come here. You see Charles Warden; Bree wishes to become the fourth member of the *Hope's* crew." Yara'el eagerly informed him.

"Oh." Ward didn't know what to say, he was completely taken aback. He didn't know what to think of the idea one way or another. He did know what Stella would think of having another woman on the team though. She would not be happy.

Yara'el continued, "Bree believes that she can offer you the benefit of being familiar with fallen culture and equipment."

Ward had to admit that would be useful, "Sorry, forgive my lack of response, I'm just in shock, that's all. I'm sure you'd be a valuable addition to the *Hope's* crew, Bree."

Bree canted her head as she detected his hesitation, "But?" she prompted him.

Ward stammered, "Well, as much as I am leaning towards giving you the opportunity to join us, I would want to talk to my wife first, she'd need to agree of course."

Yara'el raised one eyebrow, "Your what?"

"Oh, my ex-wife I mean." Ward was not handling this conversation well and he felt his face redden. Why was he making such a fool of himself?

Bree laughed, "Oh, now this I can understand. I made the boys check with me before any important decisions were made on the station as well. Go and talk to the boss, I can be patient."

Ward hadn't thought this conversation could have gotten any worse, and yet somehow it had. He almost went into an explanation as to how Stella wasn't his boss and that he was really the one in charge of the ship, but then wisely decided that he had dug the hole he was in deep enough.

*

Over the course of their first few months on New Jerusalem, Cray and Lance experienced things they could never have dreamt of previously. There was a heady mixture of enjoyment of life in the Holy City and all of the incredible new recreational and lifestyle choices that were on offer contrasted against the hard work of becoming competent marines. Their training was intense but not in the gruelling manner that life on Frixar had been. They had learnt to use pulse rifles and pulse pistols effectively, shock lances which were the primary counter to the large nephilim opponents they would face, and the iconic spirit swords imbued by the Holy Spirit Himself that would not work against the redeemed but would cut through anything else as if it were water. Aside from combat skills, they were now well versed in strategy and history. No stone had been left unturned in the pursuit of creating a well-rounded force to resist the fallen. Because of their enhanced redeemed physique, senses and cognitive abilities they learnt quickly and by the end of a few months of intense training they felt that they were ready for their first mission.

Over the course of their training the two men had developed friendships with many of the other marines, particularly the giant Titus who had become a fixture in their small clique. Mark Bastion proved to be worthy of his name and was reliable and steadfast, emerging as the most capable of the group and being assigned commander. Susan Stead was the only female marine and showed an ability to come up with creative ways around problems. Adedayo Ireti had shown himself to be prayerful and the most likely to consider spiritual warfare as a first option. Vincenzo Roccia was the deadliest shot in the group and had a wicked sense of humour, he had been a crack musketeer in the 19th century and found using a pulse rifle to be elementary in comparison. Alex Runner was a determined individual who would never give up and refused to consider any hurdle insurmountable. Lee Masters was Alex's best friend and tended to be the one to cool Alex down when he was about to run in half-cocked. Finally, making up the ten, there was Rudi Fire who was the squad's engineer and a master of both electronics and explosives, slightly nervous in disposition but able to counter it with an unshakable faith in God.

Cray and Lance were currently in one of New Jerusalem's extensive parks watching Titus attempting to catch a buffalo. Buffalo had been large on Earth, but recreated buffalo were of prehistoric proportions. Whilst it looked like he was not going to be able to keep up with the beast at first, the giant managed to leap forwards and grab onto a horn with one hand. The startled animal turned its head to try and shake him off, but Titus was determined and after throwing him around in a circle the former nephil managed to get his other hand over onto the opposite horn. Within moments the man had dug his heels in and brought the beast to halt, both panting from the exertion.

A grinning Lance turned to Cray, "You owe me a beer."

Titus wearily walked over to the two men and pointed a massive finger at Cray, his face breaking into a wide smile, "That's what you get for betting against Titus Strong, little man."

Cray laughed and held his hands up in defeat, "I owe you a beer Lance, and you a keg, big man."

It was rather easy to promise such things in New Jerusalem as all it really meant was that Cray would be the one to go up to a fabricator and request the items and then receive them for free. Alternatively, beer or other food/drink items could be acquired from someone at a market who had a passion for making them from scratch, and there was greater pleasure to be had from enjoying such a product. Even those didn't have to be paid for though, people worked for the enjoyment or satisfaction of it rather than for resources like money. Money didn't make any sense in a society where no one wanted for anything.

Their happy huddle was broken up by the sudden appearance of a portal a short distance from them, Sarah Stead's head poked through it, "Come on boys, stop mucking about with cows, we're off on our first mission!"

*

Becca looked at the clock on the wall, she couldn't believe that Cray hadn't come back from his outing with the boys yet. He was supposed to be taking Esther out for a walk and she was getting grumpy.

"Mummy? Where's daddy?" she asked for what was quite possibly the ninth time.

"Only he knows." Becca muttered to herself.

Over the last few months Becca had become fast friends with Eve and the woman seemed to have developed an extraordinary sense for knowing when Becca needed her. Almost on cue, the knock on the door came and Becca went over to open it. As expected, Eve was stood there and this time she had a huge man with long black curly hair stood behind her. Aside from Cray's friend, Titus, he was the biggest man Becca had ever seen.

"Hello Becca." Eve beamed and turned to the man behind her, "I brought someone with me, he'd like to meet the kids."

"Oh." Becca wasn't sure how to respond to this, "Matthew!" she shouted behind her. The boy came running and Esther appeared next to her magically as she always did when one of the others was called.

"Aunt Eve has someone to introduce you to." she explained to the children. They both looked up at the massive muscular man dubiously.

The giant smiled and then knelt to meet the children on their level, although even then, he towered over them. "Hello children, my name is Samson. Mother Eve has told me all about you and I thought perhaps you'd like to come for a ride on Honey with me."

"What's a Honey?" Esther asked.

"You can't ride on Honey, you eat honey, silly!" Matthew chastised Samson.

"Oh no? Perhaps you'd like to tell Honey you want to eat him?" Samson laughed. He turned and held an arm out and a giant cave lion came out from behind some nearby bushes and nuzzled against the huge man's hand. It was large enough for Samson to ride, let alone the children. "Honey, these children have something to tell you." The giant man said into the monstrous cat's ear.

The lion was in fact the same storied one Samson had killed when it attacked him, though it was now in restored form like everything else on New Jerusalem, rendering it larger and stronger. It had been gifted to Samson by Christ when they had first encountered each other in Heaven. The two had quickly become inseparable and were never seen apart.

"Erm, I'm not sure about this." Becca muttered anxiously.

"Oh, don't worry about Honey. He's already been fed." Samson smiled, completely failing to reassure Becca with this information.

"Why is he called honey? Does he eat honey?" Matthew inquired innocently.

"No, but he loves peanut butter." came the reply.

The children looked at each other, their eyes wide. "Please. Please. Please Mummy?" they asked in unison.

Becca looked to Eve for reassurance, "Honey will be good with them." the woman promised, "And don't forget, this is Heaven. What can go wrong?"

My children could be swallowed by a giant monster, Becca thought to herself. By this point both children were tugging on her arms as if intending to pull them off and then start smacking her with them, "Ok , you can go." she relented reluctantly, "But if either of you gets eaten, you'll be in big trouble!"

There were shrieks of joy and the children ran forward and promptly disappeared into the giant cat's mane as if it were a dense forest.

"Do not worry Becca, I will take good care of your babies." Samson reassured her.

"You'd better." Becca countered, "You might be the biggest man I've ever seen, but I can still make you cry, I have ways!"

This earned her a laugh from the legendary Israelite hero, and he turned to give his full attention to the kids while Eve ushered Becca back into the house, "I think you need a rest."

Becca nodded wearily as the two went into the house, "Tell me Eve, if I kill Cray when he gets here, is that still considered a sin in Heaven, even if he really deserves it?"

*

The massive metal ring being constructed in the Pillabis system had a radius of 50 miles. It had taken months of hard labour by a huge proportion of Kraan's subjects to get it as near to completion as it was. The resources required had been prodigious and had practically bankrupted the empire. Around the ring at regular points were integrated space stations where ships could dock, and which acted as hubs for the construction activity. The ship moved to a docking bay attached to one of these and slid through the hangar shield, alighting on the hangar floor inside amongst an assortment of other vessels of various shapes and size.

The station's shedim supervisor anxiously waited, flanked by two nephil guards clad in armour as the ramp of the ship slowly came down. An honour guard of the station's security detail had also been prepared and they stood in a line to one side of the hangar. Once the end of the ramp touched the floor a few tense moments passed before finally someone descended. A Grigori in an elegant red robe strode quickly down the ramp followed by two Nephilim warriors and what appeared to be a gaggle of administrators carrying data pads. They were looking about and writing notes even before they reached the bottom of the ramp.

"It is an honour to receive you, Chief Attendant," the station supervisor declared with a bow as the Grigori reached him.

"Let's dispense with the formalities, supervisor." Giska hissed. "I am here to inspect your progress, not to have my arse licked."

"We've made good progress Chief Attendant." The supervisor stammered as Giska swept past him and on into the facility. "As you will have seen on your way in, the gate is nearing ..."

Giska was unconvinced and expressed this by interrupting the supervisor, "But what of the weapons? Without them the gate is just the universe's most expensive piece of jewellery."

The supervisor hastened up a corridor after the chief attendant who appeared to be very sure of where he was going, "The weapons are working but obviously they have never been fired directly at the sun, so it is impossible to say if they will perform exactly as intended."

Giska turned on the supervisor, "When that gate opens, we will have bare moments to compel that sun to supernova before the Royal Navy realises the danger to New Jerusalem and damages the generators enough to close it. You had better be more than certain it will work supervisor, or I will make sure that before the gate closes that you are on the other side of it."

The shedim gulped, being trapped in the Sol system would be sure to result in banishment. "All the tests have given positive results my lord."

The Grigori scoffed dismissively, "Your lack of vision troubles me supervisor, small scale toys that result in the destruction of abandoned stations do not interest those of us who crave real power. We are going to destroy Heaven itself and forever tip the balance of power in favour of our cause. Make me a weapon that can achieve that supervisor, that is all."

Giska continued towards the power generators that sat beneath one of the gargantuan beam cannons pointed directly at the sun, keen to establish that the frequency fluctuations he had recorded last time had been addressed.

*

In one of New Jerusalem's massive hangars, Jonny Sharp was making some notes on a data pad and was so engrossed that the three men managed to come up behind him undetected despite one of them being over 9ft tall.

"I can't believe it looks so much like the one you showed us." Cray commented as they drew alongside the busy engineer.

Jonny muttered something in acknowledgment and made a couple more adjustments on his screen before casually glancing to one side to see who was addressing him. "Waah!" he yelled, nearly dropping the data pad in shock as he caught sight of the massive Titus.

"Don't worry, he's one of us." Lance laughed.

"Who is this *us*?" Jonny teased, "Last time I checked, I wasn't a titan!"

"He's a marine, like us, is what I meant." Lance explained.

119

Jonny didn't look convinced, "Well, keep him off the furniture. I don't have anything that can take his weight."

"Your ship is most impressive." Titus rumbled.

Jonny glanced up at the object in question. The four men were stood in one of New Jerusalem's many gigantic hangars. The ship in front of them was dwarfed by the other ships in the hangar but was still an impressive sight. It was approximately 150m long, placing it in the class of fast frigate. It was sleeker than most frigates, being flat and wide rather than high. The nose was square and narrow, and it widened towards the back where a single but very large shunt engine exhaust suggested it was capable of some speed. Two large wings extended from the rear of the ship, merging with two smaller canard type wings closer towards the nose. It had two short stubby twin tails towards the rear containing two of the window generators, the other two of which were in the ends of the wings. The cumulative effect was to make it look more like a large fighter than a small capital ship.

"Does it have a name yet?" Lance asked.

"This one is called *Wings of the Wind.* It's more of less a prototype for a new class of ship called the *Whisper* class." Jonny explained.

"Who is the captain?" Cray wondered aloud.

"At this stage, all the officers are still going to be malakim until the humans finish training and have more experience." Jonny replied. "At least that's what I've been told."

"I suppose if they've been doing it for millennia and we've only been doing it for a few months, it does make sense." Lance offered.

"I could captain it in my sleep." Titus muttered, "But, I somehow doubt Heaven is going to give me my own ship just yet." He added with a wry smile.

A pair of malakim emerged from the ship, walked down its long ramp and made their way towards the four men. They were clearly officers, though Cray couldn't have said how it was he could tell since they weren't dressed differently to the other malakim, though one of them was in armour whilst the other was not. Perhaps it was the way they carried themselves. He guessed the one in armour was a marine commander and the other one of the bridge crew.

"Greetings." the unarmoured malak addressed them as he drew close, "I am Yara'el, temporary captain of the *Wings of the Wind*. This is Eret'el, commander of the *Wind's* marine complement.

"I am guessing you are my missing marines." Eret'el looked at a data pad in his hand, "Cray Ironheart, Lance Keen and Titus Strong." The men nodded as he read their names off. "You'd better get inside, find the armoury and get into your E6 suits."

"Are we expecting action, sir?" Lance enthusiastically asked.

Eret'el looked up from his data pad and studied the man, "I can see why you are called 'Keen', it is most appropriate. We are always ready for action marine, whether there is any on this mission or not, remains to be seen."

Lance nodded nervously and made a mental note not to come across as an overexcitable child next time.

"And you must be Jonathan Sharp." Yara'el said, turning to the ship designer.

"I erm, I am." Jonny said, a little surprised to be included in a conversation centred around the *Wind's* crew.

"Your uniform isn't as crucial strategically speaking." the malak continued, "However, I do like my officers to set a good example for the crew. You will find a suitable unform in the armoury."

"But I..." Jonny was confused, he had simply designed the ship. Of course, he had fantasised about being on the crew, but he had never entertained the thought that he might actually be permitted to do so.

Yara'el's face softened slightly, "Whilst building this ship, you studied elements of stealth strategy in order to make sure the ship would be suitable for the role? Yes?"

Jonathan had in fact spent many evenings going over texts on the subject. "I did yes, but…"

"And before deciding which weapons to equip the ship with," Yara'el continued, "you studied the weaknesses of the various classes of fallen ships, working out how best you could optimise the Whisper class to exploit those weaknesses, yes?"

Jonathan just nodded helplessly this time; resistance was clearly futile.

"You even specified what skills the crew members should have and how those skills would be best used." the malak appeared to finish his diatribe and stared at the perplexed Jonny for a moment before finishing. "I could list more but we do not have the time. Suffice to say that there is no-one else more qualified to be on the bridge crew than you. I understand you still want to design ships, and maybe in a few years you'll create another, but for now you need to get into your uniform."

Jonny grinned and ran to catch up with the marines who were halfway to the ship by now.

Be brave when you face your enemies. Your courage will show them that they are going to be destroyed, and it will show you that you will be saved. God will make all of this happen, and he has blessed you. Not only do you have faith in Christ, but you suffer for him. You saw me suffer, and you still hear about my troubles. Now you must suffer in the same way.

Philippians 1: 28-30

Seven

Wings of the Wind came out of a spatial window into a four-planet star system dominated by a red giant. The arrival of the ship by window into a system was when it was at its least stealthy. Most ships could detect a window opening unless there was a planetary body in the way and there was no way to mask the signature of a tear in space.

"What do you suggest first Mr Sharp?" Yara'el asked Jonathan as they stood looking at the alien system on the monitor.

"I think we should go into stealth mode until we can establish that we weren't detected." the newly minted officer replied. As instructed, he had visited the armoury and was now dressed in the smart white uniform of a navy commander. Yara'el had designated him the ship's first officer but had assured him that it was only temporary which came as a relief, he wasn't confident in the role and would be far happier starting small and working his way up the ranks.

"Excellent, I believe that is a wise decision. Give the order if you would." The malak captain replied.

Jonathan knew the procedure; he had scripted it after all. As he rattled off the orders, the bridge crew replied with confirmations that his orders had been carried out:

"Lock down ship's hangar." he began.

"Check."

"Pulse engine to 10%."

"Check."

"Activate noise dampeners."

"Check."

"Activate skin."

"Check."

This last command meant that the hull of the ship would now begin to absorb light instead of reflecting it and would display images of any stars or other spatial features behind it onto its surface so that any ship watching wouldn't see a black shadow blotting out the view.

Finally, Sharp activated the internal comm, "Ship wide alert. We are black. Repeat, we are black."

All aboard the ship had been trained to know that this meant they were in stealth mode and that movement and noise were to be kept to a minimum. The noise dampeners were active, but it was always unwise to over rely on technology.

Jonathan turned to Yara'el as the lights in the bridge changed from bright white to a pale blue, indicating that they were in stealth mode. "We need some way to check it is working. Perhaps one of the malakim could go out and observe from space."

"Or we could use them to test it for us." Yara'el nodded his head at a ship approaching on the monitor that Jonathan had been entirely oblivious to.

It was a fallen cruiser, a vessel more than twice the size of their frigate and faster. It might have been an elegant ship, having a long neck ending in a nacelle out front and a wider main hull behind with wings extending from it. It wasn't though, as the hull, unlike that of the Wings of the Wind, was anything but sleek. It was covered in blocky protuberances which probably held sensors or similar and no effort had been made to streamline the design of the gun turrets which were placed at regular points of the hull. Whilst not beautiful, it looked deadly, and Sharp didn't doubt that it would make short work of their ship if it attacked. He watched in horror as the ship drew ever nearer and then stopped less than a mile off their prow. A mile was no distance at all in space, and Jonathan knew that they would be well within range of every weapon on the other ship. The crew of the *Wings of the Wind* watched with bated breath, waiting to see what the cruiser would do.

"This is the location your eminence." a human sensor operator informed the captain of the *Rites of Pain.*

"You had better be right, food." a nephil overseer with a whip in one hand informed the man.

"I assure you; this is where the window was." The man's back already bore a welt from an earlier mistake, and he was not eager to make any more today.

The shedim captain of the vessel, Kratos, stared at the monitor screen which showed only open space. "It was probably loyalist scum from Sol. They must have picked us up on their sensors and scurried back to safety away from the scary monsters."

The first officer, Riks, also a shedim, appeared a little concerned at this, "Scary monsters captain?"

"Us, you fool! Us!" Kratos cursed his poor luck for having a first officer who could survive for centuries and yet still present as a fool. He was about to order the ship back to their routine patrol, but he felt an unease. "Riks, have you ever been near one of the redeemed?"

Riks shrugged, "Centuries ago I encountered descendants of Abraham, I came to the stars before their Christ appeared though."

Kratos nodded in acknowledgement, "I have encountered the so-called Christians before. They exude a stench, like a disturbing of the spiritual balance of the universe. Can you not feel that now Riks?"

Riks' eyes glanced from side to side as if he would spot a believer lurking in a corner of the bridge and he tried to imagine a feeling of unease but couldn't. "I feel nothing, sir."

Kratos shrugged and pointed a taloned finger at the pilot, "Take us back to our patrol route." he ordered.

Jonathan released the breath he had been holding as the fallen cruiser turned away from them, "Praise the Lord, that was close."

Yara'el turned to him, "What do you think will happen when that cruiser captain is told that another window has been opened in a similar location to the first?"

Jonathan thought for a few moments, "He will return, but he will find nothing again."

"And?"

Jonathan wasn't sure what the malak was wanting him to answer but then it came to him, "He will guess that there was a ship here all along."

Yara'el smiled, "Exactly, and he will report it. Which may not cause any due concern, or it may be a seed that contributes towards the eventual discovery of our stealth technology."

"So..." Jonathan feared what the malak was about to suggest.

"So now would be a good time to practice a boarding operation. Take us under that ship helmsman." Yara'el instructed the pilot. The man immediately obeyed and the distance between the two ships began to close again.

"Steady as she goes Will, we don't want them to detect our pulse engine signature. Keep it under 10%."

The pilot nodded as he concentrated. Yara'el allowed a wry smile of approval to cross his face.

Jonathan activated the comm again, "This is Sharp, prepare for a boarding action. This is not a drill."

On the deck below, the marines immediately sprang into action.

"Are they serious?" Lance muttered as he checked all of his equipment for the third time.

"I reckon so." Cray replied, his voice betraying an eagerness he hadn't expected to feel when this time came. He was looking forward to striking a blow back against his former abusers.

"To the shuttle, humans. Malakim, with me." Eret'el ordered the marines. He orbed and shot through a nearby bulkhead, quickly followed by his malakim warriors, leaving his sub-commander, Mark Bastion to take over the human half of the marines.

Ten human marines and ten malakim didn't seem like much to take over a whole fallen cruiser, Cray thought to himself. It would have to go like clockwork to succeed. Briefly Cray wondered if Yara'el knew what he was doing, but then he'd never met a malak who didn't so he was prepared to give him the benefit of the doubt, for now. The marines made their way to the shuttle bay, the sleek craft were stealthy like their mother ship and were designed to slip quietly inside the shields of enemy vessels without alarming their crew. Once inside they would clamp themselves to an airlock, or failing that, part of the hull and burn a hole inside with plasma jets. Once that process started, there was no way to hide the intrusion and so it needed to happen quickly to avoid there being a very unwelcoming welcome party on the other side.

The shuttle bay was smaller than those aboard other Royal Navy vessels as the Whisper class had no fighter complement, carrying only two shuttles in a single hangar. It was not cramped however, and the marines had plenty of room to form themselves up into two orderly lines on the hangar floor before filing up the ramp into the shuttle.

After a brief conversation between Mark Bastion and the pilot, the shuttle lifted itself from the floor of the hangar and moved out through the shield, carefully maintaining the same speed as the fallen cruiser which loomed fearfully large above them. From this distance the pilot could see clearly pockmarks and scars on the older ship's surface from decades, or possibly even centuries of service. The best place for an insertion had been identified and the pilot directed the small craft towards it. There was a panel on the port side of the cruiser which had been an airlock at some point in the ship's past but had been sealed over. The shuttle came alongside it and there was a thud as magnetic clamps locked the two ships together. The plasma cutters embedded into hull of the shuttle went into action, cutting inside the magnetic seal.

On the bridge of the cruiser, an alarm sounded.

"We have a hull breach sir, on deck three." a technical station operator reported.

Captain Kratos scowled at the news and glared at Riks, "I knew there was something suspicious about that window event. Send troops to that location immediately."

Riks nodded fearfully and thumbed a comm button on his uniform, "Urga, take a squad to deck three, we may have boarders." There was no reply. He repeated the message to no avail and tried another name. "Innvagh." he was flustered now, and it came across in his voice.

"This is Innvagh." came the response.

Riks breathed a sigh of relief, "Get some guards, go to deck three and see what's going on." There was a grunt from the comm, and it went dead. Nephilim were not conversationalists.

On deck three, Eret'el stood over the dead body of the nephil Urga and watched through the open airlock inner door as the makeshift panel to the interior dropped into the ship with a clang. Mark Bastion jumped out of the shuttle and approached him down the ramp, followed closely by his marines. "We'll split into two groups, one this way and one that." Eret'el indicated with waving motions of one arm. Select five of your marines to come with me, I have selected five malakim to follow you.

Mark nodded and picked out Cray, Lance, Titus, Sarah and Vincenzo to go with Eret'el. He took the remainder and the five malakim and headed toward the stern of the enemy vessel.

Eret'el quickly assessed the five marines he had been given. "You are to provide fire support while my malakim range ahead and fill the assault role." he instructed, finding the nods he received in return to be a satisfactory indication that his order had been understood. The marines stepped over the huge body of Urga and a couple of human troops that had been with him and headed towards the bow of the ship and presumably its bridge.

Cray had spent all of his life in fallen structures, but never on one of the fighting vessels and he was disappointed to find that it was no better maintained than the facility at Frixar. There were exposed pipes and wires and here and there steam hissed from failing seals. After having been inside a few Royal Navy vessels which were pristine, he had thought perhaps that it was necessary to maintain a space going vessel to such a standard.

Next to him, Lance brushed a cluster of wires hanging from the ceiling out of his face and yelped as one of them gave him a slight shock, "Yowch!" he exclaimed, "I didn't realise how much I do not miss the good old days. Remind me why we're not sunning ourselves on a New Jerusalem beach right now?"

Cray knew that Lance hadn't forgotten the answer to that question but answered anyway, "Because there are others like us on board this ship that should be granted the same opportunity to sun themselves on a New Jerusalem beach."

Eret'el turned and put his finger to his mouth and the entire squad instantly fell silent. They had reached a junction and there were sounds from a corridor to the right. Three of the malakim orbed and disappeared into the wall whilst Eret'el and the other malak adopted a defensive stance in the corridor. Behind them, the five humans crouched and raised their pulse rifles at the corner, awaiting the order to fire.

It was a group of 7 humans being led by a nephil in heavy armour who were approaching the corner, and the giant raised the alarm as soon as he caught sight of the two malakim. Chaos suddenly erupted in the corridor.

"Rawr!" the ogre yelled and charged straight at Eret'el, drawing a huge, short-handled axe from its belt as it did so. "I will sever your wretched loyalist head from your puny loyalist body, malak scum."

The malak with Eret'el, an elegant fighter named Seta'el, lunged at the giant, but was swatted aside by a sweep of the ogre's left arm. The marines opened fire with their pulse rifles and wherever they hit the beast, the blue glowing balls of energy left black burns but the giant nephil didn't appear troubled by them.

They were sounds of a commotion from around the corner and Cray realised that the three malakim who had orbed through the wall had probably engaged the rest of the squad from behind. A fallen human appeared, walking backwards with his weapon firing in the other direction, his attention on the attack from behind and the marines quickly switched fire to him, dropping him instantly. Their weapons were on a low setting, the intention being that they would be able to revive any fallen humans and hopefully convince them to accept Christ. Titus Strong stepped forward within melee distance of the engaged nephil warrior with his spirit sword drawn. This forced the nephil to move to counter the new threat and he raised his arm enough to create an opening for Eret'el to thrust his own sword through the beast's armour and into its beast. The monster squealed in pain like a wounded boar and raised its axe in an attempt at a crushing blow but Seta'el pivoted in behind and severed the massive limb with a flick of his sword arm. There was another roar as the beast reacted to the new pain, but this was short lived as Eret'el brought his sword back around to sever the creature's head. Another couple of fallen humans came around the corner but at the sight of the two angels and the massive Titus stood over their dead nephil commander, they dropped their weapons and raised their hands. The remaining three human combatants around the corner quickly followed suit.

Eret'el indicated to a malak called Himlar'el, "Watch these men brother." he ordered, prompting a nod. At 8.4 feet the malak was slightly bigger than most Heavenly warriors and would be more than capable of managing the five captives. The men looked thoroughly beaten and were unlikely to be inspired to attack their intimidating looking captor at any rate. Cray wished he could stay and talk to the men, but he had a job to perform first. Hopefully he would get his opportunity in due course, he was itching to share with someone of the hope he had found in Christ.

Their next obstacle lay at the entrance to the bridge. The corridor widened before the double doors to the bridge creating a large open area. A makeshift barricade had been placed across the doors behind which a cluster of fallen humans had entrenched themselves. As soon as Eret'el and his squad came within sight of the men, the rebels opened fire with a heavy machine gun. The clatter of the weapon's mechanism and the boom of the rounds going off was deafening in the confined surroundings. Cray was shocked at the unfettered use of such a large kinetic weapon on board a space faring vessel. It would only take one of those rounds penetrating the outer hull to wreak havoc and possibly even result in the ship's destruction. It was an effective strategy at pinning the marines down though and they were temporarily stymied in their progress. Whilst their E6 armour could absorb the energy from small calibre kinetic weapons, the high rate of fire and heavy slugs of the machine gun would probably overwhelm their personal force fields.

Eret'el quickly formulated a strategy and turned to the humans, intending to take advantage of one of the strengths that humans possessed, "You must pray for me humans, pray that Yahweh will grant me strength."

This was more in Adedayo's field of expertise and Cray found himself wishing their African born colleague hadn't gone with the other squad, but he nodded, and the five marines bend their heads to pray. They prayed fervently and confidently that the Lord would fill their malak leader with strength and protect him. As they prayed, Eret'el's skin and armour began to glow, making him look like a large powerful living light bulb. The malak steeled himself and ran around the corner, instantly drawing the fire of the machine gunner. Bullets streaked at the malak but as they passed through the glowing field around the angelic being, the bullets simply melted and only fragments of slag metal hit the malak's armour. The marine commander rolled and as he did, let fly a pair of pulse grenades he had released from clips attached to his belt. The grenades bounded off the bridge doors and came to rest behind the barricade at the feet of the four fallen humans. One of them panicked and made to run whilst the others turned in dismay, when the two devices went off in a blue cloud of pure energy, one after the other. The men were knocked back by the concussive blasts and in the next moment lay sprawled around their now silenced weapon. Eret'el stood to his feet and was soon joined by the other marines. All that remained now was the bridge itself.

"We breach in 10." Eret'el ordered. The malakim all orbed into their semi-physical forms and the humans made use of the barricade to set up a firing line facing into the bridge. When 10 seconds had passed, the malakim passed through the bulkheads.

There were a few tense moments for the humans as the faint sounds of fighting came through the and they sat at the ready, impotent to help. Then suddenly the faint sounds turned into a cacophony as the doors opened with a clank and the swish of hydraulics in action and bullet came whipping out at them from a defender who had set up at the front of the bridge. There were two shedim who were clearly in command, five humans and three drones defending the bridge, mostly armed with pistols. Another human lay on the floor either unconscious or dead. The two shedim were trying to fight off the five malakim with their jagged dark red swords, but they were clearly outmatched. The human marines opened fire on the other bridge crew and made short work of them.

"This ship will not be yours, loyalist filth." Kratos scowled as he thumbed a button on a device, he had clenched in his left fist moments before he succumbed to a sword thrust from one of the angelic warriors.

"Was that the self-destruct?" a malak named Finn'el asked Eret'el.

The commander nodded grimly just as his comm went off. He activated it and the voice of Mark Bastion came through, "Engineering is ours."

"Any sign of a self-destruct sequence having begun commander?" Eret'el hastily threw back.

There was a brief pause as sounds of the other squad discussing something among themselves came through the comm, "Private Fire says it was the first thing he disabled, why? Did they try to activate it?"

There were relieved laughs from the marines on the bridge, Eret'el replied into the comm by way of confirmation, "You can tell Private Fire that he just made Corporal, Mark. We're not done yet though, there will be stragglers aboard that we need to mop up. Most likely humans and drones for the most part but still potentially dangerous. Post a few guards in engineering and conduct a sweep of the aft section if you would Commander." Bastion acknowledged the order and ended the communication. Eret'el turned to his marines, Finn'el, Stead and I will hold the bridge. The rest of you sweep the fore section of the ship for remnant of the crew, take particular care with the gun emplacements, there will be a crew member in each one. Sometimes there is a nephil overseer keeping them on their toes.

Cray and the others nodded and went off to search the ship. Finn'el noticed a flashing on one of the consoles and went to see what it was. "Hmm," he noted as he read the information, "We have a number of escape pods ejecting."

"Notify *Wings of the Wind*, though their sensors will undoubtedly have picked them up already." The malak commander replied.

Cray and other marines assigned sweeping duty were going through the ship room by room. The team headed down a passageway flanked by steel doors which they duly checked. At one point they passed a dead-end corridor which they went past but then Cray, who was bringing up the rear, noticed a door set in one side of the corridor, partly hidden to anyone looking from the main throughfare by a steel pipe. Cray looked at the marines disappearing up the passageway and decided, against protocol to quickly check the door on his own. He edged around the pipe and tried the handle of the door which moved easily enough but the door refused to move, as if something was blocking it from the other side. He shoved it again and it gave a little, so he kicked it with his foot.

At this point, Lance noticed Cray was missing and then heard the noises from back down the corridor. He turned back to investigate.

The door eventually gave, and Cray fell into a small storage room containing three fallen humans who immediately set on him with knives. Cray had been surprised and was lucky at first that his E6 suit's shields blocked the first few blows. He began to counter attacks as they came in using his rifle but apart from striking out with the butt occasionally, he was unable to do any real damage to his assailants despite his superior strength. The attackers were reasonably large for fallen human males, all being within the 6ft range but were undernourished and individually no match for Cray's 7ft2 body which was in peak fitness. Cray was outnumbered though and couldn't get to his sword without risking opening himself to a flank attack. It was all he could do to fight the three men off as it was. Every now and then one of them would get a blow through and weaken his shield. It was only a matter of time before the shield failed and the next strike to get through his flailing defence caused some damage. Suddenly he saw an opening though and one of the men stumbled in his attack, blocking the other two temporarily. Cray brought his rifle butt down hard on the man's back and he slumped to the floor unconscious. Now the fight was even, but at that point, Lance burst into the room with a pulse pistol drawn and the odds swung massively in the marines' favour; drastically more so when the head of Titus Strong appeared over Lance's shoulder. The two fallen men realised their predicament and stopped their attack, raising their hands in defeat, their knives dropping to the metal floor with the clatter of steel meeting steel.

"It's okay." Cray reassured them, "We're not here to harm you."

Lance chimed in, "Yeah, we were where you are a few months ago. Believe me, it's a lot better on this side."

The two men glanced at each other, unconvinced and one of them spoke out, "You serve the Tyrant. How could that possibly be an improvement."

Titus laughed in his deep nephil-like voice causing one of the men to shrink back in fear, "You've been lied to my friend, there is no Tyrant, only a loving God who genuinely wants the best for His people. It's the small gods you've been serving who are the tyrants. Look at these two men here and ask yourself if they look mistreated to you."

Again, the two men looked at each other, one of them shrugged as if to indicate that the giant had a point.

"Look," Lance continued, "you may not necessarily want to do what we're doing. But if you choose to come with us quietly and listen to what we have to say, you could be living in Paradise this time tomorrow. Your pain could be over."

Cray reached into his pocket and the two men looked at him warily, "I just want to show you something." He drew out a small data pad, flicked his finger up the screen and showed it to face the two men. On it was a picture of the street in the New Jerusalem city where Cray had his apartment. It was a wide, clean, bright, tree lined walkway with people happily milling about in gardens and sharing food and drink with each other. "This is where I live. I did nothing to deserve it, it was freely given to me when I gave my life over to Christ, the one your gods call the Tyrant." One of the men reached out and Cray let him take the data pad. The two men pored over it for a few moments and the looks on their faces told Cray that he had won them over. They handed the device back to the marine and he saw the look of hope in their eyes.

"Bring your friend." Lance told them. "I'm sure he won't hold it against you if he wakes up there."

The two marines stepped out of the room with the two fallen men behind them, their unconscious colleague draped between them. Titus reached for the man as they came out and put him gently over one of his shoulders. The rest of the squad was waiting in the main passageway, having been alerted to their absence by this time. One of the malakim with them, named Vell'el, who Cray considered to be friendly for a malak was the first to speak, "If you're finished with your little evangelistic crusade, shall we continue?" He smiled widely at the three men, clearly pleased with their actions.

The marines continued their search of the vessel, finding little of interest and no further opposition when they came across a large, locked door. It appeared to be protected by a code elected to go through and see if he could open it from the inside. Vell'el offered to reconnoitre and disappeared through the wall.

"Are we sure we want to see what's inside? What if it's full of man-eating giants?" Lance muttered as the malak disappeared through a wall.

"No problem, I'll just push you in and run away." Cray teased.

"I can run faster than you, remember." Lance retorted with a grin.

One of the freed slaves spoke up, "There were two nephilim aboard, both big evil bastards who'd eat you as soon as speak to you."

"Hmm, we've encountered them both then. You won't need to worry about them anymore." Cray assured them, earning himself a grin from one in return.

The other wasn't quite as convinced of his safety though, "What about him?" he asked, clearly meaning Titus.

"Oh, I only eat men on weekends and public holidays. Today is a weekday and I'm clearly at work so it can't be a public holiday." The giant grinned and winked.

"He's kidding." Cray explained and punched the giant playfully in the stomach.

Titus feigned pain and rubbed his belly with his free hand. "You'll make me throw up the last human I ate if you keep that up." This earned him a nervous laugh from one of their new friends. Cray rolled his eyes at the big man. The interaction had the desired effect as the slaves seemed reassured by the fact that Cray hadn't immediately been dismembered which would have been the usual result from striking a nephil.

The door then opened with a hiss to reveal a smiling Vell'el. "Please come in and don't forget to wipe your feet." the angelic warrior quipped.

A malak with a sense of humour? Here was something Cray could appreciate, he might try and spend more time around Vell'el. They stepped into a large, cavernous dark space that appeared to contain a large number of misshapen lumps of metal. One of the malakim flicked a switch and large overhead lamps came on, illuminating what now became evident as pieces of a destroyed space craft.

"It looks like a fallen freighter." Lance commented.

"We destroyed it in a one-sided battle a couple of days ago. The captain said it belonged to an enemy warlord and was fair pickings." one of the formers slaves explained.

Cray nodded and looked over at another malak near him, one called Wann'el, "Do you think we can find out which warlord?"

The malak nodded, "If you think it could prove important." He pointed at a large chunk of debris dominated by a cracked glass canopy, "That looks like part of the bridge, perhaps you could find a working console."

Having been a fallen slave most of his life, Cray did have some experience with fallen tech, and it did make him an ideal candidate to try and navigate the system he realised. Though he didn't doubt that a malak could have figured it out, nothing seemed beyond them. He got the distinct impression that they were holding back on their abilities in an effort to get the humans to develop their own. Perhaps they had even been ordered to do so. Titus carefully put his human cargo down on the floor and the three marines wandered over to the debris, "Give me a hand up?" Cray asked the giant as they reached a severed section of corridor, a few feet off the ground. Titus grabbed Cray by the back of his harness and practically threw him into the ship. A second later, Lance landed in a heap next to him, somewhat ungracefully.

"See if there's anything up there that I can read." Titus instructed the two. Of course, Cray realised, having been an ex-captain in the fallen forces it would make sense to have Titus examine any data they could lay their hands on.

Cray and Lance hunted through the ship attempting to switch on any equipment they came across, but most of it lacked power.

"Take a look at this." Lance called, prompting Cray to come up behind him. The smaller man was holding a data tablet which still seemed to have some battery power. It flickered into life and showed a manifest and some nav details.

"Let's have Titus look at it." Cray suggested to a nod from Lance. They clambered down from the vessel to where the big man waited expectantly and handed him the tablet.

Titus eagerly grasped the data pad in one big hand but found it was too delicate for his large fingers. "You'll have to go through the screens for me."

Lance smiled as finally he had found an advantage to being smaller and began to flick through the screens.

"Stop there." Titus instructed him, and then, "Go back one." As Lance went too far ahead. When the correct screen was found Titus read down it, "It appears they were hauling parts for a large construction project to a remote system here." he pointed to coordinates at the bottom of a missive.

"Can you figure out what the project was?" Cray wondered.

"It's not entirely clear, but this delivery was numbered 2403507. If the project required millions of deliveries, it must be immense." Titus concluded.

"Or perhaps they just have a continuous number system that hasn't been updated in centuries." Lance wondered.

"That would be rather foolish and unlikely." Titus answered, "Mortals come and go, and systems evolve with new management. My guess is that millions of deliveries have gone to this star system within the space of a short time."

"It sounds like it's worth taking this to command." Lance concluded.

Cray nodded "We'll let Eret'el decide I think?"

The other two agreed and Titus popped the data pad into an oversized pocket in his uniform's harness.

Within a few hours the operation was wrapped up and the two ships readied themselves for the trip back to new Jerusalem. Being the larger of the two vessels, the fallen cruiser crewed by a skeleton crew of malakim would make the window back to New Jerusalem and the *Wings of the Wind* would follow it through.

On board the Royal Navy Frigate Yara'el and Jonathan were conducting a debriefing with the marine commanders on the bridge.

"How many escape pods did we pick up?" Eret'el asked the frigate officers.

Jonathan looked to Yara'el who simply waited for the human to take the lead in the debrief, "There were 15 pods in all, all containing human occupants who were of a mind to surrender. They're in with the people you brought back with you. We haven't had any trouble from them."

Eret'el did some quick maths, "So that makes for 57 captives overall. Quite a small crew for a cruiser."

Mark Bastion sighed, "We lost some as casualties unfortunately. Whilst we used stun settings on the rifles, it's hard to keep fatalities to absolutely zero in a combat scenario."

Eret'el placed a reassuring hand on the man's shoulder, "Don't take it too hard, they may not be entirely lost. The Lord has His ways."

Mark Bastion wasn't sure to what the malak referred exactly, but he nodded and tried to take solace in the words.

"What about the nephil spirits?" Jonathan asked. He was referring to fact that when nephilim or drones occupied by nephil spirits died, the spirits were not drawn into a resting place like mortal men and wandered free as demons.

"Most of them have been rounded up and banished to the abyss but a few always slip through the net." Yara'el answered flatly. He would have preferred all of the errant demons had been dealt with as they would undoubtedly cause mischief, but it was what it was and there was no sense in agonising over it.

"And the two shedim officers you encountered on the bridge?" Mark Bastion wondered.

"Banished. They'll be spending the rest of the millennium in Tartarus." Eret'el explained with a note of sadness in his voice. Jonathan wasn't surprised at the tone, the shedim had once been Eret'el's brothers before their fall after all. The malak may even have known them once, the fact that they'd been on opposite sides for millennia could never completely change that.

Fear not, for I am with you; Be not dismayed, for I am your God. I will strengthen you, yes, I will help you, I will uphold you with My righteous right hand.' Behold, all those who were incensed against you Shall be ashamed and disgraced; They shall be as nothing, and those who strive with you shall perish. You shall seek them and not find them, those who contended with you. Those who war against you shall be as nothing, as a non-existent thing. For I, the Lord your God, will hold your right hand, saying to you, 'Fear not, I will help you.'

Isaiah 41: 10-13

Eight

Little did Cray know that his greatest challenge of the day still lay ahead. As he came down the ramp of *Wings of the Wind* he was greeted by a rather angry looking Becca. He realised in that moment that he had completely forgotten to take Esther for her walk in his excitement at getting his first mission. He ran over to her, "I'm so sorry. We were sent out on our first mission."

"Yes, I found out from one of the dock administrators, you huge doofuss." she punched him in the shoulder.

"I was supposed to take Esther out." he muttered pathetically.

"Never mind that, she'll survive, I was worried you'd get hurt. At the very least I could have been praying for you. Next time you have a mission you tell me first." She raised a hand tenderly to his cheek, "You are okay, aren't you?"

He blushed, "Yes, I'm fine. Where are the children?"

"Adam and Eve are watching them." she answered, "They said something about going fruit picking."

"Fruit picking?" Cray repeated raising an eyebrow, "Those two don't exactly have the best track record when it comes to picking fruit you know."

Becca giggled, "I'm sure they won't get the kids into any trouble."

"As long as there are no serpents involved, I'm sure they'll be okay." Cray laughed.

"We have some time to ourselves." She pointed out.

He grinned widely, "Let's not waste any time then, may I suggest a boat ride and lunch?"

Becca beamed, "That sounds wonderful."

The next few days were restful for all the newly redeemed. They settled back to enjoy their lives in New Jerusalem with a new gusto. Jonathan informed Cray and Lance of a game he loved to play, which led to them being sat on benches at the side of an outside court in a park watching something called 'basketball' taking place. It clearly required a great deal of skill and agility, and the two men weren't sure they would be able to compete effectively without some practice first. Jonathan was doing something he called 'dribbling' and in this manner he conveyed the ball from one side of the court to the other whilst evading the opposing team who were trying to take the ball from him and then dribble it themselves. The dribbling did not seem to involve any unintentional discharge of saliva from the corners of the mouth which Cray had initially found confusing. It had occurred to Cray that perhaps the activity should be called 'sweating' instead as there was plenty of that occurring, and he planned to suggest this to Jonathan at the end of the game, he felt sure his insightful idea would become the new norm. The most impressive moments were when Jonathan and the others launched themselves into the air into front of a net basket with a hole in the bottom and plunged the ball down into the basket. This appeared to be how they scored and there was great excitement in the scoring team when this happened. It was also possible to score by throwing the ball at the basket from a distance, but this wasn't quite as thrilling, though Cray didn't doubt it was a whole other skill that required learning in and of itself.

A panting Jonathan came running up to them after another successful basket. "So, what do you guys think? You fancy a go?"

The two looked at each other and shrugged. "I erm, guess we could try?" Cray offered, unconvinced it was a good idea.

What followed were the most embarrassing moments of both their lives. While their physical condition, cognitive ability and agility was at peak levels, their skills at the game were somewhat wanting and the other players ran rings around them despite Jonathan's attempts to give them pointers. The other players were good about it though and let them have a few shots at the basket occasionally, though it was obvious to Cray and Lance that they were being given an easy run. Eventually the exquisite torture was declared to be over and the two retreated to the side of the court where they thankfully found a water fountain and drank deeply of its nectar.

"Nothing like it is there?" Jonathan grinned as he jogged over.

"You can say that again." Lance quipped cynically as he mopped his brow with his shirt.

Jonathan had hoped for a slightly more enthusiastic response and his face fell slightly.

Cray had managed to enjoy moments of it; and wasn't entirely opposed to the idea of trying it again, it had been exhilarating when he had come close to scoring a couple of times and he reckoned if he could acquire some moderate degree of skill that it could become very enjoyable. "I'll give it another go, give me a few days to recover though."

He was rewarded with a wide grin from the other man, "I'll let you know when we're playing again." Jonathan turned and ran back onto the court, casually tossing the ball at the hoop and scoring another basket as he did.

Cray winced and Lance allowed himself a laugh at his friend's expense, "I'm glad you stepped into that one, I sure wasn't going to."

"And just what makes you think I'm coming back without dragging you along?" Cray retorted with an evil grin.

A look of panic came over Lance, "You wouldn't! What have I ever done to you?"

Cray laughed, "Come on, let's go and get lunch."

They wandered down a tree lined avenue towards a marketplace where there were usually a couple of food vendors offering lovingly prepared home-made delights. They stopped at a berry bush to pick a few

Chris Smithies   Millennium

raspberries along the way, because there were no diseases and no parasites in New Jerusalem it was perfectly safe to eat them directly after picking. Each one was like a sensory explosion to the men who had grown up on watery gruel.

*

On Earth, things were not as peaceful and idyllic for the redeemed who had volunteered to be stationed there for a season. Whilst the unredeemed peoples of Earth did not have the flawless bodies that the redeemed did, there were no diseases or parasites, just as in Heaven and so people lived long healthy lives. There was no poverty or famine, and no war or crime. And the last was a large part of the problem, because people felt like many of the things designated crimes in this new utopian society should not have been. Any form of pornography was illegal for instance and any sexual relations which were contrary to God's original intention. Thus, it was that David stared out of a first-floor window of his palace at a massive protest, with flags and banners waving and people chanting. A man was stood on the bonnet of a car mimicking performing an illegal sex act on himself. A line of malakim stood between the protesters and the palace and each time on of the protestors approached the line, they were effortlessly tossed back into the crowd. David turned to the being stood next to him and sighed, "I wasn't expecting Paradise to be quite like this."

"You can take a sabbatical on New Jerusalem any time you like your highness," Gabri'el replied, his brow furrowed, clearly just as disturbed by the protests as the king.

"And give up after only a few months? Imagine what the newspapers would say! Whose idea was newspapers anyway? He must have been a mad man." David huffed.

"He was certainly not a politician." Samuel, king David's chief advisor added, coming up behind the two.

Gabri'el merely raised an eyebrow at the jest, the archangel was the epitome of the trope that malakim had no sense of humour although his brother Uri'el was clear proof that this was not always the case.

David however, allowed himself a brief laugh and clapped his vizier on the shoulder, "It is good that you can bring some light to this troubled occasion my old friend."

They turned back to the window just in time to see a malak in a winged battle suit pluck the exhibitionist from the roof of the car and drop him at the back of a police van where he was quickly apprehended by two other malakim. David had previously pondered whether there should be humans in the police force, but he could see from this experience that malakim were better suited to it. At some point he would have to go out and address the crowd and he was not looking forward to it. The word from the Lord, brought to him by Gabri'el was to be firm, there was to be no tolerance of sin in Christ's new world, none whatsoever. David sighed; this was not going to be fun at all. He glanced aside at Gabri'el and saw the archangel was looking at him expectantly. He gathered that it was time and so declared as much. They made their way to a pair of double doors a short way along the wall which led to a balcony from which he could address the crowd. There was no microphone, but David was not concerned, if GOD wanted these people to hear him then they would. He noted the presence of reporters and cameras. That was good, there were similar riots going on around the world and he wanted all of them to hear his message.

"People of Israel and of the New Earth." he intoned formally. He hated formality but he felt that if he must be firm, then he might as well be formal as well. Formal and firm went well together he thought. "The Lord recognises your concerns, as do I. Your wishes are however in contravention of the new covenant and will not be granted in any form. You have five minutes to disperse, or you will be apprehended and charged with the crimes which you have requested be legalised. The Lord has seen your minds and knows that you are already guilty in your thoughts, and this is sufficient for you to be processed under the law."

A man in the front colourfully shouted to David what he could do with his laws and a malakim promptly plucked him out of the crowd and flew the flailing man to the van already containing the exhibitionist. David guessed that they would probably have some things to talk about. It would not last though, because they would be separated once they reached prison. The Lord understood that prisoners fed off each other's ideals and often exited prison with a more ingrained criminal ethic than they had when they went in. This was not something permitted in the New Earth and criminals were exposed only to caring volunteers, many of whom were redeemed people giving up time that would otherwise have been spent on New Jerusalem to work with the offenders. Having seen their foul-mouthed compatriot so efficiently dealt with, many of the others in the crowd began to slink quietly away. A man wearing a long coat was accosted by a malak officer and found to have nothing on underneath it, so he too was arrested and led towards an awaiting van along with some young women who were not covered sufficiently enough to meet clothing laws. David stood and watched until the crowd dissipated to the point where there were a few stragglers only and then noticed a man stood stock still in the middle of the yard just staring at him. David felt disconcerted by the stare and turned his head to Gabri'el seeking reassurance.

"We are watching that one, his heart holds much hatred. He intends to assassinate you." Gabri'el explained somewhat too offhandedly for David's liking.

"I assume you're not going to watch while he shoots me. And then watch while he walks away." David responded tartly.

"Your highness…" Samuel started in shock at David's lack of deference to his revered guest.

"It's okay Samuel." Gabri'el said placatingly, a hand raised. "I understand your concern for your safety your highness." he continued, turning to David, "But I personally assure you, you cannot be permanently harmed."

David turned back to the courtyard, but the staring man was gone now, probably having blended in with the leaving crowds. The king knew that if he were to be killed that his soul would be resurrected into a new body in the New Jerusalem hatchery moments later. It wasn't an experience he wanted to embrace though, and he'd prefer it be avoided. Not to mention that it would make the government appear to be vulnerable and he'd rather display a robust front of invincibility. Invincibility tempered with humility and a paternal nature of course, but invincibility, nevertheless. David ben Jesse was determined to show that he was not a man to be trifled with, although you'd think his well-documented history would have been sufficient. Perhaps he needed to find another giant to slay, but in front of the interminable press this time.

*

Giska lay on a bed in his opulently appointed bed chamber. His naked golden finely scaled skin exposed as his bed's coverings lay in a twisted heap on the floor. He was moderately weary from his nightly activity but had not been completely sated. At the foot of his bed lay the sprawled form of a beautiful human woman, her long hair splayed out from being cast there once his voracious desires had been met. Like most Grigori he was inextricably drawn to the human form, particularly the women, although he enjoyed men occasionally as well. Like many before, this woman had not survived his attentions which was a pity as she had been entertaining. His nephilim guards would be pleased though, as they would appreciate her soft flesh in a very different and final way as to what he just had. He wondered briefly where her soul would be now, unlike some others before she had shown no sign that she had been tainted by dreams of a saviour. He felt it most intrusive and unsportsmanlike that the so-called Beloved was creeping into his minion's dreams and stealing their allegiance away like a thief in the night. In a fit of petulance, he kicked at the woman's body and sent it sprawling onto the floor. There, let the Creator see how little Giska respected his precious favoured race.

He was in a foul mood despite having enjoyed quite a pleasant evening. Once again, he had been required to simper to that pompous buffoon Kraan earlier. How he had not managed to unseat the wretched cretin yet was beyond him, he was clearly the more cunning and intelligent of the two and yet any time he had challenged his Grigori master in the past he had been bested in humiliating fashion. Kraan was of the more robustly built strain of Grigori with greater marshal skill and his dragon aspect was fearsome. Giska was of the more slender and cognitively superior genus with an extended cranium but still somehow unable to leverage his superior cunning into a victory over his relatively brutish master. Pulling himself from this frustrating thought, he rang a bell next to his bed and a door across the room opened to admit the giant head of one of his guards. The creature's eyes lit up as it perceived what had occurred and it eagerly responded as its master waved a dismissive hand, indicating that the nephil could remove the body. It moved quickly for a giant as it lumbered in and grabbed the fresh corpse with its clumsy oafish hands. Giska though he saw drool appearing at a corner of the nephil's wide mouth before it turned back to the door, and he reflected on how disgusting the creatures were. Thankfully the beast was gone quickly, and he could enjoy his quiet civilised solitude once more. He winced as a crunching sound came from beyond the closed door indicating that the foul beast hadn't even waited until it reached the kitchens but then gratefully heard the clomp of retreating footsteps.

Giska was still trying to figure out how he could leverage the building project into a way to unseat the warlord and subsume his seat. He had the loyalty of a number of followers but nowhere near as many as Kraan. He felt sure a great many would change their allegiance once Giska showed his superiority once and for all though. That he was the overseer of what was looking to be a successful venture helped his cause somewhat. As the Watcher nearly singularly responsible for destroying the new Heaven, he would surely garner a great amount of fame and respect. It was something he was greatly looking forward to and he could not wait for the project to reach completion. It was well that it was only a couple of weeks away, he didn't think he could wait much longer. He reflected on the fact that New Jerusalem would only stand for a mere few months rather than the thousand years it had been designed for and he chuckled. The Creator was going to pay dearly for his creation of the humans, very dearly indeed.

*

The *Wings of the Wind* had activated its gravity wells and was hovering a few meters above the hangar floor between two of the larger Hunter class cruisers. It was not due to leave as yet, as on board a discussion was taking place.

"That wasn't a request Captain Sharp, it was an order." Yara'el insisted, his exasperated voice betraying emotion rarely seen in malakim.

Jonathan bowed his head and accepted his fate, "Yes sir."

"I've never seen anyone fight so hard not to be promoted." The comment came with a chuckle from a woman who Jonathan had just a few minutes earlier been told was now his second officer. Mei Song was relatively short for a redeemed woman but no less striking for it and her huge personality more than made up for her diminutive height. The Japanese woman had requested a posting aboard the Whisper class vessel as soon as she had heard of its existence.

With her long dark hair which reached to her waist and her big blue eyes, Jonathan had found it hard to take his eyes off her when she had first entered the bridge. Redeemed men had been freed from the bondage of lust and no longer felt the overwhelming sexual drive that they had endured in life on Earth, but it was still possible to be drawn to particular forms of beauty and Mei's was like catnip to the newly minted captain. He would have to be careful not to make a fool of himself in front of his new subordinate, "Well, since I am captain, however I might feel about it, I had better issue an order hadn't I." He turned to the pilot, "Take us out Shamus."

"Aye aye, cap'n." the pilot, Shamus Godson grinned as he manoeuvred the vessel towards the hangar shield. Like many of the smaller royal Navy capital ships, the whisper class was piloted like a fighter with the pilot sat in a reclined position having a joystick between his legs. As a denizen of 14th century Ireland during his time on Earth, Shamus had never encountered anything like a star ship during his lifetime but as soon as he heard of their existence, he knew he wanted to fly one.

"I'll leave you to it then, Captain Sharp." Yara'el commented before orbing and zipping out through a nearby bulkhead.

"I hope it's not a sin to hate an angel." Jonathan muttered under his breath after the malak had gone.

Mei laughed again, a sound that seemed musical to Jon, "I'm sure you don't really hate him, and you'll get over it once you get your sea legs."

"We should probably get focussed on the success of this mission." Jonathan responded, as much an instruction to himself as to those around him, "It's possible that beyond our next window lies an answer as to what the large construction project the fallen are working on is. I don't know about the rest of you, but I'm somewhat interested to find out."

The *Winds of the Wind* approached its exit point, a part of the Sol system near New Jerusalem rich in the entangled atoms necessary for window creation. The window generators in the tips of the *Wind's* farthest extremities blazed into life and cut a hole through space itself, creating a bridge into a star system 100s of light years away. Jonathan ordered the ship into stealth mode and then through the window which closed behind it. In front of the ship in the alien galaxy was a dead planet, one that possessed little enough resources that even a technologically advanced coloniser would find little worth in it. It was on the very edge of the system and portalling on the dark side of it would mask the window they created from detection. There would be no nasty surprises this time. The ship moved to the edge of the planet where its long-range sensors would be able to scan the rest of the

152

system without detection. They knew there would be something here, as this was the destination for the parts on board the pirated freighter.

Commander Song hovered behind one of the sensor officers, scanning the data as it came in, "What is that there?" she pointed at an anomaly as it came up on the screen.

The sensor officer had already noticed it, but he was a patient man and did not take offense at her subsummation of his role, "It's a structure of some kind, reasonably large. It looks like its planet bound." He meant that rather than being a floating station in space, the structure had been constructed on a planet, but was large enough to be detected from space.

Overhearing this, Jonathan knew that he should order the ship to make way for the structure in stealth mode, but he was plagued by uncertainty. He felt the responsibility for the people on his ship keenly and the fact that their souls would be reconstituted into new bodies if their current ones died did little to reassure him.

"Captain?" Mei prompted him, clearly a little troubled by his hesitation but hiding it moderately well. "Shall we investigate?"

"Shamus, take us closer on 10%." Jonathan ordered. "I know it's going to take a while to get there, but we can't risk discovery."

Mei had studied the Whisper class ship's data sheets closely, and knew that at this distance, the shunt engine's thruster, which had been inset deep into the hull for purposes of masking its energy discharge from sensors would not be detectable at anything below 30% power. She also knew however, that if there was a fallen ship between them and the station that they'd be grateful they'd kept the thrust to 10%. She thought that their highly capable sensors would have detected such a ship by now, but she wanted to trust her captain's judgement and kept her tongue. At least for now. So it was that it took the ship nearly an hour to cover the distance between the outer planet and the third planet in the system upon which lay the station. It was an hour which

Mei found excruciating, and she suspected Sharp had too, but he had ignored any hints to increase the power and she had continued to resist the urge to challenge his decision directly, barely. "Have we been detected?" she asked the sensor officer as they fell into a high orbit.

"I see no signs that we have." he replied in a confident tone, "We're invisible to them. The launching of the shuttle will be a big test though. Let's take the shunt engine offline and use our momentum to turn the ship to face away from the planet. That way the shuttle bay will be facing away from their sensors, and it'll be less likely to be picked up on scanners."

"We could just send the malakim marines." Mei suggested tentatively. They didn't need a shuttle to make the transit to the planet's surface and an orbed malak wasn't likely to show up on any sensor screen.

Jonathan pondered the suggestion, but only briefly, "No. It's important to the Lord to have the human marines learn their roles. I'm sure by now you've noticed I'm trying not to take any unnecessary risks..."

Boy, hadn't she just. She thought to herself.

"...but I think that's one risk we should take." He continued, not missing the brief look that had crossed her face, confirming his suspicion that she had wearied of his overly cautious approach. He suspected she might be impressed if he loosened up a little, which he had to admit might have influenced him. A slight smile appeared on her face briefly, but long enough for him to guess his gambit had achieved the desired effect.

It was as well for the human marines that he had made his choice thus because Cray, Lance and Titus were rearing to go in the armoury on the deck below and their eyes were fixed on Mark Bastion, expecting an order any second to move out. Their nerves were on edge as the marine commander cocked his head, indicating he was probably receiving a message from the bridge.

"Right marines, let's get moving." Bastion said and stood to his feet, much to the relief of the others.

Eret'el and his malakim were likewise on the move suddenly, indicating they had heard the same order. The malak commander addressed the human one, "We'll await you on the surface Bastion."

Mark nodded to the imposing elohim and turned to lead the way out of the armoury. The armoury had been placed just adjacent to the shuttle bay to facilitate rapid deployment and the marines soon found themselves facing the two shuttles in the hangar. The one with its ramp lowered and a man in a flight uniform stood expectantly at the rear seemed the obvious choice and Bastion led his marines to it. The pilot, another human recently out of training was Raymond Tracer. When he'd chosen the last name for himself, he'd done so because he thought it sounded cool for a pilot but then he got the nickname 'CGI' very quickly whilst in flight school and he'd only afterwards found out that ray tracing was a computer graphics technique from the 21st century. He'd died in the 1970s before such things were possible, how was he supposed to know? He wanted to change it, but he had a feeling that he was probably stuck with the nickname either way.

"Hey CGI, we good to go?" Bastion quipped as the marines reached the ship.

And there it was, Ray winced. "Yup climb aboard, Castle." he addressed to marine captain cheekily.

"Bastion. It's Bastion." Mark responded wearily, as if for the umpteenth time, which is fact it was.

"Wasn't that the name of the hero from a children's movie?" Susan Stead chimed in, then regretted it instantly as she received a stern look from the beleaguered commander.

"Don't ask me." Cray shrugged; "I've never seen a movie. I've heard about them though."

"You've never seen a movie? Right. My house, straight after this mission." Susan said in a commanding tone. "Bring popcorn. You can come too" she said turning to Titus, "But stay off my furniture this time."

Titus sighed, "You crush one sofa, and it follows you your entire life."

"Anything but Never-ending Story." Mark insisted.

"Gotcha boss." Susan replied, nodding emphatically, then turned to Cray and whispered conspiratorially, "Don't worry, it will definitely be Never-ending Story."

"No one is ever allowed to talk about Never-ending Story again." Mark muttered half under his breath as the marines took their places.

As the ramp at the rear of the shuttle was lifting, Susan bravely took one last irresistible dig, "Wait, we're not leaving without Artax are we?"

*

The large facility on the planet below was an assembly plant. Components were sent to it from all over Kraan's empire either by portal or via freighter vessel. It had been built on this particular world because it was rich in lithium, a material used liberally in the construction of the batteries in many of the products the facility created. The planet was littered with micro mines, small mining facilities equipped with advanced technology which permitted the valuable lithium to be removed from the crust without extensive labour required. A dock was attached to the facility, currently accommodating a large fallen freighter which looked as if it was centuries old. The stealth shuttle from the *Wings of the Wind* came to land just outside of the perimeter of an energy shield bubble around the base. Eret'el and eight malakim were already waiting on the planet surface when the shuttle landed. The malakim commander orbed inside the shuttle and activated the portal generator inside, "We've identified a suitable spot just outside the building to portal you to." he explained.

"Why not just create a window inside the building?" Lance asked.

Titus chuckled, "Do you trust a schematic to make sure you don't end up inside a wall?"

Lance went a little white, indicating he had just pictured such a scenario.

"Will CGI be okay waiting here?" Cray wondered.

"He can always retreat back up to the *Wind* if there's trouble." Bastion reassured him.

The human marines quickly filed into the portal generator and stepped out of it a bare metre from a steel door. We need to get inside quickly, if we loiter for long in the open, we could be detected, and our insurgency discovered." Eret'el instructed.

It seemed Titus was thinking similarly, "I'm surprised we haven't been seen already, you'd think they'd have someone watching a bank of screens somewhere linked to external cameras."

"There probably was." Eret'el commented meaningfully from directly behind them. "Finn'el has already been inside to take care of the surveillance system."

The door opened from the inside and Finn'el's head appeared. He ushered them closer with a wave of his hand. As they pressed past him into a corridor he explained, "The cameras are disabled for now, but it's only a matter of time before the body in the security room is noticed and my interference with their system is corrected. We'll have to be quick."

"I wish I could work a console like that, perhaps you could teach me some day." Lance whispered to the malak.

"If I taught you all I know about machine code, it wouldn't take long." The malak laughed quietly under his breath.

A look of confusion crossed Lance's face, "How did you disable the cameras then?"

"I pulled the plug out." Finn'el answered simply. When he saw this only deepened the confusion in Lance's face he explained further, "There's a saying: Don't use advanced mathematics to solve a problem when a wrench will do."

Lance nodded his understanding; this was logic he could relate to.

"It does mean that all someone has to do to fix it is plug them back in though." Titus noted.

The angel raised an eyebrow, "True, then let us not tarry, hmm?"

Susan Stead turned to the four, "Could you lot be a little noisier please? We haven't been discovered yet so if you're trying to get shot you need to try harder." She was rewarded with sheepish faces, at least from the humans.

The marines split into two groups, a mob of twenty was hardly conducive to a successful covert operation. Mark Bastion led one squad of 5 humans and 5 malakim while Eret'el took the other. Cray and Titus found themselves with Eret'el's half as they had on the fallen cruiser, but Lance was placed in the other group. Cray gave his friend a reassuring nod as they parted ways, he realised they hadn't spent very much time apart since becoming marines and it felt wrong to be separated now. He sent a quiet prayer that his friend would be alright as the other squad disappeared up a passageway. The malakim in their squad were out front as usual, being the most proficient at melee combat. Malakim could use their pulse bows for ranged support and humans could use their spirit swords in melee, but it was felt that the best results would be obtained If the physically larger malakim rushed the enemy when possible and the human marines provided support with prayer and rifle fire. The strategies involving malakim and humans working together were in their early stages, but they had been formulated by elohim with thousands of years of combat experience and were unlikely to require much improvement.

In Cray's group which had headed into an engineering section of the facility, two of the malakim, Finn'el and Seta'el had orbed and were scouting ahead through a maze of machinery. Their remit was to quietly take down any obstacle encountered if it were possible to do so. Already, Seta'el had rendered an engineer unconscious who had been working alone on a leaking oxygen line. The man's slumbering body had been so quickly concealed that the forward progress of the party had been unaffected.

Suddenly Eret'el put his hand up and the squad came to a halt, "Do you hear that?" he quietly asked Himlar'el next to him.

The big malak was quiet for a moment and then replied, "Gunfire."

Cray looked at Titus who shrugged, apparently, he hadn't heard anything either.

The squad took the next available junction and headed towards where the malakim had heard the sounds. It wasn't long before Cray could hear the shots in the distance as well, it sounded as if Lance's squad had run into some serious trouble, and he was overcome with worry for his friend.

As they approached the distant sounds, a comm message came through: "Three cruisers have just come out of a window, if you haven't completed your mission yet, I suggest you do so quickly." Captain Sharp informed Eret'el.

Eret'el could overhear Commander Mei in the background informing the captain that they appeared to be conducting sweeps of the system. He stopped to consider their options and eventually reached a decision, "Bastion." He barked into his comm, breaking radio silence.

Suddenly the sounds of gunfire became much louder as the comm line opened, "Commander Eret'el." Bastion shouted over the noise, "We've been engaged by a large squad of fallen. They have armoured nephilim warriors; I don't think these are factory guards."

It was a trap, Cray thought to himself. How had the fallen known they were coming though?

Eret'el knew that he couldn't risk losing both squads, "Retreat back to the portal Bastion. We will hold it until you arrive."

"Order received." Bastion replied and cut the communication.

"What about Lance and the others? They need our help." Cray blurted out, overhearing Eret'el's side of the exchange being enough for him to realise his friend was in serious trouble.

Eret'el's face was as hard as stone, "The best thing we can do for your friend is make sure that portal isn't taken, and the shuttle is there for them when they reach it."

Cray gulped and nodded nervously, he suddenly realised how much Lance meant to him and how afraid he was of something happening to affect their friendship. He hadn't had the opportunity to conduct a proper friendship on Frixar and aside from his relationship with his newfound saviour, nothing meant more to him.

"I have found them!" a throaty yell broke the relative silence and suddenly Lance's squad wasn't the only one fighting to escape as an armoured nephil warrior appeared at the bottom of a hallway and opened fire on them with an automatic kinetic rifle causing their shields to glow blue with the impact of the large calibre rounds. Another pair of nephilim joined it and the squad was suddenly embroiled in a bitter fighting withdrawal.

One of the malakim threw a pair of pulse grenades and as they exploded and stunned the nephilim briefly, Eret'el shouted, "Standard retreat marines! To the exfiltration point, now!" They automatically fell back upon their training and every first two marines who reached cover immediately knelt to provide covering fire for the other eight as they fell back behind the firing position. Eret'el drew his bow, the arms of which flicked out as it was raised. It was a highly accurate malakim weapon in the hands of an experienced user, with a large selection of ammunition types and the marine commander put an explosive bolt straight into the eye of the closest nephil warrior. He had already run past the two marines providing the covering fire when the stricken beast's head exploded, and it gave them the distraction they needed to fall in behind Eret'el and allow Cray and Titus to lay down the next layer of covering pulse fire. Titus' weapon was a heavier pulse cannon, not as large as the ones mounted on spaceborne vessels, but still possessing a larger calibre and higher rate of fire than a standard pulse rifle. Another nephil warrior succumbed to the barrage but to the pair's horror a full squad of human fallen were now racing to back the remaining giant up. Cray tossed a grenade down the corridor and the two quickly left cover and ran up past where Alex Runner and Lee Masters were crouched, firing down past them. They were about to turn and encourage the two marines to follow behind them when a fragmentation grenade exploded between the two and Cray was flung down the corridor by the blast. Even Titus was left staggering, and he stumbled as he reached down to take Cray's hand and help him up. Cray was horrified to see two bright streams of bright blue light whip past his head, indicating that his fellow marine's souls had been called back to New Jerusalem. He hated the thought that they would now have to leave their mangled bodies behind, but they had to keep going or join them. Thankfully they were not far from the exfiltration point now, and they could see Eret'el beckoning to them from the open door. Titus cried out in pain as his E6 sit shield finally failed and he took a kinetic round in the shoulder just as they made it through the door and the portal beckoned to them.

"It is nothing." the big man rumbled as Cray tried to inspect the wound.

"Both of you, through the portal now." Eret'el ordered.

"We have to hold it for Lance and Bastion." Cray objected.

"Their squad came through just before you." The angelic commander yelled over the noise, "Now go!"

The two men stumbled through the portal into the back of the shuttle and were horrified to see how few marines were waiting for them inside. Rudi Fire was lying in a pool of his own blood, a large gash down one of his arms and groaning in pain and Susan Stead was applying a healing pad from one of the shuttle's med kits. Cray immediately saw that Lance was not one of the few members of the other squad in the shuttle. He hoped beyond hope that his friend would be waiting for him in New Jerusalem.

Eret'el came in through the portal and it closed behind him, "Get us back to the *Wings of the Wind* Tracer." he ordered without preamble.

The shuttle, still in stealth mode, took off from the planet and headed up towards the seemingly empty stretch of space where they hoped the *Wings of the Wind* was still waiting. Cray watched over Ray's shoulder as they changed course to stay out of the sensor range of an approaching fallen cruiser and then moved back onto the original heading. Without warning it suddenly seemed to Cray as if the space in front of them had been framed, and he realised it was the faint outline of the nearly invisible *Wind's* hangar becoming opaquer as they drew closer. As they penetrated the hangar shield, the shuttle bay suddenly seemed to fully materialise and the shuttle made a safe landing, albeit with a much smaller load than it had left with.

"They're aboard." Commander Mei announced on the frigate's bridge.

"Let's not waste any time then." Captain Sharp declared, "Shamus, take us back to the outer planet, steady as you go. Let's not attract any attention."

The cruiser that had come close to the shuttle had moved away, but another was approaching on a different vector, and it would pass within a mile of them. Shamus decided the best course of action was to quietly maintain their heading, as they were unlikely to be detected at such a distance. His decision proved to be the right one and the cruiser passed by them with no signs it had detected them. Soon they were moving away from the patrolling ships and towards safety.

"Look at the way they're combing the area." Mei observed, "They clearly know we're here."

Jonathan nodded sombrely, "I know, but how?"

Mei fingered her lip as if holding onto a thought she was reluctant to say.

Jonathan guessed she had something to say and prompted her, "Out with it, Commander Song, I can see you have a theory."

"It's not a theory, more a suspicion. Maybe not even that." Mei replied evasively. Jonathan stared at her expectantly and she resigned herself to explaining, "Well, it's just that you have a marine on board who I understand used to be a nephilim? Not only that, but a captain?"

Jonathan was taken aback at first, but then after a moment's thought nodded, "I suppose it's a possibility, but if he hadn't truly given his heart to the Lord, I don't think the Holy Spirit would permit his continued presence on New Jerusalem."

"You have a point there." Mei admitted. "It was just a thought."

"Let's keep the thought to ourselves for now. I don't want it getting about that we don't trust our own marines." Sharp suggested.

Mei nodded in acceptance, "We still need to figure out how they knew we were coming though."

Jonathan simply nodded; the entire stealth program suddenly seemed to be in jeopardy. Their first mission was supposed to be a smooth information gathering exercise on a sparsely guarded factory and they were barely escaping with their lives.

*

Giska grinned at the news he had just received. An infiltration by warriors of Heaven had just been foiled at a facility producing small parts for the Pillabis project. His elaborate plans to safeguard against

163

the recent pirate attacks by rival fallen by bolstering defences had borne much riper fruit than he could had hoped. Not only had they repulsed an attack by the much-vaunted Royal Marines, but the factory administrator had said something about a gift. Giska did like gifts and he had a feeling this was going to be a good one. He made his way down to the receiving room, a large empty vaulted chamber designed to provide a large enough open area to safely receive portals of various sizes from all over the empire. It was unlikely that a portal would accidentally open in a wall in a room of this size and the floor's panels could be raised if a portal opened above ground level. He hadn't informed Lord Kraan of the exciting events unfolding as he hoped there might be some advantage to be gained from withholding the knowledge. He waited with four nephilim guards at the edge of the room as a portal opened in its centre. As he watched, a nephil warrior came through dressed in battle armour and brandishing a large kinetic automatic carbine. It stood off to one side of the portal opening and was soon followed by another giant, similarly clad, who moved to stand at the adjacent side. The next being through the portal had clearly been pushed because it stumbled as it came through and nearly fell to its knees. It was followed by another who made a better attempt at staying on its feet. The final being through the portal was a tall shedim in a dark cloak, no doubt the administrator of the factory.

"My dear administrator, what have you brought me?" Giska hissed.

The shedim smiled widely, knowing that he had brought a significant prize to the chief attendant and would be rewarded handsomely, "I suspect, in your wisdom, that you have already surmised what these are my lord."

Giska licked his lips, they were glorious. They appeared human, but taller and more heavily muscled which was easy to see as they had been stripped of most of their clothing. Their facial features were perfection and as hard as he looked, he couldn't find a single flaw in them. So, these were the redeemed he had heard so much about. He walked up to them and performed a circuit of them, inspecting every curve of their perfect bodies and savouring the experience.

"See something you like?" one of them taunted him. He was the shorter of the two and had short cropped blonde hair.

"Silence food!" the nephil warrior closest to him bellowed and hit him in the back with his rifle, causing him to stumble forward onto his knees.

Lance winced at the pain but then stood back up to his feet, determined to show these fallen that servants of the Lord could not have their spirit broken so easily.

"Hmm, this one has some backbone." Giska reached out and stroked a clawed finger down Lance's back, causing him to cringe despite attempting not to react.

"You are disgusting." The other redeemed man commented icily, "To think you used to serve Yahweh."

Giska spun on the man and grabbed his dark hair in one clawed hand. He put his face right next the redeemed man and his forked tongue flicked out against the man's cheek. "You might think so now human, but you may think differently once you have experienced an evening with me. You might be surprised at my ability to meet a man's needs." the Grigori suddenly seemed as if he was melting as he transformed himself into the form of a beautiful dark-haired human woman dressed in a flimsy transparent outfit seemingly made entirely of gauze. Whilst being undeniably beautiful, Mark thought it was a kind of beauty that was crude compared to the redeemed women he was used to spending time with. Even so, he was grateful his redeemed chemistry didn't react to sexual stimulation any longer.

The transformed Grigori turned on his heels and strode towards the door, "Bring them!" he demanded in a voice a somewhat too deep for its currently chosen form, breaking the illusion.

The four nephil guards roughly grabbed Lance and Mark and picked them up off the ground by their upper arms without barely any effort, their legs dangling in the air. The smell of the nephilim was rancid and although the redeemed constitution was strong, Lance found himself feeling nauseated by the stench. He wondered to himself as they were dragged away if anyone in New Jerusalem would be able to figure out where they had been brought.

For so says the Lord Jehovah: Behold, I Myself will search for My sheep and seek them out. As a shepherd seeks out his flock in the day that he is among his scattered sheep, so I will seek out My sheep and will deliver them out of all places where they have been scattered in the cloudy and dark day. And I will bring them out from the peoples, and gather them from the lands, and will bring them to their own land and feed them on the mountain of Israel by the rivers, and in all the places of the land where people live. I will feed them in a good pasture, and their fold shall be on the high mountains of Israel. There they shall lie in a good fold, and in a fat pasture they shall feed on the mountains of Israel. I will feed My flock, and I will cause them to lie down, says the Lord Jehovah. I will seek the lost, and bring again those driven away, and will bind up the broken, and will strengthen the sick. But I will destroy the fat and the strong; I will feed them with judgment.

Ezekial 34: 11-16

Nine

Cray had rushed straight to the Hatchery when he had arrived back at New Jerusalem and had been horrified to find out that Lance and Mark were not amongst the marines being resurrected. As someone who had lived in a fallen colony most of his life, he knew the kind of depravity his friends would likely be facing right now. He had been reassured by Eret'el, who had been with him, that a plan would quickly be made, and now he had been summoned back to the navy yard to be prepped for a new mission. When he arrived, he was guided through a door in the covert operations section and found himself in a room with Eret'el, Titus and a determined looking redeemed woman he had not met before. Arrayed on a table were various pieces of fallen equipment and clothing.

Cray assessed the situation and came to the most obvious conclusion, "I hope this means we're going after Lance."

Eret'el nodded slowly, "You are, along with Titus and Shannon here."

The serious faced young lady nodded at him upon mention of her name.

The malak commander turned to a holographic projector behind him and activated it. An impressive structure appeared on the surface of a planet surrounded by multiple habitation domes, likely the work of centuries of gradual expansion. "We believe the likeliest place for Mark and Lance to have been taken is Lord Kraan's palace on the planet of Obelis in the Hannuk system. We are going to insert you three into the palace disguised as fallen in the hopes that you will be able to locate your missing brothers and bring them home." he indicated to the young lady with his arm, "Shannon here has lived and worked in the palace and knows her way around." the malak regarded her sternly, "I'm not entirely happy about her going with, she hasn't been with us long and I would have liked for her to be more focussed on her recovery from her traumatic past."

The young lady looked suitably chastened, "I'm sorry and I will try to settle once I've completed this mission, but Giska must be stopped and if I can help then I want to do it."

Cray suspected this woman had endured some trauma at the hands of Giska. As a redeemed woman, he didn't want to think that her motivation for what she was doing was revenge and it was likely that she wouldn't be permitted to go on this mission if it was. He hoped her determination stemmed from a desire to prevent other people from going through what she went through. It occurred to Cray that he was very different in appearance from what he had been as a fallen though. "How am I going to pass as a fallen now though? You don't get many who are 7ft tall. I assume we're going to try and pass Titus off as a nephil as well and he doesn't look very much like one now, apart from his size of course." he queried.

Eret'el smiled and took the marines over to the table and waved an arm over its contents, "All of these are replicas of fallen equipment, but made to be 15% larger than the originals. From a distance, you and Shannon will appear to be in scale with what observers will assume are normal sized weapons. Your clothes have been designed to have haphazard colours that will break up your profile to the eye and make it harder to assess your size."

Clever, Cray thought, "But it will only work if I don't get close to anyone."

"Indeed. Try to avoid particularly close contact." Eret'el confirmed.

"And what about me?" Titus wondered.

Eret'el walked a little further down the table, "We've created nephilim style armour with bumps and ridges in the metal that will make it appear as if there are horns and other deformities underneath. Your gloves have 6 fingers each, the 6th of which are prosthetics." the angel addressed them all, "It's unlikely that anyone will look at you too closely once you're in the palace, they probably haven't encountered an insurgent in there for hundreds of years and the guards will be complacent."

"That does sound like the fallen." Cray observed. He'd been them around enough to know.

Eret'el continued to instruct them while they donned the fallen gear over their marine jumpsuits, "This portal generator will take you into the lower palace which tends to be quieter and you're less likely to be spotted going in."

"There are no malakim on this mission?" Titus wondered.

"Only a very skilled malak would be able to stay undetected considering the number of shedim and Grigori in the palace." Eret'el responded.

The three acknowledged this with nods but Cray's concern was evident on his face.

"You are troubled Cray Ironheart, what is it?" Eret'el inquired.

Cray took a moment to align his thoughts and then responded, "It's just that we're all ex-fallen. It surprises me a little that you are trusting us with this mission."

Eret'el laughed dismissively, "You have the Holy Spirit in you. Don't you think He would have informed us if one of you wasn't true to your commitment to the Lord?" His expression became warmer and for the first time, Cray suspected that the malak commander might actually have become fond of them, "We have the utmost confidence in the three of you and you are our brothers and sister as much as any redeemed here."

This unexpected reassurance warmed Cray's heart greatly and he suddenly found himself more able to focus on the objective rather than his self-doubt, "Let's go and get our friends back then."

"Indeed." Titus agreed, "If anyone has hurt Lance, they will answer to me."

For a moment, Cray was tempted to feel sorry for the fallen captors, but then he thought of Lance and Mark and dismissed the idea. He was happy for them to get everything that was coming to them.

They were dressed now and Eret'el activated the portal. "Go with Yahweh saints of God. Do not neglect to pray when the situation demands it. Now go quickly, before someone sees the gate on the other side."

The marines nodded and Cray led them through the window.

They had been sent to what appeared to be a storage room of some kind. It was large and empty apart from a few scattered empty boxes and had probably been selected for just that reason. Shannon and Titus followed him through and as he watched them come through the portal he started and just how much they appeared to be fallen. It was sad to him in a way that they'd had to revert to type for even such a short time. Being redeemed was glorious and he would never want to return to this his previous life for any longer time than necessary.

"Let's get out of this room so I can get my bearings." Shannon suggested.

The two marines nodded in agreement, though neither of them was particularly in a hurry to enter the halls of the palace and be exposed to the company of their previous fallen comrades.

The door opened into a dim corridor which comfortably accepted Titus' size, probably due to the need to use Nephilim to move whatever had been stored in this area. It was dusty and the smell of disuse and neglect piqued the heightened senses of their redeemed noses.

"We should head upstairs." Shannon suggested, "I'm sure I'll be able to find my way once we reach the busier parts of the palace."

"Makes sense." Cray muttered, not particularly interested in the minor logistics of their mission. He didn't feel that Lance would be that hard to find. Redeemed hostages probably held the interest of many here and word would have gotten around about them. The first guard they asked would probably know exactly where they were.

The three made their way up a flight of stairs to a door on rusty hinges. With some effort Titus managed to heave it open, creaking as it did. They found themselves at the end of a hallway in an area that was clearly used more often than the one they had left.

"When did Eret'el say the portal would be opened again?" Cray asked, he had been focussed on something else when that particular part of the briefing had taken place.

"An hour from when we arrived. You really should pay better attention to your officers." Shannon chastised him as Cray set about creating a timer on his suit, pointedly ignoring the jibe.

"We'd better be quick then." Titus interjected, keen to not let the atmosphere between the three of them get strained.

"I have an idea of where we are now. The holding cells are in the west wing of the palace and should be at the end of this hall and to the left. I think the guard's quarters lie between us and them though." Shannon explained.

"We'd have to talk our way through. Is there another way around?" Cray asked.

"Hmm, we could go through the kitchens, but it will take us a little longer." Shannon offered.

"I like that idea better; we'll be less likely to be stopped." Titus replied, "Though I hope they're not serving anything questionable."

"In my experience, all fallen food is questionable." Cray commented.

"I wasn't referring to the quality, I was referring to..."

Titus didn't finish as Cray interrupted, "We know what you were referring to, let's not talk about it."

Titus shrugged and headed down the hall, "My nose is telling me it's this way."

After they walked a few paces Cray added, "Ugh, mine is telling me the same now. Are we still sure this is a good idea?"

As they turned a corner a couple of human guards were walking up their way. The redeemed insurgents moved to one side of the hallway so that when they passed it wouldn't be as obvious that they were taller. The guards were locked in what sounded like quite a heated conversation with each other and didn't pay the three any attention. Cray had forgotten a time when an 11ft nephil could walk around without getting attention. He wasn't particularly glad to be back in a place where the giants were commonplace.

"This way to the kitchens." Shannon said, guiding the two toward the left. They went do a short flight of stairs and stopped in front of a pair of large doors on robust industrial swing hinges. "Steel yourselves. I'd try not to look at what's on the counters if I were you."

"My plan exactly." came Cray's reply.

Titus pushed the doors open and the three were instantly assailed by steam, smoke and the smell of boiled and roasted flesh. They headed straight for the other side of the kitchen, their heads down. There were people working in the kitchen, mostly humans, but also a few of the slender grey skinned drones. They were hard at work and didn't appear to care that they had visitors.

"Ugh." Cray muttered as he accidentally caught sight of something unpleasant.

"What is it?" Shannon asked.

"Trust me, you do not want to know." was the curt reply. Cray was not keen to have his mouth open for too long, it was hard enough keeping his bile down. After what seemed like an eternity to the three, they came to a pair of double doors at the opposite end of the kitchen to the ones they entered through. Gratefully they pushed their way through the doors and came out into a long corridor ending in an iron latched door with a large nephil guard in armour next to it. They shared a glance to each other and walked down towards the door.

"Halt." The nephil grunted as they approached. "What is your purpose here."

Cray had been mentally preparing for this moment, "We're here to take the humans to be interrogated."

The nephil laughed, "Which humans? I have forty-five. Are you planning to take all of them?"

Cray cursed himself for having used a term to describe his friends that also fit most of the population of the palace. "I meant the redeemed humans, sorry."

The nephil eyed him strangely, "What is redeemed?"

It hadn't occurred to Cray that the fallen wouldn't be referring to the denizens of Heaven in the same way that they referred to themselves, he tried to think how he might have described them before he became one himself if he had known of their existence but came up with nothing, "The two tall ones? One is blonde, one has dark hair."

"Hmmph." The giant grunted, "You mean the chief attendant's favourites. They went straight to his rooms. He will be enjoying himself with them. They may be brought down here alive eventually for you to get your answers, they may not." The monster shrugged and grinned.

Cray nodded at the guard and turned to his friends, indicating with ahead motion that they should move away. Once they had walked far enough to not be overheard, Cray turned to Shannon, "Do you know where this chief attendant's apartments would be?"

She blanched briefly, but then seemed to recover and a look of determination cross her face, "I know only too well. Follow me." She set off at a pace up the corridor and the two men picked up their feet to keep up. Their journey took them up into the more heavily populated levels of the palace and the décor became more elaborate as they ascended. Fortunately for them, the only people they encountered were human slaves who had little desire to interrogate a trio of guards as to their intentions. Eventually Shannon brought them to the end of a corridor lined by a number of doors. A fearsome looking nephil guard stood outside one. "He'll be in there with them."

"I'll take care of this." Titus declared. He sauntered up to the nephil guard and grunted casually, "I'm here to take over."

"It's not time yet, you fool." the guard chastened him.

"Very well, I will go down to the kitchen and enjoy that tasty looking human female I saw on a slab down there." Titus shrugged and made to move away.

"Wait." the nephil grabbed him by the arm and pulled him back, "I will go to the kitchen, you guard the door."

Titus shrugged again and made to stand by the door. The nephil hurried past the two humans who were pretending to be discussing something with each other.

"Nicely done." Cray commended his friend.

Titus grimaced, "I know what motivates my ex-brethren. Let's go and get our friends before they suffer any more than they already have."

Inside the room, Griska was frustrated. He had discovered that it was far harder to incite arousal in a redeemed male than it was in a fallen one and he had exhausted his usual tricks. He was angered now and had just decided to turn to the pleasures of torture instead of sex when three idiot guards burst into his chamber.

"What in the Devil's name are you doing in here?" he yelled angrily, then he noticed Shannon and despite her transformed redeemed body, found her to be familiar to him. After a moment it dawned on him who she was: "You! It can't be! You're dead, I handed your corpse over to the nephilim myself."

Shannon had suspected that her old body would have been disposed of so, but it sickened her to have it confirmed anyway. "It turns out that bodies can be replaced and that is all of me that is within your power to destroy, my soul belongs to someone else, monster."

It occurred to Cray that this moment of distraction was probably the only chance they would get. They were faced with one of the most powerful spiritual beings in creation and any moment now he might decide to annihilate all three of them. Titus was a step ahead of him though.

"Excuse me a moment." the giant man stated casually and stepped past Shannon to throw a massive punch at Griska's face. The Grigori was as tall as Titus but nowhere near as well built and hadn't been expecting to be assaulted in his own quarters. The powerful punch landed square on his elegant nose and instantly rendered him unconscious. He slumped to the ground in a heap.

Lance was physically weak from a lack of nutrients and had just endured a great deal of emotional distress, but he managed to summon a smile regardless, "You arrived just in time. I can't tell you how glad I am to see you."

"Mark?" Cray asked him intently.

Lance cocked his head in the direction of the bed, "On there. I hope he's okay. That wretched creature was pretty rough with him." Although he'd been fallen for most of his life, Lance had never encountered a Watcher before now and had no idea what one was.

Cray went over to the bed and beheld his marine commander sprawled across the sheets. He could see he was alive, but probably barely. The Grigori would have known that killing him would result in him being resurrected back in New Jerusalem and wouldn't have wanted to lose his prize in such a way. He's going to need your help big man." he instructed Titus.

"In a second." Titus replied.

Cray turned to see what could possibly be holding him up and was shocked to see Titus standing between the unconscious Giska and Shannon brandishing a knife she had taken from a table of food.

"It's not worth it Shannon." he cautioned her.

She gritted her teeth, "He deserves to die for what he did to me. In this very room he took my sanity, and he took my life. And then he fed me to his pets like a piece of meat."

Titus nodded, "And then the Lord restored it all to you through His grace and mercy." She looked up at him and tears came into her eyes, "Come sister." he urged her and held out his massive arms. She ran into them and began bawling. "Jesus can remove all of your pain. You should let Him, just let it all go." Her head nodded where it was buried in the small of his huge chest.

Cray let them have the moment for as long as he felt he could, but he was concerned someone else would come into the room, or worse, that the Grigori would regain consciousness. "We should go if we want to get out of this place alive guys."

Titus nodded and opened his arms. Shannon got the hint and began to compose herself while the giant pulled a backpack off he had been carrying. "We brought fallen disguises for you and Mark, Lance." He explained as he tossed the bag at Lance's feet. "I suggest we leave Mark as he is, though." He walked over to the bed and picked up the unconscious Mark as if he weighed nothing and tossed him over one shoulder while Lance quickly donned one of the outfits. They left the bag where it lay and walked to the door. As they did, Cray noticed a data tablet lying on a nearby table. It occurred to him that it might have something useful on it and he quickly picked it up and thrust it into a pocket. He peered out into the corridor and indicated to the others that the way was clear, prompting the others to follow him out as they began the long walk back to the storeroom.

"We're not going to be able to go back through the kitchens, genius here sent that guard down there." Cray commented in mock critique of his friend.

"I could have left him for you to deal with. He might have been sufficiently distracted if I'd let him gnaw on your bones instead." Titus hit back with a vicious grin.

"That leaves the guard room." Shannon commented, "You don't really think they're going to let us through there like this do you?"

Cray had to admit she had a point. He wracked his brains for an idea, "Okay, I'll deal with it. Just give me a minute before you come in."

"I hope you know what you're doing Cray." Titus cautioned his friend, "My kin are not to be messed with."

"They're not your kin anymore my friend, we are." Cray reminded him, earning himself a smile from the giant. "Wait here."

Cray pushed through into the kitchen and immediately noticed the nephil stalking up and down the slabs, disappointedly looking for the plump woman he'd been promised. He made sure he was well beyond the dangerous creature before making his move, "Hey moron!" he shouted. It took the nephil a while to realise that he was the object of the jibe, but eventually it looked up and glared at Cray. "I knew nephilim were stupid, but I still can't believe you fell for that one!"

The beast roared and fumbled in its belt for its axe, "I will gut you fool! And I will feast on human after all!"

Titus, Lance and Shannon came through the doors just in time to see Cray run out of the opposite end of the kitchen with the enraged giant in pursuit.

"He's brave, your friend." Shannon commented to Lance, she regarded the rescued marine with a wry smile, "Incredibly stupid, but brave."

"Aye." Lance replied, "That's my Cray."

The three hastened through the disgusting kitchen, getting a few more looks than they had the last time.

"I think we're getting more attention than we did on the way in." Shannon observed.

"Aye." Titus grunted. "I hope that portal is open when we get there. We might be getting some friends soon."

The three left the kitchen and found the rusty door to the lower levels.

"This is your plan, to hide in the basement?" Lance commented concernedly.

"There will be a portal opening down here soon, but you can go upstairs and wait on the roof for a miracle if you want." Titus commented acerbically.

"Er no, that's fine." Lance replied, "I just thought maybe the *Wind* was here, and you'd come by stealth shuttle."

"You thought a whole Royal Navy frigate would be sent into danger just for a runt like you?" Titus teased with a laugh.

Lance feigned chagrin, "I will have you know that I am a child of the Almighty God!" he scoffed, "Runt indeed."

They reached the storeroom and just as they had hoped, the tell-tale glow of an open portal emanated through the crack of the partly open door. Just then they heard running footsteps behind them.

"Run!" Cray yelled as he came up on them from behind.

The three looked back to see Cray come around a corner followed closely by an enraged nephil wielding an axe and then not far behind that another two nephil, a shedim and a crowd of fallen humans.

"We should go." Lance commented dryly.

"I concur." Titus agreed and kicked the door to the storeroom open. The three ran across the room toward the welcoming open window to New Jerusalem. Inside it they could see Eret'el standing with his arms out as if he was going to pull them inside, flanked with two malakim with drawn bows. The three ran inside the window just as Cray reached the door and sprinted across the storeroom with the three nephilim warriors close on his heels. The two malakim immediately opened fire on Cray's pursuers and he ducked his head down as pulse fire whipped past him on either side. It didn't slow the pursuing nephilim much although it did discourage the other fallen from entering the room. Cray reached the portal a fraction of a second ahead of the leading nephil that he had originally teased, and it reached its arm for him in a last desperate attempt to catch its prey. The portal snapped shut and there was a sickening squelching sound as the severed head and arm of the beast dropped to the floor, the rolling head coming to a stop at Eret'el's feet.

"A successful mission then?" the marine commander commented.

*

Once again Becca found herself worrying about Cray as he had not returned from his mission when she was expecting him. She wondered what it was about his work with the marines that kept him away from them so much. She knew what he did of course, and that it was important, they had spoken about it many times. But she still didn't quite relate to his sense of priorities. He was off fighting to save people he didn't know at the expense of the people that he cared about. Not that they were suffering without him, they wanted for nothing on New Jerusalem. Becca had to admit to herself that part of her reason for wanting him there was selfish, she loved being around him. She enjoyed his company and felt somehow incomplete without him, though a counter to that was that most of the incompleteness she had felt before coming to Heaven was fulfilled by Christ. Being close to GOD gave her the reassurance that life had meaning, that she had a purpose and that whatever might happen, that her and her children would emerge unscathed. Still, she liked being around Cray and wished they could be together more. She half-heartedly wondered to herself if she would have to join the marines in order to spend more time with him. Following this train of thought she started wondering about the roles aboard the space craft and whether or not there was one which would suit her. She'd heard that there were prayer teams aboard the ships, which interested her. She liked the idea of praying for the safety of the marines as an occupation. For now, though, the only occupation she wanted was being a mother. She'd pray about the situation though; she loved the idea that she could speak to GOD whenever she wanted and know that He was listening. She knew this was the case, because ofttimes when Christ had visited, He'd brought up some of the things she'd asked Him about in prayer. Other times he'd send someone like Eve as an answer to her prayers. Right now, she felt like she could talk to Eve actually, but she didn't dare pray it as she knew that God might send her, and she didn't want to feel that the mother of mankind was at her beck and call. What an odd thought to have, she told herself. Being a Christian could be complicated sometimes. She was about to start wondering if she should pray at all when there came a knock on the door, and she immediately began to worry if GOD had sent Eve after all and she hoped she hadn't interrupted her day with her silly worrying. She opened the door and found it wasn't Eve at all.

"My beloved Becca," Jesus smiled, "You worry far too much."

*

David ben Jesse hung his jacket up and stretched his arms out to relieve some of the tension of the day. He was grateful that his redeemed body didn't become sore like his old one did after a hard day, but he still felt it was wise to stretch his muscles to stay as limber as possible. Like he had many times before, he reflected on how different his life might be now if Samuel hadn't come to his father's farm that day and anointed him as the future king of Israel. He'd probably be happily wiling away the millennium on a comfortable smallholding up in New Jerusalem with maybe a few sheep to tend and a small vegetable garden. People coveted roles like his, being King of Israel in a world where the country was the most important on Earth. They didn't realise that what he really was, was a servant and a hard working one at that. He was practically a slave to the entire population of the planet in one sense. No, he didn't fetch and carry for each one of course, but each of them was his responsibility, if they were malcontent then it was his job to figure out why and try and negotiate with the kingdoms of the world to cooperate in order to smooth out the issues. And there were lots of people in the world who were discontented with the events of the past few years. Even the most well-meaning people were chaffing a little under the strict laws that had been introduced to govern the Earth under the millennial reign of Christ. Most people hadn't realised just how many lies they told on a daily basis until lying had been made illegal and fines began to be doled out. No-one got remonstrated for telling a colleague they looked great when they really didn't, or for convincing their children they weren't getting the bike they wanted for Christmas and then surprising them with it. No, it was the small lies to assuage guilt or subtly pass blame that people had quietly gotten away with in the past and had always been able to justify to themselves that they now suddenly found themselves being condemned for and they did not like it. David sighed, he was only a few months into the millennium, and he was already exhausted. He might take his father up on his offer to spend a few days up in New Jerusalem at the farm. Two of his brothers, Eliab and Nathanel had been trying to talk him into going pterosaur riding with them which sounded a lot more interesting to him than he'd been willing to admit to them at the time.

The red dot first appeared on his desk and had crept nearly to his waist before David realised what he was looking and dove to one side. He expected a bullet to come zipping through the window, but none did, and he crept on all fours up to the window and hid beneath the sill. He looked around the room to see if the red dot was on any of the walls or room's contents, but he saw nothing. Could he have imagined what he saw? He was still crouched below the window when Gabri'el orbed through the wall and materialised in the centre of the room.

"We've caught him your highness, it is safe to stand." The archangel informed him.

David sighed with relief and pulled himself to his feet, "Is he in custody? I want to talk to him and find out who he is and why he wants me dead."

"He wanted you dead for the same reason everyone like him wants you dead your highness, you are the face of the law." Gabri'el informed him.

David was taken aback, "Wanted in the past tense? Are you saying he's dead?"

Gabri'el nodded in affirmation, "Did you really think we'd leave a man who would try to assassinate the King of Israel alive? That would be sending the wrong message. We need to be firm in upholding the law."

David sighed, "While I agree in principle, he can't be questioned now."

Gabri'el laughed, "Oh, I'm sure he's being asked plenty of questions where he is."

The assassin was in fact dead, having been shot with a bolt from the pulsebow of one of the palace guards as he was preparing the pull the trigger on a sniper rifle that had been carefully hidden during the tribulation. He didn't feel dead though, to his mind, he was stood in the middle of a country lane that ran through the grassy plains of his home country wondering how he had gotten there. He turned around to get his bearing and spied a tall man in a white linen suit walking up the lane towards him. As he drew closer, he recognised the man's face, "You!"

Jesus stopped when he came within arm's length, "Yes, it is I."

"Why have you brought me here pretender? Where is the craft you brought me in?" the assassin cried. "Take me back to Jerusalem immediately."

"There is no craft, I have no need of one. This is a realm between life and death, and you are here temporarily because you were killed trying to assassinate my appointed king." Jesus explained.

The assassin just laughed, "You have no power to raise the dead, though you would certainly like us to think you do. I believe you have me tied to a table somewhere with some kind of exotic mind device attached to my temples showing me these images. This is not real."

Jesus continued regardless, "You believe that I am an alien from another planet, sent to try and fool people into following me instead the one you consider to be the true god."

The assassin scoffed, "That is so, but it would be easy to guess it is the case."

"What if I told you that it is in fact the god you serve that is the imposter? That I created him and that he served Me until such a time as he decided he wanted power and riches for himself and betrayed Me." Jesus informed him.

The man faltered as it took a while for his brain to register what to him was a preposterous idea, "You cannot seriously expect me to believe that."

"He is currently in chains in a prison we call Tartarus." Jesus continued unabated.

"If this is so, show me." the man challenged.

"Very well." Jesus created an oval portal in the air in front of the man and beckoned for him to step though. When he appeared to be reluctant, Jesus stepped through first and then beckoned from the other side. The would-be assassin then followed him into the portal, finding himself in a small dark room with a window at one side.

"Where have you brought me?" the man asked.

"Beyond that window is the pit of Tartarus, where Heaven keeps its criminals." Jesus explained, "One of whom is your supposed god."

"Even if you could show me my god through that window, how would I know it was he?" the man scoffed, "This will not convince me."

"I did not offer to bring you here to convince you, you asked." Jesus pointed out. He walked over to the window, "Come." He beckoned.

The assassin walked to the window and looked out into the darkness beyond. Whatever cavern or room lay out there was too big to see across, looking down he could just about see figures moving about on a rock floor. Looking up, he could see fierce clouds swirling and a faint yellow light penetrating through them. Every now and then there was a flash of light as lightning flickered and occasionally an explosion as it ignited a pocket of air.

"Hydrogen gas." Jesus explained. "Do not be alarmed, this glass is unbreakable. Which is just as well because..."

There was a mighty crash as suddenly a large lizard-like dragon crashed into the glass and then an unbearable screeching sound as it dragged its claws across the window.

"The so called Beloved." It hissed, "Come in here, let me hold you in my warm embrace." It put its head to the glass and belched hot plasma at it.

"This is a Grigori, or what some call a Watcher." Jesus calmly went on, as if the dragon was no threat at all. "He was once placed in a position of authority in Europe, but then rebelled and exalted himself into a position of godhood, claiming that he was their creator rather than I, and inventing a history based on half-truths and outright lies. Eventually, one of my loyal servants, an archangel named Uri'el, defeated him and banished him here."

"And I suppose you would have me believe that this monster is my god?" the assassin laughed dismissively, though also somewhat nervously.

"No." Jesus answered calmly, "This watcher was known as Zeus, though his name in Heaven before he rebelled was Jeppiter."

The assassin had no answer to this and choose to simply stare out of the window at the dragon until his next argument came to him, "And what of my family? Have they all been condemned for not believing in You?

"Come." Jesus stepped back through the portal with the assassin flowing behind and this time it led to a hilly vale in New Jerusalem. A redeemed woman was sat on the grass a way off, reading a book, lazily twirling a flower in her fingertips. The assassin looked at her for some time, trying to figure out why the Lord had brought him to this person, when he suddenly saw through the changes that redemption had wrought to her features and recognised his own sister.

"Mariah." he gasped, "This cannot be real, she would never serve you."

"Like you, she died unbelieving, but she decided to follow Me after I had a conversation with her similar to the one that I am now having with you." Jesus informed him, "You see, she never had any real faith in your god, she was following the religion because it was expected of her by your parents, whom she loved very much."

"And they are here too I suppose?" he asked Christ.

Jesus' face fell, "Your mother is." He uttered, the implication of the omission of the assassin's father clear.

"Can I talk to my sister?" the assassin asked.

Jesus shook his head, "I would not want her to think that you had decided to follow me and then have her heart broken were you to ultimately decide otherwise."

"Or you know that she wouldn't put on a convincing performance because she is not my sister." the man accused.

Jesus smiled, "And what would you ask her that would convince you that she was your sister?"

He thought for a moment, "I would ask her where we went for my 13th birthday." the man answered. "And when…"

"And when she replied 'Dubai', you would believe it was her?" Jesus interrupted him.

"I…" the man faltered, "How do you know that? What trickery is this?"

"No trickery, I know that, because I am GOD." Jesus stated.

"That is blasphemy!" the assassin roared.

"Not if I AM." Jesus countered.

"Pffah!" the man muttered and turned back to the portal, "Take me back to the road, pretender. I will walk to my village from there."

"No. I'm afraid that you are not going home from here, that life is over. If you do not choose to follow me now, then you will be cast into Hades until the time for your judgement by the Father." Jesus cautioned him.

The man flailed with his arms, "So typical! An ultimatum from the one who claims to be fair and just, and yet I am not allowed to believe what I wish to believe."

"You have to believe in Me in order to receive forgiveness." Jesus explained, "If you do not, you will be judged on your own merit and deemed a sinner. My substitution is the only way to conquer sin."

The man sighed in exasperation, "You have an answer for everything don't you? I suppose you can tell me why my father left my mother when we were five. And why, if you are truly GOD, you didn't stop him."

"He left because he felt unable to care for her in the manner in which he felt she deserved. He went to labour on a mining rig in the hopes of returning someday a wealthier man, but he died in an accident there." Jesus sighed, "And I could not bring him back to you because He did not open his heart to my Holy Spirit to hear my warnings."

"What? My mother always believed he left for another woman." The assassin blurted, no longer thinking to question the validity of Jesus' statements.

"Not any longer she doesn't. She knows the truth now and has forgiven him." Jesus assured him.

The man laughed, "For all the good it does her now that you have separated them."

Jesus shook his head in sorrow, "I did not choose for your father to go to Hades, he chose to go himself rather than follow me. He was a good man in so many ways, but his heart was ever full of pride, much as yours is."

A tear broke from the assassin's eye, "So now my mother has to spend eternity without the man she loved."

"She could still have her son." Jesus pointed out.

And whatever you do, do it heartily, as to the Lord and not to men, knowing that from the Lord you will receive the reward of the inheritance; for you serve the Lord Christ.

Colossians 3: 23-24

Ten

Stella sat at the back of *Hope's* bridge with a data pad on her knee, pretending to be studying it, but surreptitiously observing Bree who was operating the navigation computer. She was certainly a beautiful woman now that she was redeemed, but for Charles to have thought that Stella might be jealous was ridiculous. He hadn't said as much, but she knew it was what he had been thinking due to the careful way in which he'd broached the subject of Bree joining the crew. She knew him well enough to know when he was treading on eggshells, and he had been earlier. She'd agreed immediately of course, not just to prove him wrong she told herself, but because she was a redeemed woman and jealousy wasn't part of her make-up. Besides, her and Charles had a special bond even though they were no longer married, and nothing could compare to that. She looked at Bree again and wondered if it were possible for the Lord to make someone too beautiful. The woman looked aside and caught Stella's eyes, she smiled warmly. Stella gave a reluctant half smile in return. Bree had a lovely smile, why did everything about the woman need to be beautiful? Yes, the Lord had definitely overdone it with her, it was indeed possible to be too good looking.

Ward came into the bridge; he had been inspecting the generous care package for their next mission before they took off. He immediately sensed the tense atmosphere in the room and decided to get everyone's attention focussed on the task at hand. "I've checked the cargo; we can disembark as soon as Men'el has finished his pre-flight checks."

As he said this, a shining orb rose up through the floor and then materialised into the form of the big angel, "We are ready to leave, *Hope* is as flightworthy as she was the day she left the shipyard." Men'el advised them.

"I'd have hoped so, since she's only a few months old." Ward grinned.

"We're all dialled in for the Wodda system." Bree announced.

Men'el began settling himself in the pilot's chair, "I guess I'd better get us moving then."

"What do we know about this system?" Stella inquired.

"As far as I can tell, it's not significantly different to Hobar in terms of human inhabitants. It's another populated entirely by disaffected humans." Ward offered.

"Ripe for the harvest then." Bree commented. "They'll grab Jesus with both hands."

"GOD willing." Ward added as the sleek craft lifted from the hangar floor and began to edge towards the open entrance, "I don't like to count my redeemed before they've hatched."

Hope slipped out of the hangar through the shield and into open space. As soon as it was sufficiently clear of New Jerusalem the window emitters sprang into life, cutting a gateway through into the Wodda system. A few seconds later, and the small ship was in a completely different part of the Milky Way.

"There's no station here." Bree said, looking at the scanner reports.

"There's a large ship though, from what I can tell it's derelict." Stella observed from the data on her console.

Men'el piloted the craft towards the large object on the scanner. As they drew closer it became more obvious that it was a stricken fallen destroyer.

"I hope that thing doesn't have active weapons systems." Ward commented. "We'd be severely outmatched."

"Doubtful." Men'el replied reassuringly, "Scanners detect minimal power readings, they're lucky if they have life support."

There was no challenge as *Hope* drew closer to the derelict.

"They're not responding to hails." Stella reported.

"They'd be very vulnerable to attack with such low power reserves." Ward pointed out, "My guess is that they're laying low, playing possum."

"What is a possum?" Bree asked.

"An earth creature that acts dead to avoid predators." Men'el helpfully replied.

"I can't imagine that strategy being particularly effective against scavengers." she wondered.

Ward laughed, "Hmm, I'll ask a possum next time I see one. Not that it's a problem that possums have anymore with there being no carnivores on Earth."

Stella forced a laugh as well; she wasn't going to be left out of their fun even if Ward's corny sense of humour had long since ceased to genuinely amuse her.

Men'el pulled *Hope* close to the hull of the destroyer, they could see the name *Monstrous* in faded letters stencilled on the side of the ship. "Take over." He instructed Ward, "I'll orb over and try and get an idea of what we're facing."

Ward slipped into the pilot's seat as Men'el orbed and disappeared through the front of the hull. A few tense minutes passed before the communicator beeped.

"Men'el?" Ward answered the hail.

"Affirmative Ward, you need to get in here quickly. There is a hangar on the other side of the ship that is available." the malak responded.

Ward applied some thrust and turned the ship to navigate around the hull of the large floating wreck. Before long he had swung the manoeuvrable *Hope* around the bulk of the destroyer and was entering the hangar. Even while they were landing the ship the crew could see through the canopy windows that the destroyer was in even poorer shape on the inside than on the outside. There were loose panel covers everywhere and wires dangled out of uncovered compartments, some of them showering sparks everywhere. Flames licked from a damaged conduit and black smoke tendrils wound their way across the hangar ominously.

"Perhaps you two should stay with the ship." Ward offered, as he got out of the pilot's chair, having precariously landed the ship between two crippled shuttles.

"Not on your life." Bree responded, "There will be people in here needing our help."

"You're not leaving me either, where you go, I go." Stella announced determinedly.

"Very well; but arm yourselves. We have no idea what's out there. Whatever did this damage could be on board." Ward cautioned them as he threw a pulse rifle over his shoulder that he had collected from a locker on the bridge.

Bree reached into the locker and selected for herself an identical rifle which she brandished in her arms. Stella elected for a pulse pistol.

The three lowered the ramp and exited the ship to find Men'el waiting for them at the bottom of the ramp.

"You won't need those." he said, when he saw the weapons. "What you will need is med kits."

Ward nodded and patted a case by his side. "Already thought of that." He left the rifle propped against the landing gear and followed the malak out of the hangar. Bree shrugged and left her rifle too while Stella hurried behind Ward, her pistol still in the holster.

"What are we dealing with?" Ward asked the malak as they walked, "How many?"

"I've counted six humans so far, all injured. I don't believe there are any other living beings on the ship." Men'el scowled in disapproval as he gave the report.

Ward shared his attitude; it looked like the injured had been abandoned to fend for themselves after a battle of some kind. *Hope* wasn't exactly equipped to be an ambulance, but it was more than capable of acting as such, missionaries had to be prepared for anything. They turned a corner into a fallen medical bay that half of the roof had collapsed in. Ward was taken aback by just how crude the equipment was, it bore more in common with a civil war medical tent than a modern clinic. As Men'el had reported, there were six humans in the bay, four of whom were on beds with the other two tending them despite their own injuries.

"Thank Gogon you came." One of two standing humans declared, "Is that a med kit? We need morphine desperately."

"It's a New Jerusalem med kit, it doesn't contain morphine." Ward informed the woman. He moved to the side of one of the gurneys and opened the case he was carrying. It contained a probe which he began to run up and down the body of the groaning patient. He watched a screen as he did which displayed the scanner's findings. As he did Bree and Stella came in with a med kit of their own and immediately went to one of the other beds to repeat the process. "He has a broken leg and two broken ribs." Ward reported, "He has a punctured lung as well."

"That explains his laboured breathing." the woman replied as she looked on interestedly.

"Run this down his leg while I hold this over his chest." Ward advised her.

"What about sedation?" she queried.

"The devices sedate as they heal." He informed her as he placed a pad over the man's chest and activated a switch on it. "He won't feel anything." he added as the machine began to hum softly. While the device worked, he went to the next bed and began to examine the patient there. The woman continued to run the machine up and down the leg as the man suddenly declared he could breathe properly again.

"Are you sure?" she asked him.

"Pretty sure." he replied with a smile. "And the pain in my leg is gone. See if that thing will work here." he suggested, pointing at his bruised midriff. She began to work the device over the area he had indicated, and he sighed contentedly.

"This technology is incredible." she called to Ward at the next bed over, "Where did you say you're from again?"

"New Jerusalem." he replied over his shoulder as he continued to examine the second patient.

"I've never heard of it. It must be quite a place." she commented wonderingly.

"You can say that again." Ward smiled.

He began to explain about the history of the universe and the reason they were there. By the time he had finished all the patients were physically healed and they were sat up on their beds listening keenly.

"And you say this GOD can free us of disease completely?" one man asked. He was clearly not in the best of health and Ward was not surprised he had been the first to ask such a question.

By way of reply, Ward responded, "You must have noticed that we are physically different to you. We have renewed bodies, And Yahweh can do the same for you if you choose to accept his Son."

"Would he do this for us though? Your society has followed Him in the past. Ours exists in rebellion to Him. We in this room have been serving a god you say is a rebel to His Kingdom. Surely your God would resent this?" another fallen woman stated sombrely.

Bree laughed, "I was just like you until a few months ago. I too was serving a fallen Grigori false god and living only for myself. I turned from my ways and look what Jesus did for me." She turned herself in a circle with her arms extended out to better let them see her perfect physical condition. "Not only that, but He has placed enough faith in me to let me do the work I am now doing after such a short time. He is truly an incredible GOD."

This was greeted with sighs of amazement and the six fallen began to chatter amongst themselves. Eventually the woman who had first addressed Ward as he came into the room spoke for them, "We would all like to offer our lives to this Christ."

Men'el grinned widely, "Hallelujah to the Lord."

"Then let's not waste any time in getting you to your new home." Stella suggested.

They chatted on the way back to *Hope* but nervously on Ward's part. He had managed to forget in the excitement of witnessing that they were aboard a dying ship that could potentially explode any moment and kill them. "We should probably not tarry." he told the others and picked up his pace.

The woman who had announced the group's decision came up next to him, "Thank you for rescuing us, my designation is 487."

"Please to meet you 487, my name is Ward." he answered, "I was wondering, how did your ship come to be stranded here?"

She sighed, "We were conducting a sweep of some of the systems adjoining ours. They belong to the warlord Kraan but are outliers and are usually poorly defended."

"This time they weren't though?" Ward probed.

"No, we entered a system called Pillabis and came upon a massive construction project. Some kind of ring-shaped structure." She informed him, "Half of Kraan's fleet must have been there, hundreds of ships, and those within range fired on us immediately doing the damage you've seen. We barely managed to window to a random destination with the ship as battered as it was. Fortunately, they had no idea where we portaled to otherwise, I feel certain they would have followed us and finished their work. As if our situation wasn't already dire enough, the uninjured crew and the higher races all used the shuttles to make their way back to Gogon's space, leaving us behind."

Ward placed a reassuring hand on her shoulder in an empathic response to her woeful tale. Mentally though, he was making a careful note of what she had told him; a fallen building operation being staunchly defended might be significant. He'd inform Yara'el upon their return, just in case the ring structure 487 had mentioned was something of interest to the navy.

*

The human marines spent their first few days back on New Jerusalem recovering from their ordeal. Lance had decided to stay at home and recover and Cray visited him regularly. Titus was conspicuous in his absence and Cray suspected he was spending time with Shannon; she had taken to the big marine and seemed to find his presence therapeutic. Cray suspected it had something to do with how changed he was from his previous self and if the Lord could transform the heart of a nephil, then He could heal anyone.

On the morning of the third day, there was an unexpected knock on the door of Becca's lodge, where Cray was spending most of his time, and he opened it expecting to find Lance, but instead Eret'el was stood there with Jonathan Sharp

"Commander? Captain?" Cray greeted the marine officers.

"Good day Ironheart, may we?" Eret'el asked after an awkward delay, by way of requesting to come in.

Cray suddenly remembered his manners, realising he was just standing in the door like a dumbfounded lump, "Oh I'm sorry, yes please, come

Chris Smithies   Millennium

in." He left the door open and picked up Esther, putting her on his hip while his guests looked about.

"Humans love their trinkets." Eret'el observed as he picked up a scale model of the *Wings of the Wind* and turned it over in his large hands.

"Don't you be calling months of my hard work a trinket." Jonathan commented in mock chagrin as he wandered over to a bookshelf and started looking at the titles. "Have you read all of these?" he asked as he picked out a copy of *The Screwtape Letters* and flicked through it.

"I'm trying." Cray replied, "Reading in English is still a skill I'm developing. Most of those are Becca's."

"Oh of course. Your first language is the tongue of the planet you grew up on. What was it called again?" with the Holy Spirit's gift of tongues, it was easy to forget that the people on New Jerusalem were speaking different languages that were being supernaturally translated.

"Frixar." Cray dutifully replied, though he preferred to try and pretend those years had never happened.

At this point Becca came into the room and saw that she had guests, "Oh, I'm sorry." she blurted, "I didn't know anyone was coming."

Eret'el apologised in turn, "It is I who am sorry Becca, we gave no warning of our coming. You have a lovely home."

"Of course, I do." she answered with a cheeky smile, "The Lord built it."

"Well, as you might imagine, we are not here to reminisce." Eret'el stated, as he perched himself on the edge of one of the sofas., somewhat awkwardly. Malakim were not inclined to recline.

"Of course, what can I do for you?" Cray asked, somewhat apprehensively. He was secretly hoping he wasn't being sent on another mission quite yet. He had planned to go fishing with Lance tomorrow who had finally agreed to leave his house. He thought it would be good for his friend to get outside into nature.

"Mark has recovered from his physical injuries quite nicely." Jonathan informed Cray, although the marine was already aware of this. He had been keeping tabs on Mark's status keenly. Cray simply smiled and nodded politely as if it was news to him.

"He has however decided not to come back to the marines." Eret'el elaborated, which was news that Cray wasn't privy to.

"Poor Mark." muttered Becca. Cray had informed her of what had happened, and she had been praying for the marine commander.

"That's a shame," Cray replied, "He's a good leader."

"So are you, apparently." Jonathan added.

"I am?" Cray retorted, suddenly wary of the conversation.

"According to the rest of Razor squad, yes." The captain assured him.

"Which leads us tidily into why we are here." Eret'el smiled.

"Oh no, I see where this is going." Cray responded wearily, "I'm not the man for the job."

"The General believes you are." Eret'el informed him, in reference to the archangel Micha'el.

"He does? Micha'el himself sent you?" Cray asked in wonder.

"Not exactly. I decided we should come and inform you." Eret'el elucidated somewhat pedantically, "But he did agree with my recommendation."

"And mine." Sharp interjected. "When I read the reports."

"I don't know what to say. I didn't think I'd really done anything extraordinary." Cray sat down on the sofa placing Esther carefully on his lap and Becca sat next to him with her hand on his shoulder. Cray's mind was a whirl, and he found her presence comforting.

Eret'el laughed, "You don't think risking your life mocking a 12ft nephil and then kiting it around an enemy palace while your comrades escape is extraordinary? Well, that tells me that you are definitely the right man for this job."

"I er…" Cray mumbled, somewhat overwhelmed. He'd been so worried about Lance and Mark that he hadn't really dwelt on his actions of that day much. Now that he thought about it, he supposed he had been quite brave. He didn't know he'd had it in him.

"Well, I'm not surprised." Becca put in, "It's the man you are. It's why I worry about you."

"Wouldn't being a commander take me away from Becca and the kids more?" Cray asked.

"No more than it does right now." Eret'el replied. "The malakim are increasingly starting to refer to the human marines by a new name as well." he informed Cray.

"Oh really? What's that?" the human asked.

"They're calling you the mighty men. Or in our malakimic parlance, the Gibborim." Eret'el proudly shared with a grin.

"The Gibborim." Cray repeated as if testing the feel of the word on his tongue. "I can live with that." Then he quickly rethought his words. "I'm sorry, I can more than live with it, it's very flattering. Please let your malakim know that we're proud to be honoured by them so." He decided after some deliberation and grinned.

Eret'el smiled, for he knew that the kind of pride Cray was referring to was not that of an exaggerated view of one's self-importance like the sort that had led to the downfall of many of his peers, but rather being proud of a job well done, which was edifying.

"He'll do it." Becca asserted, "You will, won't you my dear?" she added to Cray with pride in her eyes. "It looks like the galaxy needs you."

"I guess I'm taking the job." Cray decided, still somewhat unsure he was doing the right thing, but beginning to feel very cornered.

"I'm glad, Cray Ironheart, Commander of the Royal Navy Gibborim Marines." Eret'el declared, "Now rest, for we have a new mission in two days, and you and I will be leading it."

*

On the other side of the galaxy, Giska raged. They had come into his own residence and had humiliated him. By now probably most of the empire had heard of his humbling, even though he'd had all his servants killed as a precaution. He'd not invited a human to his quarters last night at first, until he had realised that he was afraid of creating another vengeful harridan. He'd then ordered an orgy in his rooms, just to prove to himself that he was not a coward. Then, paradoxically he'd cursed himself afterwards for having his actions influenced in any away whatsoever by that witch, he should have just carried on as if nothing had happened. However hard he tried; he couldn't get the events of that day out of his head. The woman had clearly given her life to the tyrant upon her death, hence her ability to cheat fate and return in a new body. Giska firmly believed it was against all laws of conduct for the Christ to consort with souls after they had passed and recruit them to his cause. An inordinate number of fallen slaves had become redeemed in this very manner and supposedly had their sins washed away. Giska was planning to create a decree stating that any of these defectors who were caught should be tortured in the most brutal way possible in order to discourage the practice. He also reflected on how poor the Christ's taste was to have taken that slut he had killed. He truly must be desperate for followers the Watcher thought. He also couldn't understand why they'd let Giska live, if he'd been in her place, he'd have murdered her in the most painful way possible and burned her body to ash. He tried to calm himself down, there was no point in tormenting himself about it. He'd bury himself in his work to forget, at least it was purely a personal attack and hadn't jeopardised his pet project which would have been far worse. He could take some solace in that. Now where did he leave that data pad with the schematics for the ring weapon in it?

Giska's howl of fury as he realised that Heaven had his project notes was heard across the palace, causing servants to cower in terror as they realised that another night of horror lay ahead.

*

The briefing room contained some of the most powerful elohim in Heaven, Cray realised as he stepped inside. He felt intimidated to be in the presence of such honoured company, even the General was there. It occurred to him that something very big must be happening to warrant such attention. He sat down at the table between Jonathan and Eret'el as Micha'el acknowledged his arrival.

"Ah, our guest of honour is here." the archangel commented mysteriously.

Cray was completely oblivious to what was happening here and Eret'el could tell, "The datapad you brought back from Kraan's palace contained the full schematics of the project we've been looking for. And thanks to one of our missionary teams we now know exactly where it is as well." He explained. Suddenly it dawned on Cray why he was being made a fuss of, and to think he'd only picked it up as an afterthought.

"And it's just as well you did, because the project poses a serious threat to New Jerusalem and not only that, but it's nearly complete according to these figures. It's already being tested." Micha'el continued. He activated a holographic projector in the table which produced a 3d image of the Pillabis system showing its dying sun at the centre. All eyes were on the graphic as he manipulated it to zoom in on an area of space near the glowing orb. As he zoomed ever more, the image of a ring became clearer and details such as weapons towers and docking ports began to become evident.

"What is that?" Jonathan queried.

"According to the documentation on the datapad, it's a portal generator spanning 100 miles across." Yara'el answered from his place across the table from the humans.

The *Wings of the Wind* captain breathed out sharply, "What would require a gate so massive?"

"It's not intended to transport ships or goods; it's intended to convey pure energy." Micha'el answered. He zoomed out again and began a simulation.

Those sat around the table watched in great interest as the beam weapons around the ring began firing into the sun and then gasped in horror as the gate opened in the same moment that the sun went into supernova. Energy from the supernova washed over the ring's shields, overwhelming them within seconds and destroying it utterly, but a mass of energy also poured into the gate during those few seconds, essentially turning it into an immense directed energy weapon. The image on the holoprojector changed into a hypothetical view of New Jerusalem being on the other side of the open window. Mere seconds after the window opening, a 100-mile-wide lance of pure supernova energy poured through the gate and into the side of the Holy City. It punched a hole through the city's shields and burned into the structure, causing a cataclysmic level of damage in the seconds before the ring was destroyed and the window closed.

The archangel ended the simulation and addressed the room, "So you see what our enemies have been planning for us. I calculate that we have approximately three hours to act before the events you have just witnessed in the simulation take place. Perhaps less if the fallen decide to take short cuts."

This news was greeted with gasps of horror from around the table. "So, we are going to send a fleet to destroy it?" Jonathan asked.

Yara'el responded, but not with the answer Jonathan had hoped for, "We are, and a big one at that, but there's another problem."

Micha'el continued, "We have recently intercepted communications from Lord Skaan's home planet to numerous other fallen warlords, begging them to send ships to help him defend his gate. They have obviously realised that we have these plans now and are anticipating an attack."

"Surely Royal Navy ships are more than a match for a rag tag fallen fleet though?" Cray stated hopefully.

Yara'el nodded to Cray's relief, "Of course they are, but the shields on the rings are likely to be incredibly strong and will take time to reduce using weapons fire. We cannot take the chance that we'll be able to bring them down at the same time as fighting off what is likely to be an appreciable enemy fleet presence."

Jonathan sighed at the inevitable, "Which is where we come in."

Micha'el smiled grimly, "Exactly. The *Wings of the Wind* will enter the system with the rest of the fleet but in stealth mode. While the fleet fights the enemy and draws their attention away, you will approach the ring and insert Eret'el and Cray's marines. They will prevent the ring's engineers from completing their work, allowing the Royal Navy the time it needs to defeat the enemy fleet and then destroy the ring."

"Will we have time to exfiltrate?" Cray wondered.

"We hope so." Yara'el reassured him, "It will take some time for the fleet to destroy the ring's shields once your work is done. That should give your marines a chance to get out."

Cray nodded grimly. At least if the worst came to the worst, they would wake up in the hatchery in New Jerusalem in new bodies. "Let's do it then." It was only after he'd said it that he realised that if the fallen were successful, there might not be a hatchery.

"Good." Micha'el pointed at a highlighted part of the ring, "This is the incomplete section. They do not have time to fully complete the structure before we strike, but we anticipate the gate will work regardless. What they must achieve though, is to finish installing and connecting the power generators. The incomplete section will be your point of entry and from there you can proceed to your targets. You can destroy the power generators, eliminate the engineers, or obliterate the section entirely if possible."

"Whichever proves the easiest to achieve at the time, got it." Cray surmised.

"And that kind of deduction shows we were right to promote you." Eret'el smiled.

"Do we have to destroy all the generators? There must be a great many of them?" Cray wondered.

Yara'el shook his head, "You only need to destroy enough that the beam weapons will lack the power to bring the sun to nova. The fleet will protect you until that is achieved."

"It's going to be Armageddon in space." Jonathan groaned.

"I fear the battle ahead may well be on that scale," Micha'el agreed to Jonathan's horror, "but we won that battle, and we will win this one."

"We had the Lord Himself alongside us at that battle." the star ship captain pointed out.

"The Lord is always with us my friend, be ever sure of that." Yara'el asserted.

Jonathan allowed himself a smile, of course the malak admiral was correct, and he shouldn't have allowed himself to forget that.

Eret'el ended the briefing, "This is time sensitive, so let's get moving."

The horse is prepared for the day of battle, but deliverance is of the Lord.

Proverbs 21: 31

Eleven

The Fortress class vessels were ungainly looking craft. Based on the hull of a standard destroyer, their prow had been enlarged to accommodate a massive solid ram of metal designed to absorb enemy fire, particularly during the crucial vulnerable moments of window transition. Behind this ram, mounted along the flanks of the ships were outsized shield generators, which when activated projected an incredibly powerful shield a mile across around the ship. This created a safe zone inside which other ships could operate safely, at least until such a time as the shields were penetrated, even the strongest shield couldn't absorb fire forever. The shield could be penetrated by supernatural beings such as shedim or dragons and as such, any fleet stationed inside was vulnerable to melee attack. Invulnerability to ranged fire, even if only for a small amount of time, gave a fleet a huge advantage in any battle, however.

So it was, that when windows opened into the Pillabis system, The Fortress class vessels Kathenoth and Petra were the first through. Weapons fire began to strike their rams almost as soon as the link to the alien system was established, a sure indication that the fleet's arrival had been anticipated. The rams of both ships soon began to show wear from the sheer weight of fire inflicted upon them and chunks of metal were scythed away as the ships made the transition from one system to another. Their resilience was to prove sufficient for the purpose however, as they lasted long enough for the slow-moving ships to get through the windows and activate their shields. The shield generators sprang into life and a small pale blue bubble appeared around each generator but then grew and combined with the shields of other generators to form a spherical energy wall which continued to expand and absorb the fire from the enemy fleet until they reached full size. Once the shields were activated, each Fortress class vessel provided a safe spherical area into which other ships could safely make the transition from the Sol system into the Pillabis system.

First through were the mighty Judah class battleships, Bethlehem, Masada and Jericho, these were followed by the equally impressively sized fleet carriers, Goshen, Shiloh and Gilgal, each equipped with a hundred Crucifix fighters, ready to tangle with anything foolish enough to come through the shield. After the capital ships came a host of smaller vessels, Hunter and Lance class cruisers, destroyers and frigates. These last two ship types had no long-range weapons and were there to engage any enemy who drew near the fleet. Last through the window, just before it closed, was *Wings of the Wind.*

Looking at the view screen Jonathan found it hard to believe there was a massive enemy fleet out there. The ring was visible, but the ships were too far away to be seen with the naked eye.

"*Wings*, show basic sensor data on view screen." he instructed the ship. Suddenly the screen filled with tiny glowing square showing the locations of each enemy vessel. There were hundreds. "Highlight capital ships only." he ordered, attempting to filter the results down to a manageable amount. A great many of the squares disappeared but still too many remained to be easily counted.

"We appear to be vastly outnumbered." Mei observed from next to him.

"Just how Yahweh likes it." Jonathan responded, referring to the many times in history God had intervened to allow an underdog to win in a fight, thus showing that it was His presence that made the difference, not that of the physical combatants. The Royal Navy fleet would have a technological advantage though, the beam weapons of the Lance class cruisers could hit the fallen from a much greater distance than the fallen could respond from. As if to confirm this thought, the order was given to open fire, and a series of red laser beams shot out from the cruisers towards the enemy fleet.

"We should get moving while they're distracted." Mei prompted him.

"Navigation, plot us a course to the ring, keep us as far away from any enemy ships as you can manage." Jonathan ordered.

"I'll try sir," the woman at the navigation console responded, "but they appear to have a tight formation of frigates around the ring structure."

"Then we're going to have a serious test of our ship's stealth abilities." Jonathan replied.

Mei raised an eyebrow, "And if we're detected?"

Jonathan's was stony-faced in his reply, "Against that many ships, we wouldn't last more than a few seconds."

Mei grinned mischievously, "Well, a little incineration by pulse cannon fire will make an otherwise boring week more interesting. Take us in if you would, Shamus."

At stealth speed, it took *Wings* a few minutes to cover the distance between the Navy fleet and the ring weapon during which time there were a few close calls as errant shots from the ongoing battle came uncomfortably close. Having one hit their shields could potentially give their presence away if the impact was observed.

"Is it me, or is it getting hot in here?" Mei commented as the system's giant sun loomed large on the screen.

"I wonder how the construction crew of the ring cope with working in these temperatures." Jonathan pondered aloud.

Mei scoffed, "My guess is that they aren't offered any other choice."

"That would have to have some impact on their work efficiency." he continued as he watched the structure in question looming closer and closer on the viewscreen. He was starting to gain an appreciation for just how big it was.

"I have no personal experience, but I'd guess that a nephil with a whip is a good motivator." Mei commented, "That thing is really massive, isn't it? Are those beam weapons on those turrets? I never imagined they could be constructed that large."

"Apparently once the ring is complete, the beam weapons will fire on the sun and then the ring will open a portal to New Jerusalem allowing the energy of the explosion to be transmitted through the portal into the city." Jonathan shuddered at the thought.

A look of surprise crossed Mei's face, "The ring will surely be destroyed in the process."

He shrugged, "Yes, but I think the hope is that a significant amount of damage will be done to the Holy City before the ring's shields are overwhelmed."

"So, it's basically going to come down to who makes the strongest shields then. My bet in that case would be on Heaven." Mei decided.

Jonathan sighed, "If only if were that simple. The ring has been built knowing that it will need to withstand the force of a supernova for as long as possible. New Jerusalem's shields were designed to defend against an attack from a hostile fleet, not an exploding sun. It's hard to say how they would hold up against the blast of a nova. It's likely enough heat would be transmitted through the shield to seriously harm a great many of the inhabitants at the very least."

The navigation officer interrupted their discussion, "We're nearly upon the ring's defensive perimeter, sir."

"Here goes nothing then." Mei quipped, "If this doesn't work, I'll see you back at the hatchery Captain."

Jonathan gave her a scathing look, "It'll work. I designed this ship myself. It will work."

"Who are you trying to convince, me or yourself?" she countered cheekily.

"Entering the perimeter now." the officer informed the bridge crew.

All eyes turned to the viewscreen as they watched a fallen frigate that was holding station near the ring loom closer. Not far off its port bow was another ship and close behind that yet another. The *Wings of the Wind* was trying to fly through a grid of ships and one wrong move could cause them to be detected.

"There." Jonathan pointed at a space between two of the enemy vessels. "That gap is slightly wider; we'll go through there."

The pilot pointed the ship at the gap indicated, but as he did, the enemy frigates shifted slightly and the space between them was reduced.

"Don't worry." Jonathan reassured the pilot, "Adjust course 30 degrees starboard."

The pilot did as he was instructed and found a clearer passage near the point one of the frigates had just left.

"We're through." The navigation officer advised them.

There was a collective sigh of relief across the bridge as the *Wind* moved beyond the defensive perimeter of ships and proceed towards the ring itself.

"Our insertion point is near that beam cannon there. There's a shield generator on the opposite side of the emplacement." Mei pointed at a section of the ring that protruded on the outside and was clearly still under construction, although any visible gaps in the outer skin of the ring were being closed fast by construction crews desperately trying to finish their work before the approaching Heavenly fleet could destroy it.

"Let the marines know we're here. It's all up to them now." Jonathan ordered. It wouldn't be hard to keep *Wings of the Wind* hidden until the marines had done their work, as they were not moving and could power down to minimal levels. It would still be an anxious wait as the soldiers went about their work though, and Captain Sharp wasn't looking forward to it. He was grateful to have Mei to wait it out with, he was impressed with his new second officer and had decided she was someone he could get along with. He told himself it wasn't at all because she was exactly the kind of woman he would have fantasised about as a young man back on Earth. He found himself briefly wondering what kind of men she would have fantasised about in her previous life and then remembered he was deep inside enemy space inside a ring of hostile ships holding station next to a super weapon, and he was daydreaming about a pretty girl. Get a grip, he scolded himself. He stalked to the viewscreen and stood there with his hands crossed behind his back staring out at the ring.

Unlike Jonathan, Mei was completely focussed on the task at hand and was taking readings from a nearby console. This is what she was telling herself at any rate. She wasn't taking note at all of how handsome her captain looked right now with that intense look on his face and commanding stance which had caused his uniform to stretch ever so slightly over his well-built frame. She glanced over the readings on the console for the third time, determined to actually read what she was looking at instead of just looking for somewhere to put her eyes instead of on him. Surely it was acceptable to find someone of the opposite gender intriguing even if there were no marriage as such in Heaven?

On one of the lower decks, the marines were preparing to leave the *Wings of the Wind* on their shuttle. There was a new member on the marine squad who was filling the position left open by Cray when he had been promoted up to Commander. This was Gordon Light who had joined the marines a couple of months after Cray and Lance had. He was therefore a little greener than the rest of them but appeared to be a good man possessed of a calm, confident demeanour.

Cray looked over at Lance and Titus and gave them a thumbs up. They looked back at him oddly. He had never given anyone a 'thumbs up' before and had recently seen people doing it on New Jerusalem. He'd been told it conveyed a sense of confidence and reassured people but it didn't seem to work on his friends.

Lance leaned over to Titus and whispered, "Did you see anything wrong with Cray's thumb?"

Titus shrugged, "It's very small, but other than that no."

"Why did he hold it out to us?" Lance asked.

"I do not know. Perhaps he is seeking reassurance. You should hold out one of your fingers in return as a gesture of solidarity." the giant suggested thoughtfully.

There were gasps of shock from the other marines as Lance did what Titus suggested with a finger selected at random.

"What?" Lance asked the others.

Susan Stead could barely contain her laughter, "You two are banned from holding any digits out to each other from this point onwards."

The laughter broke the tension only briefly as Adedayo presented the question: "Is there a backup plan if we don't manage to get the ring shield down?"

The marines looked around at each other worriedly and eventually every eye landed on Cray, as if he would have an answer but he hadn't been briefed on any alternative strategies that might have been formulated. He found himself wishing that the malakim were in the shuttle, rather than making their way stealthily to the ring inside the spiritual realm. One of them would quickly reply in a characteristic malakim baritone, "GOD will make a way." or something like that. Then it occurred to him to simply say that. He uttered the words as confidently as he could and there were nods and beams of approval from the marines.

"God will make a way, where there seems to be no way." Adedayo completed the phrase for Cray. "You are learning your bible quickly Cray Ironheart."

That was from the bible? Cray thought. He hadn't realised when he said it, it had just come to him. Perhaps spending so much time with malakim and long-time Christians was rubbing off on him.

"Well at the moment there does seem to be a way, and it's Razor Squad." Titus grumbled. "So, I suggest we stay on task until such a time as that ceases to be the case. Then we can worry about alternatives."

"Well said, big man." Adedayo affirmed, "We are the instrument of GOD's will right now so let's be the best instrument we can be."

The shuttle slowed perceptibly, and an orb appeared through the hull and morphed into Eret'el. "We have arrived Gibborim. We need to remain as silent as possible as there are workmen in this area of the ring." The marines nodded their acknowledgment of his words as the rear ramp of the shuttle dropped onto a half-finished platform. Cray stepped out and was initially surprised to find an atmosphere in a section of the ring that was exposed to space, but then remembered they had flown through a shield which would have been holding the air in place.

"What a charming establishment." Vincenzo commented as the marines congregated on the platform amidst the dangling wires and piles of yet to be used construction materials.

The 9 other malakim warriors were already there waiting and came up to the marines. "Very good, we are a combined force of 20 again. This is going to need to be a combination of stealth, speed and strength. We will not always be able to avoid combat and so we will have to overwhelm any hostile forces as efficiently as possible." Eret'el instructed them.

"Overwhelming is my specialty." Titus muttered to muted laughter from those around him.

One of the malakim was at the end of the platform near a metal doorway working on a console panel. As the marines approached this door, the malak succeeded in overriding the controls and the doors slid open with a hiss.

Eret'el gave one last order before they entered the ring, "Once inside we will revert to hand signals only, until we engage the enemy."

As they entered it was immediately obvious that this was no ordinary structure. There were no doors other than the one they entered in, only a long uninterrupted passageway that disappeared into the distance in both directions, almost imperceptibly curving upwards as it went. Eret'el motioned with a hand signal for the squad to move up the corridor towards the right. The marines felt very exposed as they moved along, despite the intention to be stealthy, they could be plainly seen from hundreds of metres away. For this reason, Eret'el had placed Vincenzo Roccia and Lee Masters at the front of the squad, as the two best snipers in the group with orders to neutralise any targets that came into view. Cray was bringing up the rear when he heard the first two pulse rifle shots go off. The pulse rifle was a relatively stealthy weapon as its retort was nowhere near as loud as a kinetic rifle. The squad continued moving and soon Cray was sidestepping past the unconscious bodies of two engineers who had been working on an open panel in the wall. They encountered no other obstacles before coming to a large set of double doors in the right side of the corridor. Eret'el made the sign to get ready as Finn'el began working on the door controls.

The door opened into a large area where several relatively small generators were pumping power into a larger structure in the centre of the room which appeared to be sending a stream of blue energy up a conduit into the ceiling. It was instantly recognisable as being one of the shield generators. A number of drones and humans were milling around checking readings and performing maintenance with a pair of fallen human guards standing watch from a platform off to one side.

"Engage them." Cray ordered his gibborim, indicating the two guards.

Chaos erupted in the room as pulse rifle fire was exchanged briefly before the two guards dropped. The engineers took to hiding behind machinery for fear that the marines would target them next but any that did not present a direct threat were ignored.

"You can plant your charge here, Corporal Fire." Eret'el indicated a location on the shield generator's lower casing.

Rudi Fire darted forwards, removing an electromagnetic charge from his bag, and placed it where Eret'el had indicated. Some of the engineers took it upon themselves to flee the room while they were working, and the marines let them go. There was no point in trying to prevent them from warning their compatriots, as when this generator went down it would signal to the entire operation that they had saboteurs not to mention pinpointing where exactly those saboteurs were. Rudi finished deploying the charge and nodded to Eret'el.

The angel indicated for the marines to exfiltrate the room before addressing the engineers, "Remain where you are until the blast goes off and you should be safe. Do not attempt to call for assistance, your communicators will not function. I would strongly suggest that you try to get off this structure within the next twenty minutes if you can find a way." He turned and strode from the room, as Rudi activated the detonator from his position at the door. Nearly invisible pulses of energy radiated out from the device and all the generators in the room fell silent, followed by the shield generator in the centre of the room losing power and ceasing its operation. As an added advantage, the lights in a large section of the corridor went out which would assist them greatly in terms of making them harder to target.

"Let's move on to the next one." Eret'el ordered the squad as he stepped out into the now darkened corridor.

"Stay on guard, they'll be aware we're here now." Cray added.

Once again, Vincenzo and Lee took point and the squad continued moving around the structure.

*

"I'm reading power fluctuations in the ring. The shield strength has dropped significantly in the target area." A sensor officer on board the Royal Navy battleship *Bethlehem* informed her captain.

Bethlehem, like her sister ships *Jericho* and *Masada* was not unsimilar to a World War two battleship in configuration, possessing a long sleek hull which was flattened on top and had five huge rail gun turrets mounted on it, each boasting 4 large guns. Currently its rail cannons were laying down a steady stream of fire into the opposing fleet, wreaking havoc on larger ships. A fallen frigate was unlucky enough to stray into the path of a rail gun slug and the heavy large calibre shell overwhelmed its shields instantly and passed straight through the hull and out of the other side without barely losing momentum. The combined result of loss of compression on both sides of the ship and the catastrophic damage the slug did to a fuel conduit on the way through caused the vessel to shatter and explode.

"The marines must have begun disabling the generators." the captain, currently a highly capable malak named Keera'el replied. "How soon before we can put shots through the shield?"

"As we suspected, the adjoining generators are picking up the slack and the shield remains in place. I estimate from the readings that we will require them to disable another two generators before they become unable to span the gap in the shielding and we will be given a window to damage the ring." the officer responded.

"What are your thoughts Mr Hardy?" the captain asked his second officer, a future captain in training who had a great amount of experience in ship-to-ship warfare, but none of it in the past two centuries and certainly none of it in space.

Unlike many other redeemed, Thomas Hardy had not changed his name as it had been deemed by his Lord to already be an appropriate descriptor of the man. "I believe we should continue to batter the defensive line for the time being. I am as much a believer in bold actions as the next man, but if we move in towards the ring too soon, we will be moving our ships into the range of their smaller vessels which will reduce the time we can stay in the area. Back here at extreme range we can bide our time more effectively and give the marines time to get those shields down."

Keera'el nodded approvingly, this human would indeed make a good captain for the *Bethlehem* when the time came, possibly even an admiral in time. "Very good Mr Hardy, my thoughts were much the same. Instruct the fleet of the success of the marines thus far, but that we intend to hold station here at least until the next generator is disabled."

Hardy took note of how much faith his malak captain put in the marines, apparently, he was accustomed to expecting success of his kin.

*

On the ring, the marines that so much counted on were bogged down in a firefight in the long corridor. The way ahead had been barricaded with a makeshift pile of construction materials and behind it a group of fallen humans were dug in with a pair of nephilim, one of whom had a pulse cannon. The marines couldn't progress any further without inviting a withering hail of fire from the rapid firing high calibre weapon.

Eret'el took his malakim out through the hull of the ring in order to sweep around the obstacle whilst Cray was left to command the human section of the squad. He had pulled Vincenzo and Lee back as they couldn't maintain a stable stance long enough to get accurate shots off. He had considered rolling smoke down the passageway to give them some cover, but the likelihood of one of them being hit if the pulse cannon was fired blindly into the smoke was too high. He decided to bide his time, despite time not being something they had a great deal off. He was relieved when he heard the recognisable sounds of melee combat echoing down the ring and he urged his marines to move up again, hoping desperately that the malakim had neutralised the cannon first. As the barricade became visible Cray noted that nearly all the fallen were locked in combat and very few were free to continue firing at them. He quickly ordered a firing line and then the gibborim began to pick off the fallen at the edges of the melee. From where they were positioned, Cray felt sure he saw at least one malakim drop to a blow from one of the nephilim. He hoped that if that was indeed the case, that the malak in question would be able to make it to the fleet in the spiritual realm and not end up stranded in this sector. Eventually the way was cleared, and the marines hurried to the next target before more reinforcements could arrive and delay their progress.

*

"A second shield generator has fallen on the ring my lord." the nervous servant who had just run into Warlord Kraan's throne room informed the ruler and his first attendant.

"There must be more ships we can send." Griska pleaded, "We cannot afford to let this opportunity die when we are so close to our objective."

"And achieve what exactly Griska?" Kraan berated him, "It is not the space battle that is the issue, it is the progress of what appears to be a handful of Heaven's marines around the ring. Surely a 100mile wide structure has enough guards to stop one marine squad?"

"They were slow to respond to the unexpected threat my lord." Giska explained, "We don't know how they got there. It is possible the marines will not reach the third generator, but landing reinforcements on the ring would make it even less likely. If they manage to destroy a third shield generator, then the shield will likely fail."

"Very well, send a full contingent of shedim in a fast cruiser. Their marshal prowess should be enough to overwhelm the insurgents." Kraan allowed. "Is it not possible that the ring can be activated before the third generator can be destroyed?"

Giska paused before answering, "A premature firing of the weapon could result in the ring being destroyed by the nova before enough energy was transferred through it to damage the city. All of my, I mean our work would be destroyed for naught."

Kraan leaned forward, "And the enemy fleet?"

Giska faltered, "Well, it would be destroyed of course, along with ours, but that is not our objective, the holy city is."

"Our objective is to hurt Heaven and losing their fleet would do exactly that. Fire the weapon immediately. If enough energy is transferred through the ring to cause even a little damage to the city, then that will have to suffice along with the loss of their precious fleet." Kraan ordered in a tone that strongly suggested the debate was over.

Giska bowed obediently and activated his communicator to issue the order.

*

"Something is happening." Hardy informed his captain as the massive beam cannon turrets on the ring were raised.

Keera'el took a moment to guess what was about to happen, "It's going to fire on the sun early." he uttered in horror.

"But that will destroy both fleets." Hardy replied in disbelief.

"Issue the retreat order to the fleet, we're leaving this system now." Keera'el ordered.

"But New Jerusalem!" Hardy protested.

"There is nothing we can do about that now. Even if the shield was to fall in the next minute, we would be unable to damage the ring significantly enough before it activated to stop it. Saving the fleet is all we can achieve here now; the rest is in the Lord's hands." the malak captain explained.

*

A similar degree of panic was taking place aboard *Wings of the Wind* once the order to retreat came in. They had observed the deployment of the beam weapons and were the best positioned in the fleet to see that the surface of the sun had already begun to react.

"How long will those beams take to bring the sun to nova?" Mei asked.

Jonathan hazarded his best guess, "It's hard to say without having more data, but I wouldn't have thought we have much time."

Mei frowned, "Should I order the marines to exfiltrate?"

"Let me think." Jonathan said stalling her. "The two shield generators in this section of the ring are down. How much damage could *Wings* do to the ring from our position this close?"

"To a structure this size? Not much. Unless we hit something volatile that could cause a chain reaction." Mei answered thoughtfully.

Jonathan shook his head, "That might work in the movies, but in real life there aren't any convenient targets to hit that aren't shielded."

"What if we were inside the shield?" Mei suggested. "We could fly into the unfinished section and…"

"Open a window! You clever, wonderful, gorgeous woman!" Jonathan blurted.

"I was going to say open fire, but…" Mei stammered, "Where are you suggesting we open a window to?"

"The ring!" Jonathan shouted, beside himself with excitement, "Pilot, take us inside the structure, slowly so that the shields don't kick us out."

Mei was totally flummoxed now, not able to comprehend what he was planning. Also, had he just called her gorgeous?

"And get our marines out of there, now!" Jonathan ordered.

*

On the rings chaos erupted as the marines received the order from *Wings of the Wind* to exfiltrate as soon as possible.

"We can just enter the spiritual realm to avoid the blast Cray Ironheart, but you need to get your men back to the shuttle." Eret'el explained.

Ray Tracer had been listening in, "What if I brought the shuttle to you?"

"The frigates wouldn't let you get more than a few metres CGI." Cray objected.

"The frigates are pulling out, along with every other ship in the fallen fleet." Tracer responded. "It doesn't seem like anyone wants to be here when that sun explodes, whatever their orders might be."

"Well in that case, get your butt over here!" Cray yelled with a grin.

The marines were in a corridor deep inside the ring at this point. Even though the shuttle was coming closer, they still had the problem of reaching an outer airlock. Finn'el found a console and accessed a map of the ring. "There's a large conduit leading to the surface nearby, but it has no atmosphere. You'll have to use your suits' breathing system." He informed Cray.

"So be it." the marine commander responded. "Whatever gets us out of here the fastest."

"Guys." CGI's voice came through the comm, "A fallen cruiser has just entered the system."

What now? Cray thought to himself.

*

Wings of the Wind manoeuvred its way inside the shield and held station inside an unfinished section of the ring.

"Deactivate stealth mode." Jonathan ordered, and the ship which had previously been invisible to the naked eye flickered into sight. "I want you to make a window to here." he pointed on the navigation officer's computer.

Mei had been observing over his shoulder, "But that's inside the structure, we can't travel to that point!"

"Who said anything about going through it?" Sharp responded with a grin.

The navigation officer followed his instructions, and the window emitters began to work on opening the window. The view that appeared through the portal was that of a cross section of the ring's interior with severed corridors, conduits and rooms. Immediately, without any supporting structure to hold it in place, pieces of the ring's interior began to break off and drift through the portal aided by the sun's gravitational pull, including pieces of machinery.

"What's the status of that beam cannon?" Jonathan asked, going over to the sensor officer and pointing at his screen.

"It's still, no wait, it's shut down sir! I think it burnt out." the man reported.

Jonathan laughed and pointed at a piece of equipment that had just floated through the open window and bounced off their shield, "I do believe that was its power regulator."

"You've turned the window emitters into a weapon?" Mei realised.

"Hey, you use what you're given." he grinned back as he went back to the navigator, "Now open a window here." he directed.

*

There was a rumble and the floor underneath the marines trembled as they were taking turns to work their way into the conduit through an access panel.

"It feels like this thing is tearing itself apart." Lance commented.

"Perhaps that is exactly what it is doing." Titus responded as he squeezed his massive bulk through what was for him a tight fit.

The squad had found themselves in a large cylindrical conduit not dissimilar to a large sewage pipe but containing outsize electrical cables running from the centre of the ring to the outside surface. There was just enough space for the squad to walk up the conduit between the cabling and its curved wall. There was a metal platform which seemed to have been used during construction as there were discarded implements, packaging and offcuts scattered about on it. The malakim had remained with the gibborim and planned to leave them only at the last minute. It was just as well because the conduit suddenly began to fill with orbs.

"Shedim!" Eret'el yelled, instantly recognising the subtle difference between these orbs and those of malakim, "Draw swords!"

The enemy began to de-orb and materialise as the malakim's twisted fallen brothers. They were not interested in shooting at the marines from a distance and rushed them immediately with sinister looking black curved blade scimitars.

Cray and the other gibborim could not match the marshal skills of beings who had 1000s of years of combat experience, but they did have vastly superior weapons in their spirit swords. The shedim had to avoid parrying with their swords because the weapons of the marines would cut clean through them. The malakim on the other hand had both superior skill and superior weapons and attempted to put themselves between the de-orbing shedim and the humans, cutting their fallen kin down in defence of their gibborim squad mates.

One human who was proving a handful for the shedim was Titus strong. He flailed left and right with a spirit axe, a weapon normally reserved for the largest malakim. He caught an unfortunate shedim on the edge of its spirit imbued blade and cut through it entirely as it were made of soft butter.

"You will not prevail here!" the large malak Himlar'el bellowed as he kicked one of the shedim across the platform towards Eret'el who skewered it with a quick thrust to one side.

There was a yell of pain as one of the fallen angels managed to cleave Alex Runner across the chest, causing Lee Masters to scream as if his friend's pain was his own. There was a blue flash of light as Alex's soul was pulled back to New Jerusalem in an instant. Lee took the shedim's head off with a clumsy swing but then was felled himself in the next moment as another shedim came up behind the first and pierced him with a quick thrust of its dark sword. His spirit was taken mere seconds after his friend's, and they would wake up in New Jerusalem's hatchery in new bodies moments apart. Despite these losses, the forces of Heaven were gaining the advantage. The shedim were all engaged now, having apparently exhausted their reserves and their numbers were being whittled down by the malakim. The eminent swordsman, Seta'el, was like a whirlwind of steel and had cut down 10 of the fiends himself. Wann'el had managed to banish three of the attackers before being sent to the spiritual realm himself by a lucky blow where he found the previously defeated Bola'el who had been following the squad since the skirmish at the barricade.

"Well met brother." he greeted him.

"I'm not sure 'well met' is the right phrase considering we're here as a result of defeat in battle. Badly met might be more appropriate." Bola'el grumbled.

The final shedim was finished by a sword thrust from Eret'el and he immediately ordered the remaining members of the squad to continue up the conduit. The structure shook again and there was the sound of a distant explosion. They were running out of time and Eret'el was starting to think that it might be all of his gibborim squad mates who would be waking up in the hatchery. He wasn't intending to let that happen if it could at all be avoided.

*

Wings of the Wind had disabled four beam cannons now and the effect the two remaining ones were having on the sun was far less pronounced.

"I don't think the two remaining weapons are enough to make it nova." The sensor operator reported.

"Which is just as well, because we have a fallen cruiser incoming." Mei announced, pointing at another part of the screen. The ship shook as incoming fire from the cruiser struck their shields. "As much as I appreciate your ship's great qualities, I don't think it's a match for that thing." she added.

"I fear you're right, get us out of here." Jonathan instructed Shamus.

"What about the marines?" Mei asked.

"I haven't forgotten about them, but we can't do them any good scattered in pieces across the sector." he responded.

Mei came up to his side, "What's the plan?"

"For now, outrun them." he responded as the Whisper class frigate pulled away from the ring and shot out into space, accelerating as fast as possible without harming the occupants, the larger fallen cruiser falling in behind it, weapons still firing.

The distance between the two ships grew ever larger as the smaller, faster vessel pulled away from the larger one. The cruiser showed no signs of giving up though, clearly determined to exact vengeance for the damage exacted on the fallen super weapon. Eventually Jonathan decided they were far enough ahead.

"Stop here and make a window to New Jerusalem." he ordered.

"We can't leave our marines." Mei objected.

"Do it." he barked at the wavering navigation officer who then quickly obeyed.

The window was quickly formed. and Jonathan ordered the ship through. A short while later the window closed leaving the fallen cruiser crew staring at the empty space where the window had been. The captain ordered it to turn around and go back to the ring.

Jonathan breathed out slowly as he watched it go on the viewscreen.

"They don't know we came back through before it closed." Mei said with a grin. She turned to Jonathan, "I can see now why you were drilling us on getting the stealth mode activated quicker."

"I'm full of tricks today." He answered with a weary smile. "Let's go and get our marines."

Therefore He [Jesus] said: "A certain nobleman went into a far country to receive for himself a kingdom and to return. So, he called ten of his servants, delivered to them ten minas, and said to them, 'Do business till I come.' But his citizens hated him, and sent a delegation after him, saying, 'We will not have this man to reign over us.'

And so it was that when he returned, having received the kingdom, he then commanded these servants, to whom he had given the money, to be called to him, that he might know how much every man had gained by trading.

Then came the first, saying, 'Master, your mina has earned ten minas.' And he said to him, 'Well done, good servant; because you were faithful in a very little, have authority over ten cities.'

And the second came, saying, 'Master, your mina has earned five minas.' Likewise, he said to him, 'You also be over five cities.'

Then another came, saying, 'Master, here is your mina, which I have kept put away in a handkerchief. For I feared you, because you are an austere man. You collect what you did not deposit, and reap what you did not sow.'

And he said to him, 'Out of your own mouth I will judge you, you wicked servant. You knew that I was an austere man, collecting what I did not deposit and reaping what I did not sow. Why then did you not put my money in the bank, that at my coming I might have collected it with interest?'

And he said to those who stood by, 'Take the mina from him, and give it to him who has ten minas.' (But they said to him, 'Master, he has ten minas.') 'For I say to you, that to everyone who has will be given; and from him who does not have, even what he has will be taken away from him. But bring here those enemies of mine, who did not want me to reign over them, and slay them before me.'"

Luke 19: 12-27

Twelve

Giska was more furious than he had ever been with Kraan. As far as he was concerned, it was Kraan's ill-fated decision to fire the weapon early that had led to its eventual destruction before it was given the chance to inflict any damage on New Jerusalem whatsoever. Now it lay in ruins, its structure ripped in numerous places by what appeared to have been some kind of razor-sharp cutting tool. It could be repaired, but he very much doubted Heaven would sit by and allow that now that they knew both where it was, and its schematics.

No, Giska would have to abandon any hope of rising to prominence by destroying New Jerusalem. He would just have to do it the old-fashioned way, by killing the current king and stealing his throne. Then he would build the empire into a truly frightening power. Thankfully the fleet had mostly been saved bar those ships that the Heavenly fleet had destroyed in battle. He would be able to use those to further his interests once he took power.

Suddenly he heard gun fire and shouting from outside the room. He called to his loyal nephil guard who would have been stood outside the room, "Grugh! What is happening?"

There was more gunfire and then a brief silence before a tremendous bang came on his door, followed by another. Someone was trying to break in! It was obvious to Giska what was happening, Kraan had clearly had the exact same thought that Giska had himself had, but he was not willing to enact his decision himself. Giska took the only action he felt he could at this point, he dove for the window and crashed through the glass into the artificial atmosphere outside the building. It was a long fall from his tower, but he was not concerned as he quickly morphed into his dragon aspect. He was not out of danger yet though, a second later a nephil with a kinetic assault rifle appeared at the window and began firing at Giska's retreating form from it. The Grigori desperately attempted to put as much distance between himself and the fortress as possible. Nephilim were not the best shots even when the target was right in front of them, and he was confident that it would not hit him,

229

but he took evasive action regardless. He dove down into the city and lost himself amongst the buildings. He kept low, swooping through the busy streets until he came to the shield at the edge of the colony and burst through it. By this point any pursuers were far behind and by the time they located him, he was halfway across the desert.

Later in the day after traversing some thousand miles on the wing, he found a cave and transitioned back into his Grigori self to recharge his energy. He had contemplated his new circumstances and remaining options carefully whilst in flight and had decided the best course of action was to strike out into space, find a small colony with some pathetic humans to dominate somewhere and go into hiding there. Tomorrow he would start his journey, he would begin by waiting out in space until one of the many ships ferrying cargoes between Obelis and the colonies passed. Then he would escape this star system and begin the creation of his own empire. It was probably what he should have done eons ago but better late than never.

*

Cray Ironheart stood at a hatchery window dejected. He had been grateful to be reunited with their lost comrades a few minutes earlier, but as far as Cray was concerned, they had failed in yet another mission. Being a marine was harder than he had imagined and being a marine commander harder still. He looked out of the window at a group of laughing children playing in a park behind the building. He had been told that children were not conceived on New Jerusalem and that these were resurrected children who had never gotten the chance of a childhood on Earth, so they were being given that chance now. Apparently, they had the option of growing old as quickly or as slowly as they wished. Cray had been shocked to hear why most of these children had not enjoyed a long childhood and how many of them had not even been allowed to survive to birth. Apparently, some practices had been as barbaric on Earth as they had been in the fallen colonies. Right now, whatever horror their past had held, he wished he was one of those kids playing light-heartedly in the fields of GOD's Kingdom. His thoughts were interrupted by a familiar voice from behind him.

"You appear deep in thought, commander." Eret'el noted as he came to stand at Cray's side.

"Commander..." Cray greeted him perfunctorily in return. He did not turn from the window.

"You seem somewhat downcast Cray Ironheart despite our success in destroying the ring weapon." Eret'el commented.

Cray wordlessly continued his vigil of the children as the malak looked on.

"They appear very carefree." Eret'el observed. "You'd think anyone enjoying the bounty of Heaven would be so light of burden. Apparently not though."

Cray sighed, realising the malak was going to continue to pass pointed comments until he explained the reason for his mood, "We failed again Eret'el. We have been given two chances thus far to serve our Lord and neither time did we bring Him glory."

"Our captain destroyed the ring, should we not bask in the achievements of our colleagues? We cannot expect for every single crew member aboard *Wings of the Wind* to play a crucial part in every engagement. This time it was Captain Sharp who won the victory, perhaps next time it will be the marines. The important thing is that New Jerusalem is out of danger." Eret'el chastised him.

"Of course, I am glad that the city is safe." Cray responded hastily, horrified at the thought that Eret'el might think he felt otherwise, "But I want to be the good and faithful servant and return to my Lord bearing the fruit of my labour to offer to Him. Right now, I feel like that man in the parable who hid his coin instead of investing it."

Eret'el laughed, "The message of that parable is not that the man did wrong by not earning as much, it is that he did wrong by taking no action at all. He was too cowardly, and possibly also too lazy to do what his lord expected. Now can you Cray Ironheart, possibly say that you have been actionless or lazy since you came to New Jerusalem?"

Cray shrugged, "I guess not?"

"No, you most certainly have not. You have laboured tirelessly for your Lord since you arrived and believe me when I tell you that He loves you for it." Eret'el spoke with a confidence that told Cray he was not just saying these things. "And He wishes for you to take a well-earned rest when our mission is completed."

"What do you mean when our mission is completed?" Cray responded in confusion, "The ring is in pieces and the threat to New Jerusalem is gone. Surely our mission is complete."

"Oh no, not at all." Eret'el countered, "The ring is gone, but the threat remains very real. The architects of the ring project are still out there and if they are not stopped, they will continue to plot against our Lord. Despite his losses, the rebel Kraan is still a powerful force in the galaxy and as such represents a threat that cannot be tolerated."

A small smile crept across Cray's face, "So we're going after him?"

Eret'el nodded, "You have a couple of days to recover from yesterday, and then yes, we're going after Kraan. May I suggest you spend that time with your own children?"

"I think I'll go and do just that." Cray smiled in reply, his spirit somewhat uplifted by the news. He would be given a fresh chance to show what humans could offer to the marines.

He made his way to Becca's lodge and when he came through the door the kids immediately jumped up and ran to him and threw their arms around him.

"Our hero has returned." Becca announced proudly.

Despite the hope of being given a chance to redeem himself on another mission, Cray was still not willing to accept any praise for his previous actions, "I'm afraid I wasn't the hero this time, Uncle Jonathan was." he informed the family.

"You silly man." Becca admonished him with a loving smile and taking his hands in hers, "You're not our hero because you go away and do great things, you're our hero because you keep coming back to us."

*

Two days later, far away across the galaxy, Kraan was pacing up and down his throne room, furious that Giska had escaped, but also fearful of retribution from Heaven. Kraan had just carried out a direct attempt to physically attack New Jerusalem itself and had failed. He had tripled his guard, and the fleet was now stationed around his home planet, but he knew that if GOD wanted to carry out judgement, then there was little Kraan could do to stop him. His hope was in the fact that Yahweh rarely intervened Himself, preferring to let what Kraan saw as His pathetic human creations do things for themselves. It was a fatal flaw that could result in Kraan being permitted to continue to run his empire for as long as he could match the humans in strength. So it was that the ships patrolling Kraan's home system were anticipating a massive fleet arriving and not the advent of a small window opening behind one of the smaller uninhabited planets. *Wings of the Wind* therefore slipped into the system unnoticed despite it being on high alert.

"You're sure we haven't been detected?" Jonathan Sharp asked his sensor officer.

"It's impossible to be 100% sure sir, but I see no indications on sensors that our arrival is being responded to in any way." she replied.

"Perhaps we should lay low for a few minutes to make sure." Mei suggested to her own surprise. Jonathan's cautious nature must have been rubbing off on her.

Jonathan nodded his assent, "We hold station here for now." The bridge crew monitored their consoles anxiously for a short while.

On the deck below the marines were experiencing some anxiety of their own as they went through the routine of checking their equipment in the armoury.

"How are you doing big man?" Lance asked Titus, "I imagine this is hard for you."

The former nephil shrugged, "The fact that Kraan is my father isn't as significant for me as it might be for another. Fathers don't play a role in nephilim culture in the same way that they do in human cultures."

Lance nodded, "I get that. I have no idea who my father was, and I can't say that it interests me that much, because of the way things were run on the station, he was basically relegated to being a sperm donor. My father is Yahweh as far as I'm concerned."

"It becomes a little different once you find out their name though and have some knowledge of them." Cray pointed out, "You start to wonder things like how much of them is inside you."

"My father's genetic seed was purged from me by the Lord." Titus informed them, "As far as I can surmise, there is nothing of me that is of him now. My existence is due to a decision by him to enter into one of his human slaves one night and I suppose he provided the framework for my upbringing with his resources as he did many other nephilim. I do not feel I owe him anything for that. His motivation for creating nephilim spawn was to fill his ranks rather than to father sons."

"It comes across as being very cold when you explain it like that." Lance muttered.

Titus nodded, "The fallen Grigori are very cold. Dead inside, like centuries old spiritual corpses. Like Lance, I consider my father to be Yahweh, and you to be my brothers. This is my family." He smiled at this.

"So, bringing Kraan to justice will cause you no difficulty?" Cray queried, looking for a final reassurance.

Titus shook his head sombrely, "None." He went back to checking the diagnostics on his pulse cannon.

Captain Sharp's voice came over the comm, "Commanders Eret'el and Cray Ironheart to the bridge please."

"That's my cue." Cray commented, standing to leave.

Lance waved to him as he left, "Tell the captain I said 'hi' and thank him for so kindly bringing us to all these delightful exotic places."

Cray just laughed the comment away and strode out. A few moments later he was walking through the door onto the bridge, "Reporting as requested." He said formally as his eyes went to the viewscreen which showed the approaching planet. Eret'el was already there, no doubt having orbed through the bulkhead.

"Good to see you Cray." Jonathan smiled. "We'll be in orbit soon and then the shuttle will depart, but before then I wanted to brief you on the latest developments."

Cray frowned, "Oh good, I do so love developments."

Eret'el stepped in, "It would appear that the defences have been bolstered since your last visit."

"Well, that's understandable." Cray responded, "There's nothing like a bunch of marines portaling into your base and running off with a couple of prisoners to make you re-examine your security."

"It's more than just that I'm afraid." Jonathan added, "Nearly Kraan's entire fleet is berthed on the other side of the planet."

"Oh." Cray muttered, "I didn't realise we'd humiliated them quite that badly."

"It's likely a response to the events at the Pillabis system. Kraan will be afraid of the repercussions of his actions." Eret'el explained. "You don't normally expect to get away with threatening the most powerful force in the universe. He'll be expecting a response and is preparing for the worst."

"How does this affect our plans?" was Cray's response to this uncomfortable news.

"We can expect the palace to be heavily manned with guards, making it nearly impossible to get through it unnoticed." Eret'el explained, "So I think a diversion is called for."

"What do you have in mind?" Cray wondered.

Eret'el pointed at a cluster of buildings displayed on the holographic projector, "There is a vehicle depot which forms part of the palace complex and one of its features is a fuel dump. I propose that you take your gibborim and sabotage the depot with explosives whilst I take my malakim and capture Kraan."

Cray pondered this proposal, "It would split our forces..."

"Which would make each section easier to hide." Eret'el interjected, "With the number of troops stationed here currently, we'd never be able to hold out in an all-out battle anyway. Stealth is our only option today."

"Hmm, or subterfuge. We still have our fallen disguises from the hostage mission." Cray suggested.

"Very good. You won't need a full squad in order to destroy the fuel dump, but you will need Rudi Fire to manage the explosives." Eret'el reminded him.

"Rudi isn't ex-fallen though. He will find it harder to blend with the locals." Cray said thoughtfully. "Perhaps we could have him school Lance on how to use the explosives."

"I do see your point. Very well, we'll have Rudi show Lance how to activate the charges from a safe distance." Eret'el declared.

"It sounds like we have a plan." Captain Sharp declared, "Eret'el and his malakim will secure the objective while Cray, Titus and Lance create a distraction."

So it was that Cray, Lance and Titus found themselves being shuttled down to the planet by Ray Tracer half an hour later after Lance had been given a crash course on how to set and then activate the standard marine explosive charge. It was something they'd all done in training, but a refresher was never a bad thing.

"Remind me how we're getting into the facility." Titus rumbled; his voice slurred due to the false tusk he'd shoved over his lower teeth.

"Why don't you take that thing out for now so that we can understand what you're saying?" Lance ribbed him.

"Because if I take it out, I might be tempted to stab you repeatedly with it for being such an ass?" Titus shot back.

"Erm, I changed my mind, I think you should leave it in." Lance allowed.

"We're going to land on the surface and then infiltrate a supply truck. There is a steady stream of them coming in from a nearby mine." Cray replied in answer to the original question.

"Why don't we just portal in like last time? Surely that would be easier and safer." Lance suggested.

"Because they're onto that little trick and they'll have set up window dampeners. The sensor officer detected some tell-tale readings." Titus explained.

"We couldn't have tried anyway? Just in case?" Lance persisted.

Cray shook his head, "They'd have detected the attempt and then we'd have put them on their guard. This way is better this time, we're less likely to be detected."

Lance sighed, "Well, at least this way is more colourful."

The shuttle set down next to a rock outcrop and the ramp dropped, "Welcome to the desert, don't say I never bring you anywhere nice." Tracer said with a chuckle.

"Aww gee, thanks. We'll get you a souvenir while we're here. What kind of rocks do you like? Sandstone or shale?" Lance sarcastically replied.

"I feel like your heart is not really in the whole gift giving enterprise Lance." Ray complained.

"We could bring you the severed head of the first fallen we slay as an alternative?" Titus offered with a tusk enhanced grin.

Tracer raised his hands in protest, "You know what? A nice piece of sandstone would look great on my mantlepiece. Thanks Lance. Now get down that ramp, keeping it down is breaking my whole invisibility mojo. If someone sees us and we get shot at, I'm blaming you and your corny jokes."

"Says the man who changed his name to Ray Tracer." Lance muttered.

"I heard that! You can keep your exotic overvalued sandstone artifacts!" CGI yelled as the ramp rose, cutting off his complaints. The shuttle vanished to their eyes and soon it was as if they were alone on the planet's surface.

Cray pulled a small device from his pack as a desert wind howled around the rock, forcing them to raise their arms over their faces to protect their eyes. The device was designed to look like a fallen data pad but possessing heavenly levels of technology. After consulting it for a few seconds, he pointed in a direction adjacent to the rock outcrop they had landed behind. "The mine is this way." he informed the others.

The three set off in the direction Cray had indicated, fighting through the strong desert storm.

"Couldn't we have come when it was better weather?" Lance muttered.

"This is good weather for this planet." Cray shot back, "On a bad day we'd have been stripped to bare skeletons in seconds."

Lance responded to this with his usual enthusiasm, "Nice, I'm seriously starting to question certain recent career choices."

"I am not." Titus grunted, "I find the challenge invigorating."

Lance grinned, "You can have my share of the challenge as well if you'd like. You could be twice as invigorated, think about it."

The giant responded with a coarse laugh, "Perhaps you'd like to walk behind me Lance Keen. I will shelter you from the storm using my vastly superior size and resilience."

"Ooh, I will take you up on that." Lance slowed his step and fell in behind the giant and began whistling a merry tune. His merriment lasted but a few moments before he cried out in distress, "Good grief Titus Strong! What on earth did you have for breakfast?" he dramatically put his hands to his throat, "I can't breathe. This is the end dear friends!"

"I am quite sure I do not know what you mean Lance." Titus objected innocently.

Lance continued unabated, "You could at least give some warning, like a distinctive trumping sound so that people know to evacuate the blast radius."

"The mining camp is just ahead." Cray cautioned them and they fell silent. The ground gradually began to taper downwards, giving them some respite from the wind. They came to a set of steps carved into the side of a rock wall and began to walk down. They had descended a few meters when the dust they had been forging their way through suddenly cleared to a great degree and they found themselves looking across a huge pit in the ground full of workers and busy machinery.

"I think we found the mine." Titus commented.

Cray pointed to a roadway leading up the opposite side, "There's the road, and I think I see the trucks at the bottom. That's how we're going to get into the outpost."

Lance grimaced, "Travelling in style as always."

"All the tickets for the luxury space liner were sold out." Cray retorted.

"Yeah, I hear those tickets are really popular on this planet on account of all the wealthy slaves." Lance commented acerbically.

Titus was already making his way around the side of the pit and the two men had to jog to catch up to the giant's strides. "Has anyone ever told you two that you talk too much?" their hulking colleague berated them as they came up alongside him.

"I don't know." Lance made a display of appearing to ponder the question intensely, "Has anyone told you that Cray?"

Cray smiled mischievously, "Oh I don't know, I just don't think it's the case that we talk too much, so why would anyone pass such a hurtful untruthful comment?"

"I have a theory on that as it happens if you'd like to hear it..." Lance began.

"Enough! I get the point." Titus bellowed and the two men finally stopped, grinning at each other.

As they drew nearer to the transports, they adopted more of an air of professionalism appropriate to the increased level of risk. There were guards at the trucks and one of them turned and studied them at their approach.

"Who are you lot? What are you doing here?" the guard challenged them.

"We're part of the night shift guard; we got trapped on the other side of the pit last night when a sandstorm hit. We've been hiding out there until we had the opportunity to get back." Cray explained. He had no idea if there had been a sandstorm or not last night, but he suspected they happened all the time.

The guard looked at their dust covered uniforms and must have decided the explanation was plausible, "Hah." he laughed, "I knew you night shift idiots were stupid, but you've outdone yourselves this time." he stared at them critically for a moment before relenting, "Well, you'd better get on one of the trucks. You'll be able to get a couple of hours sleep before you go back on shift." He began laughing again at that.

"Gee, thanks." Cray muttered, "Remind me to return the favour some time."

The trucks were large units, designed to carry heavy materials as well as workers which would regularly include nephilim. There was plenty of room for the three in the back. They sat anxiously for a few minutes before the engine rumbled into life and the truck lumbered away with a rocking motion. A force field came up over the rear entrance as they approached the edge of the shield dome over the mine to protect any occupants against exposure to the atmosphere between the mining complex and the outpost.

*

As the three gibborim marines were transiting between the mine and the outpost, things remained settled in a palace still unaware of the ongoing operation to rob them of their emperor.

A nephil guard stood watch on one side of the throne room. It was a 10ft tall behemoth of a creature clad in black leather covered in gunmetal armour plating. As Vell'el approached it, he caught a stench of filth and sweat, and he had to work hard to avoid wrinkling his nose

241

and giving himself away. "I am here to relieve you; you are required to assist in the armoury." he informed the ogre.

The nephil stared at the malak, seeing a being much like himself except a little shorter and less well muscled. "And why can you not help at the armoury?" the monster rumbled.

"They have requested the strongest of us. You were on the list. I think it should be me, but I do as I'm told." Vell'el responded slyly in an attempt to play to the creature's vanity.

The ploy clearly worked as the nephil replied, "Hah, you are clearly not my equal fool. I will go and be useful while you stand here like the useless cretin you are. Later we will wrestle and see who is the strongest." The guard left his post and wandered off, still laughing to himself.

Vell'el took his position in the throne room quietly. A minute later he observed while a similar interaction took place between Wann'el and a guard across the room. That was five of them in place already and five less guards to contend with when they struck. The plan was going well so far. Now what they needed was for the humans to provide their distraction before the guards had a chance to realise that they'd been duped and return.

*

Cray accessed his data pad once more to get his bearings. They were now inside the complex, having ridden straight through the guard post in the back of the truck. Apparently searching trucks was not an activity nephilim guards could be bothered with. "The fuel depot is this way." he informed the others.

"Let's not waste any time. I believe we are slightly behind schedule." Titus informed them.

"Can't we rest for a minute, just one minute?" Lance muttered, his face a slight tinge of green. Having grown up in space, Cray and Lance had never been aboard a wheeled vehicle before and the long ride on a makeshift road through the rocky desert had not been kind to Lance's stomach.

"If you need to vomit, do it now and get it over with. We need to keep moving if we're going to make up for lost time." Cray urged him.

"No, I'll be fine. Let's go and blow stuff up." Lance assured him unconvincingly.

"Blow stuff up or throw stuff up?" Titus laughed, and slapped Lance on the back with predictable explosive results.

Cray looked down at his boots which were now covered with what a second ago had been the contents of Lance's stomach, "Well, that was useful you two." he chastised them as Lance wiped his mouth. To their credit, both Lance and Titus managed to look sheepish in response to the reproval. "Can you keep up with us?" Cray asked Lance.

"Yeah, I feel a little better after getting it up. Thanks Titus, I'll always be there in future to make you hurl when you need it." Lance promised.

"Oh, I have a cast iron stomach Lance Keen." Titus punched his own belly as if in demonstration of this fact, "But the sentiment is appreciated." he commented unironically.

"I was being...I'm not actually going to...oh, never mind." Lance sighed and started off in the direction Cray had indicated.

The three men made their way towards the fuel depot, trying to blend in. There were plenty of guards amongst the population which made that job easier, especially since fallen guard uniforms were anything but uniform.

Eventually they reached the fuel depot and found a position under a sloping roof from which they could survey the area. After a minute of observation, Cray identified the fuel tank that had been designated as the best target for creating a chain reaction, thus leveraging the amount of chaos they could cause.

"Rudi said to affix it firmly to the side of that pump housing." Lance said, pointing at a box from which piping was leading.

"Well, get to it then." Cray muttered impatiently.

Lance made to move out from their cover, but then scurried back as a nephil guard passed by. "That was close." he muttered.

"You're in fallen uniform, why would he see you as being suspicious?" Cray challenged him.

"Because not a lot of guards go around attaching devices to the sides of volatile containers?" Lance shot back.

"I suppose you have a point. He's gone now anyway." Cray noted.

Lance slipped out again and strolled nonchalantly to the side of the fuel tank. He slid the explosive device out and used its magnets to attach it to the side of the pump housing. He pressed a button on its surface and a green light came on. Taking the detonator out of his pack, he examined it and noted that the green light on it was also glowing. He ran back to the awning where the other two were waiting. "That's it, let's get out of here. It should work from 200m away, so I suggest we make the most of that distance. This thing is going to make a real mess."

They quickly strode down an alley between two buildings, trying to avoid drawing attention and took cover behind a corner. "Do it." Cray urged Lance.

Lance produced the detonator and held it up, but to his horror the green light had gone out. He pressed the button anyway, but to no effect. "It's been disabled." he complained.

Cray looked around the corner and saw to his horror that the nephil guard had returned and was holding the device in his hands, turning it over and over as if trying to figure out what it was.

"That wretched guard has come back. He must have pushed the button." Cray informed the others.

"Does he look like he knows what he's doing?" Titus wondered.

Cray looked again, "No, not really. He seems puzzled by it."

"Keep trying the button, Lance. Perhaps he will reactivate it again?" Titus suggested.

Lance did as he was told and began repeatedly pressing the detonator, "Fine, but I don't think anyone could possibly be that stu…"

Lance's final word was cut off by a tremendous noise as the device exploded and a second later another as the fuel container went up as well. This was followed by a dull thud as one of the nephil guard's severed arms landed next to the three men.

"I guess someone could be that stupid." Lance noted.

"It's time for us to leave." Cray adjured them and the three men made for the edge of the outpost.

*

Kraan heard the explosion and stood to his feet. "What in the name of all that is holy was that?" he yelled. He turned to Eret'el who was stood before the throne in the guise of a nephil. "Go and see what it was." Kraan ordered him.

"At once my lord." Eret'el said with a nod, turning to leave, but then stopped and turned back."

"Well? What are you waiting for?" Kraan roared.

Eret'el feigned confusion, "I'm sorry my lord, what is it you want me to do again?"

His attempt at distracting the Grigori was successful and Kraan was filled with rage, "I want you to see what that explosion was, you bumbling…" Suddenly Kraan cried out in excruciating pain as three shock lances, wielded by disguised malakim who had snuck up behind him while his attention was on Eret'el, were pressed into the bottom of his spine. Whilst the Grigori constitution was incredibly powerful, it could not stand up to that treatment and Kraan slumped to the floor unconscious. The other malakim ran in and soon the Grigori warlord was bundled up in a tarpaulin.

"Now comes the hard part." Eret'el remarked.

The malakim, still in their nephilim guises, made their way out of a service door in the back of the throne room, leaving the space very obviously devoid of its usual occupants. It would not be long before the fallen discovered their emperor was missing.

*

Another blast rocked the outpost as the next closest fuel container to the first exceeded its maximum heat parameters and detonated. The gibborim marines were reaching the edge of the outpost now and began to look around a quick way to exfiltrate.

"There must be a truck or something around here somewhere." Lance fretted.

"We'd be sitting ducks in a transport anyway." Titus noted. "We should leave on foot."

"Three guards trudging across the desert will be too obviously out of place and we'd be even more vulnerable than in a vehicle." Cray countered.

Suddenly, as if sent by GOD Himself, a truck similar to the one they had come in on turned a corner and rumbled towards them. A familiar face poked out of the window, "You three idiots. I hope you've gotten some sleep already because we're going to need you to help put out those fires." The day shift had clearly been pulled from the mine to help with the disaster, because in front of them was the same guard that had put them on the truck into the outpost in the first place.

"Of course, can we get a lift?" Cray responded.

*

The malakim had managed to procure for themselves a small truck in which to place their unconscious prize and took great care to hide the bodies of its previous occupants. Eret'el took the wheel and the other malakim orbed around it. The truck pulled out into the street and Eret'el unhurriedly drove it towards the edge of the outpost. It would not be a good idea to be seen to be fleeing the scene of the chaos in a hurry. Whilst he had already formulated a good excuse to be leaving the outpost during a crisis, he felt it would look too suspicious to be racing towards the outskirts like criminals fleeing a bank heist.

When they finally reached the gatepost, he explained that he was going to the mine to fetch more slaves to help control the fires and was allowed through. When a large truck followed the smaller one a few moments later and the same explanation for leaving was given, it made sense to the guard, and he allowed them through also.

Tracer was waiting impatiently in the shuttle when the two vehicles pulled up and he quickly lowered the ramp. "It's about time. The desert is not the most exciting place to camp out and wait."

"You should have brought a crossword." Lance suggested in jest as the malakim carried the unconscious Grigori emperor into the shuttle and dropped him unceremoniously on the floor.

Ray shrugged, "I'm more of a sudoku man."

"I have no idea what that is, but it sounds absolutely fascinating. Definitely do that next time." Lance teased.

"Get this shuttle back to the *Wings of the Wind* lieutenant Tracer." Eret'el instructed CGI, "They have probably already discovered him missing."

"Aye aye sir." The pilot quipped and made for the cockpit hurriedly.

Surrounded by malakim orbs, the stealthy shuttle took off and headed into orbit where their mother ship would be waiting.

On board *Wings of the Wind,* Captain Sharp was keenly waiting for word to come that the shuttle had docked. They had been monitoring the planet using low level sensors and had detected the explosion, so they were aware that the plan had at least partially succeeded. They were soon to receive confirmation of the remainder as Eret'el orbed in through the ship's outer skin and materialised in front of the bridge crew. He had discarded his nephilim disguise and presented himself in his usual form.

"Captain, the shuttle is returning with the traitor Kraan aboard." Eret'el informed him.

"Good, we can leave. These patrols are giving me the willies." Commander Song remarked, causing Eret'el to raise a questioning eyebrow.

"There have been constant sweeps of the area, increasing in intensity after the explosions started. A cruiser passed right underneath us at one point. We nearly had to change station to avoid it hitting us." Jonathan explained.

"Well then, I humbly suggest you take us out of orbit as soon as the shuttle is docked Captain." Eret'el returned.

The sensor operator chimed in, "It's approaching the shuttle bay entrance now sir."

"Shamus, take us back to the outer planet as soon as they're safely aboard." Jonathan ordered.

A few seconds later the sensor officer spoke up again, "They're in sir."

Shamus needed no further encouragement and the ship immediately turned to pull itself away from the planet. The first few moments were the most stressful as it required a boost to the shunt drive to break orbit and if they were going to be detected, that would be the time. Tense moments passed as the ship broke free of the planet's gravitational pull and headed out into space. Their mission successful, they headed back to New Jerusalem where Kraan would face trial for his crimes against Heaven.

Then Peter came to Him and said, "Lord, how often shall my brother sin against me, and I forgive him? Up to seven times?" Jesus said to him, "I do not say to you, up to seven times, but up to seventy times seven.

Matthew 18: 21-22

Thirteen

Hope came out of the window into the Copox system and headed for the lone fallen colony situated there. It was an isolated system eschewed by the fallen warlords and so was a prime candidate for a refuge for humans who had managed to escape Grigori control. As the ship approached the station, the occupants hailed them:

"Unidentified vessel, please state your purpose for being here." a voice demanded. Whilst the person on the other end was trying to sound formal and intimidating, they could not hide the nervous tint to their voice.

Bree suspected they had no way of driving *Hope* off if they had wanted to. "We are the star ship *Hope* from New Jerusalem. We bring supplies of food and drink for your people and in return request only that we be allowed to share a message of hope with you." she responded.

There was a pause on the other end of the transmission and Bree suspected that a discussion around whether to admit them or not was taking place. After a few moments the voice came back, "You may dock. No weapons will be permitted to be carried and you must remain under guard whilst here." The transmission ended abruptly.

"What a polite young man." Ward commented.

"I don't know that I like this, he sounded terrified." Stella added.

Ward agreed that there had certainly been a note of fear in the voice on the transmission but there could be any number of reasons for that, "It might be intimidating for them having an advanced star ship approach the station. They probably don't have much in the way of defensive capabilities." he guessed.

"I will scout ahead as usual and raise the alarm if I see a threat of any kind." Men'el reassured Stella and orbed out of the ship as it drew near to the docking bay.

"Here goes nothing then." Ward announced as he took the ship into the hangar. He landed it deftly in a landing bay and lowered the ramp. Ward, Stella and Bree made their way down to the awaiting welcoming party devoid of any defensive weapons. Bree felt naked without her rifle but tried to exude a demeanour of confidence for Stella's sake. Ward was carrying a crate of fruit in the hope of making an early good impression. The welcoming party was a small one, consisting of only five fallen humans, all of whom appeared to be extremely nervous. Ward put the food crate down in front of them expecting that they would descend upon it, but none moved. He identified a man out front as being a possible leader and addressed him. "We are from New Jerusalem, the Holy City. We've brought gifts and we'd like to give you news of God's kingdom if you would allow us."

The fallen all looked at each other dubiously and the man spoke after a delay, "We have our own gods, we serve them faithfully. We have no interest in yours."

This immediately struck Ward as odd. Normally the estranged fallen were very quick to decry their vicious gods as tyrants once they were out from under their control. He was starting to think that Stella might be right to be worried and he hoped that Men'el had a good handle on what was happening here.

Men'el watched the exchange from the shadows, he too felt something suspicious was going on at this station. They had been to a number of these stations now and had never before encountered a reception as odd as this. It was as if they were still under the thrall of their overlord. This idea occurred to him only a split second before a long knife went into his back and straight through his body. He wanted to warn the others, but a scaly hand covered his mouth. "My dear malak, I cannot permit you to warn them of my presence, I'm afraid you must remain confined to the spiritual realm whilst I play with your humans." a sibilant voice hissed from behind him. His spirit slipped into the next dimension from whence he watched a fallen Grigori wiping the blood off his blade. He railed against his circumstances helplessly as the watcher settled down to observe the humans.

Giska couldn't believe his luck as he watched the visitors, three beautiful, redeemed humans who had been protected only by a single malak. He would enjoy himself immensely with these delicious looking morsels. He had thought he would have to live out the next few months with only the pitiful fallen creatures he had found here to entertain him. But now here before him were a beautiful blonde creature who looked more fit and supple than any woman he had ever seen, a striking redhead who was very nearly as comely to look upon and a well-muscled male who probably looked like a Greek god under his shirt. He would make sure he had his way with them all by the time he was done, and he already had some ideas to avoid the frustrations he'd suffered with the last two. The ship was probably full of provisions from New Jerusalem as well which had already become fabled for their tastiness. Giska's luck had certainly changed today.

Ward was becoming concerned that Men'el hadn't shown himself yet. The fallen humans were starting to unload his ship and that was normally the malak's queue to come out of hiding.

He hoped nothing had gone wrong, but in the next moment his hopes were dashed.

Stella had wandered off and was unpacking one of the first crates the fallen humans had unloaded. Giska slithered out of hiding with a speed that belied his size and grabbed the unwitting woman roughly, spinning her around before she even knew he was there, and placing his dagger to her neck.

"Get your filthy hands off her!" the horrified Ward shouted. There was nothing to remind you how much you loved someone until they were in danger and in that moment, Ward realised that he loved Stella more than ever. Bree stood frozen in terror at the turn of events.

"Oh, but I washed my hands this morning peon of Heaven." Giska scowled. "I would not touch such a lovely specimen of a woman with mucky fingers." A forked tongue slid out of his mouth and across Stella's cheek causing her to try and flinch away from him, but the Grigori's grip was too strong. Giska saw the renewed look of horror on Ward's face and mocked him again, "Oh do not worry Christian, I assure you my tongue is clean also.

Ward made to move towards the Watcher, but Giska pushed the knife harder against Stella's throat, "Ah-ah-ah, not a step closer human. You are going to watch quietly while I pleasure this lovely creature on this spot. I will leave her crying for more."

Ward became aware that the fallen humans had moved up behind him, "I'm sorry." came a voice from over his shoulder, "He would kill us all if we do not do what he says."

Giska ran the back of a clawed finger down Stella's side, following the curves of her body. He had become very aroused by the fact that he had such a terrified audience and could not contain himself any longer. He reached to tear her clothes.

"You will regret this, monster. God Himself will take vengeance on you for harming one of His beloved children." Ward yelled.

Giska looked up, annoyed at the interruption, "You pathetic Christians are all the same, thinking that your love for your distant GOD will preserve you. You like to say that Jesus is in your heart when He is in fact a thousand light years away, not giving you a second thought."

Ward's face lit up and he stood up straighter, "Not exactly, I was going to say that Jesus is with us."

"Jesus is with you, Jesus is in your heart, Jesus holds you in his hand. It is all worthless rambling." Giska scoffed.

Ward looked ecstatic by this stage, causing Giska to lose some of his confidence. He even laughed as he continued, "No, I mean that Jesus IS with us." and he pointed past the Grigori's shoulder.

Giska's face went white, and he felt an ice-cold chill go through his body, he tried to reassure himself that Ward was bluffing, but then suddenly he felt a pinpoint of heat against the back of his neck.

"Let go of My daughter and turn to face your GOD traitor." A voice that he had not heard in centuries but was unmistakable came from behind him. Giska allowed Stella to slip from his grasp and she ran crying to Ward who held her in his arms briefly and then turned her to see what was about to unfold. The Grigori swivelled around slowly and the first thing he saw was the deadly blazing sword tip of Logos at the edge of his nose. Looking down the blade he saw the wrist of the hand holding it bore a scar, one of only two scars present on New Jerusalem. He looked up from the hand into the terrifying face of GOD. Below that face Jesus was clad in a white robe covered in shining armour plating similar to that the malakim wore. He was a fearsome sight and had clearly come to this place ready to dole out justice. Giska dropped to his knees and the sword point followed him to the floor.

"Lord, I…" he began.

"You what? You wish to deny to the omniscient God what you were about to do to my children? You wish to repent of your wickedness?" the Lord chastised him. "You are a foul traitor with a black heart, and I say to you that this day you will go to Tartarus." A portal opened behind Giska and through it only blackness could be seen.

"My Lord, take pity on a misguided servant. I swear I will serve you all my remaining days." Giska pleaded.

The Lord did not reply but only raised his sword to strike and Giska yelped in fear. As the blazing blade came down the terrified Watcher escaped imminent oblivion the only way he could and fled into the gaping portal. As soon as he was gone, it snapped closed leaving him trapped beyond. Ward, Stella and Bree ran forward and threw themselves at Christ's feet.

"Thank you, Lord, oh thank you." Stella wept.

Jesus held a hand to her cheek and wiped away her tears, "You are mine Stella, and I will not permit harm to come to you." He turned and reached out, his hand disappearing for a moment. He pulled it back and the hand of Men'el was now on the other end.

"Thank you, Lord." He breathed as he re-entered the physical realm with his energy restored, "I am so sorry I failed you."

"Speak not of it my courageous Men'el, you could not have known that treacherous snake had slithered his way into this outpost." Jesus reassured him. Then he turned to the fallen humans who were prostrate on their faces and trembling. "Please rise and eat." He urged them, "My children have provided you with this bounty and you are all so very hungry." He turned to one of the women, "Especially you Maya, you haven't had anything to eat in nearly a week."

The woman stared at Jesus in shock, not only had He known how long it was since she last ate, but He also knew the secret name that she had never revealed to anyone. The fallen nervously pulled themselves to their feet and looked at each other, trying to decide if any of them thought it was a trick or not. Maya was now convinced that Christ was who He said He was though and led the way towards the food. She took a tentative bite of a loaf of bread and then, finding it to be good, ate heartily of it. Feeling reassured by this, the others fell upon the crate of bread Stella had opened with gusto.

Jesus smiled at the sight of the starving people sating their hunger, "When you have eaten, Ward here will give you the option of coming back to New Jerusalem with him. If you do, you will not only eat like this for the rest of your lives, but you will have the option of following Me and entering into life eternal."

Another portal opened and this time the unmistakable sight of New Jerusalem was visible through it. Jesus stepped into it and a second later was gone. To the redeemed in the room, it was as if light itself had been snuffed out as the presence of their Lord receded back into the distance.

Ward and his team watched the fallen enjoy the first satisfying meal they had ever really enjoyed and then sat and chatted with them about the nature of their GOD, the wonders of Paradise and the full story of the Jesus they had just met in person. When they left to return to New Jerusalem an hour later, they left the outpost completely deserted.

*

Mei stood watch as the malakim carried the still unconscious Kraan down *Wings of the Wind's* loading ramp, believing it her responsibility as second officer to oversee the process and make sure it ran smoothly. The marines had placed the captured warlord in a large cradle to make their work easier. He would likely wake up in a prison cell and then the enormity of his new circumstances would dawn in him. Mei was impatient for the malakim to finish their work so that she could catch up with Jonathan who had left the *Wind* a few minutes before. She was hoping that if she conversed with him outside of the ship that it might lead to them spending some time together off duty. She couldn't stop thinking about her captain and despite being a well-disciplined person normally, had found that Captain Sharp had somehow penetrated all her defences. The marines finally marched off with the slumbering Grigori and she set off in search of Jonathan. She didn't have far to go as she found him in a corner of the hangar near the entrance talking to a woman in civilian clothing. Mei stopped in her tracks; the woman was a slender brunette with perfect porcelain skin and was quite possibly the most beautiful woman Mei had ever seen. The two of them hugged warmly and Mei cursed herself. Of course, a man like Jonathan would already have a beautiful woman in his life, how could she have imagined otherwise? She had probably been his wife in his past life, many people remained very close to their ex-spouses in New Jerusalem despite there being no marriage.

She intended to slink off unseen, but Jonathan saw her and immediately called her. "Mei, come here, there's someone I'd like you to meet."

Mei cursed her luck and put on her best smile despite the fact that her heart was breaking in that very moment. She walked over to the two and the woman spoke first.

"Is this the one you won't stop talking about Jonny?" she smiled beautifully, and Mei inwardly cursed her for being as pretty as she was.

"This is Mei, Mei Song, my second officer." he gushed. He looked as if he was very pleased to be showing Mei off and she realised how easy it would have been for anyone to mistake it for romantic affection. Likely Jonathan was proud of her for her skills as a navy officer, which was flattering if it was the case, but not that for which she had been hoping.

"You're very pretty, I can see why he's so enamoured with you." The woman beamed, causing Jonathan to blush furiously.

Mei was taken aback at her complete lack of defensiveness regarding Mei's own attractiveness, "I'm sorry?" she spluttered. The woman was behaving very oddly for a romantic partner and suddenly a hope sprang up in Mei's heart. She prodded Jonathan on the arm, "Are you going to get around to introducing this lovely woman to me?"

"Oh…" he blurted "of course, I'm sorry. Mei, this is my mother, Sharon Greatheart."

Mei felt her heart rise up into her throat as relief flooded through her like a wave, "Sharon, it's such a pleasure to meet you. Does he always forget his manners like this?"

"What manners?" his mother replied and the two laughed together at his expense.

"I'd like to invite you around for dinner Mei, if you think you'd like that?" Sharon suggested.

Mei tried not to show the joy she felt inside and stay calm, "Are you sure it wouldn't be too much trouble?"

"Not for me, I'm going to make Jonny do the cooking." she smiled. Now that the beauty of her smiles had ceased to be a threat to Mei, she found herself drawn to this woman and her clearly caring nature.

Mei feigned a cringe, "Are you sure that's safe?"

The two laughed together again and Jonathan began to wonder if he'd made a mistake introducing them to each other. He had the nagging feeling that his life was about to become a great deal more complicated.

*

David ben Jesse stood anxiously at the railing looking out over Earth exactly as he had done a short time ago with his friend, Jack Lewis. Today he was not meeting a friend though, but an enemy. He tried to control his emotions as a familiar face appeared in the doorway to the public lounge and upon noticing him, came over.

"Your highness, you asked to see me?" Moshe Zeal said nervously as he came to stand next to the king at the window.

"I was most pleased to hear that you had decided to follow Christ." David heard himself say.

"I hope you don't mind me saying so, but you don't sound convinced." Moshe responded with a sly smile.

David sighed, "Well, you did try to kill me."

"I did." Moshe replied sorrowfully, "And no amount of apologising can make up for that."

David put a reassuring hand on his shoulder, "But true repentance can. And if Christ has accepted that you have truly repented, then I must also. I have asked you to come here partly to assure you that you have my forgiveness."

An unconcealable wave of emotion crossed the former assassin's face, "My thanks your highness, I am most unworthy of your forgiveness."

David smiled, "But Christ is, and it is the life that He lived that has made remission for the one you did. Thus, you have become worthy in GOD's eyes, and therefore in mine also."

Moshe was almost in tears at this, "I never suspected just how real His sacrifice would become to me, after I denied its reality for so long."

"It will take us both a while to adjust to this new dynamic between us but adjust we must as I have an offer for you." David enigmatically informed Moshe.

"An offer? What kind of offer?" Moshe responded interestedly.

David turned to face the window, "I am sure there will be many more attempts on my life in the next thousand years. I need someone by my side who has some insight into the way any would be assassins might think. I need someone with the skills to stop them before they have the chance to strike." The king turned back to the ex-assassin, "I need you, Moshe."

Moshe Zeal stood back in shock at the king's words, he had expected something like the message of acceptance, but this went far beyond what he had hoped for. He had only to think for a moment however, "Then you shall have me your highness, I am yours to command."

*

Kraan stood before the throne of GOD for judgement. Due to his high status, he had been allowed directly into the Holy of Holies to stand before Yahweh Himself. He had explained the reasons for his rebellion against his GOD and how much of it had been justified under the circumstances. He was now preparing to defend his treatment of his slaves, although even he realised that he was defending the indefensible: "I do admit Lord, that I have engaged in what some may call cruel behaviour towards the humans. However, do humans themselves not also treat lesser beings with disdain and abuse them routinely? Think on how the human child torments ants with a magnifying glass, or how the farmer raises cattle with the only purpose being to slaughter them. Should my treatment of my human followers not be seen in the same light, since a Grigori is so very obviously a superior being to a human? I would suggest therefore that if a human can be forgiven, then it follows that a Grigori should be able to seek repentance also." Kraan looked up at GOD in expectation, knowing that he had presented his case well.

Yahweh appeared to be considering the argument thoughtfully, though the Father aspect of the Trinity was so enigmatic in appearance that it was hard to discern His demeanour from his physical features alone.

Eventually GOD spoke in a booming voice, "Very well Kraan, you have spoken well and you shall be accepted back into the ranks of Heaven and given a post commensurate with your proven worth." Yahweh addressed another figure stood near the throne, "Micha'el, escort our esteemed cousin to a luxury apartment and ensure that he is provided with his every desire whilst he prepares himself to serve."

Kraan grinned widely, his every belief confirmed, and his every wish granted. He congratulated himself for being cunning enough to live the lifestyle he had for millennia and still find favour in the eyes of GOD. Perhaps he would be able to continue to feed his base desires here under the very eves of New Jerusalem. He looked over at Micha'el who was clearly annoyed at having to wait on his former enemy, perhaps Kraan would get the opportunity to flaunt his behaviour in front of the General himself. How delicious that would be.

Suddenly Kraan started to feel a pain in his lower back which was gradually becoming more severe as he returned to full consciousness. He reached his hand around to find that something had burnt into his skin there and was painful to the touch. He sat up from where he had been sleeping and groggily opened his eyes, cursing the fact that this unexpected pain in his back had roused him from his favourite dream. As his eyes adjusted to the bright light in the room, he realised he was in a cell of some kind, white walled and with a single door. How had he gotten here? He didn't recognise this as being a part of his palace. Perhaps he had been injured somehow and taken to the hospital wing. He stood to his feet and stumbled to the door, which he found to be locked. "I demand to be released from this room right now!" he cried out in fury. The door opened and a being he had hoped never to see face to face again came into the

263

room. Kraan was so shocked that it didn't even occur to him to push his way past, out of the cell. "Uri'el!" he hissed.

The archangel grinned maddeningly, "You were expecting someone else perhaps? One of your human slaves? A loyal fallen elohim? I'm afraid you'll never be setting eyes on them again, unless it is in Tartarus."

Kraan tried to make sense of the situation, "I... How..."

Uri'el laughed, "Let me make it clear for you, in a way that your shrunken twisted fallen mind can comprehend. You have been captured by my malakim marines, you are in a prison cell in New Jerusalem and now that you are awake, you will be taken before the Council for judgement."

Kraan tried to grasp all of this, and his mind filled with questions, "Will Yahweh not judge me Himself?"

Uri'el laughed heartily, "Setting aside the fact that in your stinking sin filled condition you are not remotely fit to stand before Yahweh, you would not want to. His very countenance just by dint of its holy nature would annihilate you where you stood."

Kraan's heart sank, he knew that Uri'el spoke the truth and that he had been a fool to have ever let himself hope otherwise. Instead, he reached for the next hope to cross his mind, "I have a right to a representative; I want to see the best advocate for the fallen there is."

Uri'el laughed again and his eyes turned stone cold, "The best there is you say? Oh, you'll be seeing him soon enough, he's already been in Tartarus these past few months. I'm sure he'll be most pleased to have you added to his collection of playthings."

Epilogue

Jonathan left his luxurious country house and walked across the marvellous wild garden that stood before it. Before he went any further, he turned and gazed with righteous pride upon the home his Lord had given him for 25 years of loyal service in the Royal Navy. He waited expectantly for the one thing that could make this picture complete and didn't have to wait long. The door to the house opened and Mei stepped out wearing her captain's uniform. She looked no different to the day he had met her 23 years ago, though she was wearing her hair differently. Her redeemed body, with its perfectly functional cell replacement system hadn't aged in the slightest. Although technically the body she currently resided in was only 5 years old since her first body had perished when *Wings of the Wind* had been destroyed. Jonathan still fondly remembered them waking up in the hatchery together afterwards and her deriding him for not having ordered the tactic she had suggested. He still hadn't been able to convince her that the Riker Manoeuvre was not actually a military move.

"What? Is my hair funny?" she asked as she approached him and raised her hand, attempting to detect if anything was out of place.

Jonathan realised that he was staring at her, as he so often did, and forced himself to look away. It was always a great strain to do so. "No." he replied, "You're as perfect as always my love."

"Well then, we'd better get to work." she smiled. "One more day of testing and we can take her out."

"Cray still thinks we're making a mistake abandoning our stealth tactics." Jonathan sighed.

Mei shrugged, "He likes the security of taking his marines in unexpected. The reality is that after 18 years of being outfoxed, the fallen have adapted too well to our technology and strategies. It simply isn't safe enough for us to continue to try and slip into a fallen system in a small under armed ship unnoticed anymore."

Jonathan nodded, knowing that she was right, "Well, let's hope that *Courage* proves to be half the ship that *Wings of the Wind* was."

Mei scoffed, "More like twice the ship. You designed it, so you should know."

"With a little help from my friend." he pointed out.

"Excuse me, I hope I'm more of a friend by now. We've only been dating for nearly a quarter of a century!" Mei retorted in mock chagrin.

Jonathan took her by the hand and looked deeply into her eyes, "And I intend to date you for another 9 centuries my beloved."

She could have accepted his words of love gracefully, but it was not in her nature to surrender so easily. "Just one minute, that only makes 925 years. Who exactly are you planning on spending the remaining 75 with?" She made her face into a picture of mock scorned fury.

The pedantry of her reply was so ridiculous that he couldn't be goaded to defensiveness. He simply laughed, and grabbed her by the waist, pulling him close to him, "975 years then, you kook. You know very well that I have no intention of ever so much as looking at another woman. Why on Earth would I when there is not a single woman in all creation that can compare to you?"

Her eyes were trapped by his and her resistance melted away as always when looking into the face of her dear strapping captain. Who could have known that Heaven would be so...well, heavenly?

*

Ward looked on as another load of grateful refugees walked down *Hope's* ramp and into Paradise. He felt such a feeling of contentment and gratification from doing this work that he wasn't sure if he could ever stop. As he watched the line of people being welcomed by a greeting party of volunteers, he felt a presence by his side. From the feint scent of lavender, he guessed that it was Stella.

"Are you glad to be home my love?" he chimed.

"Excuse me?" came the unexpected response in a far deeper voice that Stella's melodic soprano and he realised he'd made yet another of his faux pas.

Ward turned and apologised to Bree immediately, "I'm sorry, it's just that you smell like Stella."

"That's because she is borrowing my perfume." Stella explained, coming up behind the two.

"You two are exchanging scents now?" he exclaimed.

"Are best friends not allowed to share things?" Stella objected.

"Yes Ward, is this some new directive of yours?" Bree added.

Ward sighed, he figured he might as well dig the hole deeper, it was after all what he did best, "Of course not, I'm just starting to struggle to tell the difference between you two. Yesterday you were wearing each other's clothes, the week before you came onto the ship sporting the exact same hairstyle..."

Stella gasped, "It was not exactly the same! Mine was styled to fall on the left."

"And mine was styled to fall on the right." Bree added, "Honestly, how could you not see that?"

"Not to mention that I'm a blonde and she's a redhead." Stella added.

Ward shook his head in exasperation and ducked back inside the ship to escape little knowing that the women had been teasing him. He could not understand what had happened these past years. He'd started out with Stella not wanting Bree around because of a fear that Ward would be attracted to her, despite the fact that his redeemed body didn't feel those kind of impulses anymore, and now he was in a situation not of his own making, wherein he felt like he had two wives. Well, one ex-wife and one…

Ward suddenly felt mentally exhausted and decided to spend the rest of the day at the Temple with the Lord. Now there was a relationship that he could rely on to remain uncomplicated and satisfying.

*

Shannon sat on a rock dangling her feet in the water of the river of life, allowing the intense feeling of peace and contentment it carried with it to flow through her. It was one of her favourite things to do and she revelled in the stark contrast between being here and her brutal previous life. She knew she would never have to endure pain like that again, partly because she was protected by GOD in Paradise itself, but also because she possessed the love of a hugely overprotective giant. Titus sat down next her and instantly her world went dark.

"You're sat on the wrong side again." she gently chastised him with a smile.

"Oh, sorry." he muttered and manoeuvred himself to the side away from GOD's temple so that he wasn't between her and the glorious light from it which illuminated all of New Jerusalem. Shannon marvelled at how fluidly such a big man could move. Titus was 9 and a half feet tall and well-muscled, so she felt tiny in his presence. She loved how safe that made her feel, no doubt due to her tragic past. Thankfully she couldn't remember the full details of what Giska and other fallen had done to her. She knew in her mind what had transpired but couldn't replay images of it as Jesus had taken those precise details away when she had been redeemed so that she couldn't be tormented by them. She slid her hand into Titus' and laid her head against his elbow. This was as intimate as male-female relationships tended to get in Heaven and they were both perfectly content with that. For both, the true great love of their life was Christ.

*

Cray Ironheart looked out over his garden and felt a surge of contentment. He had left his apartment in the city some years back for a larger place to raise the children and didn't regret it. After being surrounded by people all his life he hadn't really considered how any other life could bring satisfaction, but now that he was out here in a more rural setting, he could clearly see the attraction. It had only been made possible because of his continued service to the Lord of course. Although you couldn't purchase property in New Jerusalem, these things still had to be earned and you were rewarded if you served faithfully, as Cray had. He still remembered the conversation he had with Eret'el over two decades ago about how he felt like he wasn't bringing enough of a sacrifice of service to his Lord and wasn't bringing Him glory. Well, he had certainly corrected that, in the past quarter century he had guided many people to the Lord and had aided in bringing many fallen criminals to justice. A deer came into the garden and began munching on a clump of grass which grew around the edge of a single lovingly tended rose bush. It showed no fear as it enjoyed its meal mere feet from where he sat, even when Lance came into the garden its only reaction was to look up briefly and then continue its browsing.

"Good day to you sir." His friend greeted him.

Cray looked up at the clear blue sky, "Is there any other kind here?"

Lance shrugged in response, "Well, there are the days we're asked to go out and fight 12ft tall cannibalistic giants. Those days tend to be a little less than perfect."

The marine commander laughed, "I suppose you have a point there. Those days are less good, but certainly more exciting."

"'Exciting' he says" responded Lance with a sly grin, "Not quite how I'd describe nearly being skewered and becoming lunch on a regular basis. But each to his own."

"You know you love it, otherwise you wouldn't still be doing it after 25 years." Cray admonished his friend.

"Yeah, you believe what you want to believe." Lance commented, sitting down and reaching for a non-alcoholic beer from an ice filled bucket Cray had on a side table. "Perhaps I'm only still doing it because your ugly hide needs saving on a regular basis, and I get paid in beer for performing that service." He raised the bottle and took a long drag on its contents.

Cray chuckled, "Now who's believing what he wants to believe."

The two sat quietly for a little while and then Lance broke the silence, "What do you think they'll have us doing next? There hasn't been a major external threat in months."

"Which is just as well since we don't have a ship." Cray pointed out.

"A slight technicality. We'll have one soon enough." Lance reminded him. "And then we'll be provided with many more opportunities to die in the line of duty."

Cray reproved the comment with a tut and then added, "Whilst there have been many opportunities for a glorious death, we've only actually died once."

"And it didn't feel at all glorious. I kind of feel like that one death was enough for me." Lance grinned, clearly making fun of Cray as he took another beer from the bucket.

"Hey, that stuff doesn't grow on trees you know." Cray objected.

Lance laughed, "No, it grows on stalks, in barley fields. Sometimes massive fields stretching for miles as far as the eye can see." Lance stretched his arms out dramatically as he made this point.

This obvious comment was met with a sigh, "Yes, it does. But what I mean is, I don't feel like walking down to the brewery every five minutes to satisfy your insatiable appetite for barley-based beverages."

Lance surrendered the point, "This is my last one, I promise." Not a minute later he repented of this statement, "Well, at least my second to last one anyway."

Cray grabbed another beer from the bucket before they were all gone, "I've overheard people talking about Mars a lot lately you know."

Lance shook his head, "Don't even go there. That place is a mess."

"Which suggests all the more that it will need to be cleared out eventually." Cray countered.

Lance shrugged, "Well, as long as it's done by someone other than us, I fully agree."

A tall striking young man strode up to the house in a pilot's uniform and reached for the last beer just as Lance did, "Now don't be stingy Uncle Lance, you look like you've had your share judging by all those empty bottles." He grinned at Lance and Cray laughed out loud.

"You've raised a cheeky bunch, Cray. Why am I not surprised?" Lance complained.

Cray grinned even wider, "I think I've done a sterling job with my children; wouldn't you agree Josh?"

Joshua Ironheart grinned equally as widely, "I would agree wholeheartedly, your children are all amazing." Whilst the three children had been given the options of choosing their own names at 18, Joshua had chosen to take Cray's. His intention was to follow in the man's footsteps as closely as possible despite Cray's objections.

Becca came out of the house in that moment and beamed widely at the sight of Joshua, "My youngest has returned home at last."

"Mum, it's been three days." he groaned.

"Which is three days too many." she chastised him. "Where is your sister? Why isn't she with you?"

Joshua sighed, "We don't go everywhere together mum."

"No, but I sent her to bring you home, so I assumed she'd be with you." Becca explained.

"Her commander grabbed her just as we were leaving, I think she'll be a while." Joshua informed them.

Becca sighed, "It's a hard life being the matriarch of a navy family. I blame you, Cray Ironheart."

"I didn't indoctrinate them all, Matthew isn't in the navy." he grinned.

"No, but he works in the hatchery, which is not far off." she shot back. Her affrontery was a sham, she was secretly very proud of her children for their life choices. Whilst she had eventually decided not to join the navy herself, her children were another matter altogether with Esther Ironheart joining the prayer guard first and then Joshua following suit as soon as he was old enough. Matthew Gentle had taken his mother's name and had decided to spend his energies restoring people rather than fighting them. The children knew how proud of them she was and loved her all the more for it.

"What's all this talk about Mars?" Joshua asked.

Hearing this, Becca put her hands on her hips, "Don't you dare let them send you there, either of you."

"Whoa, we haven't been told anything yet." Cray replied defensively, "Maybe the malakim will take care of it."

"I doubt it dad, you know GOD likes…" he caught the look on Cray's face and his voice tapered off.

"Cray Ironheart, if you decide to go to Mars with the navy, the fallen won't have to kill you, I'll do it first." Becca announced.

Cray laughed in response and tried to reassure her, "Don't worry love, I'm not exactly keen on the idea myself." but in his heart he knew that if the Lord asked him, he would go. Even if the planet was widely considered to be worse than Hell itself.

*

The Council of the Holy was in session and Moses spoke forcefully, "The threat is real, and it is too close, we must take action sooner rather than later."

Elijah added his voice to that of the famed leader of the exodus, "We haven't faced danger like this since the battle at Daigar's Bane. Moses is correct, we should act now."

"This discourse has become too impassioned." one of the three loyal Grigori on the council admonished the humans, "This is Heaven and Heaven is and always will be unassailable."

Enoch scoffed at this, "Heaven has always remained strong and intact because we act out of wisdom when we need to, not because we are invincible enough to be complacent. It is GOD who is unassailable, not the city."

Another Grigori spoke out, "Their fleet was decimated in the lead up to Armageddon over a quarter of a century ago. They no longer have any teeth."

Elijah shook his head, "They have been rebuilding at a frightening rate since then. Their fleet isn't a match for ours yet, but I don't believe we should wait until it is."

Jesus interjected and the council fell silent, as it always did when the Lord spoke, "There is truth in what you all say, but Moses' proposal bears much merit, and action must be taken. The time to wrest the control of Mars from out of the hands of the fallen is upon us."

Glossary of terms

These descriptions are for the purposes of this work of fiction alone to help you to connect to the story easier. They should not be seen as being instructional although I have attempted to follow what I believe to be the best research on these subjects in establishing their nature for the purposes of the story. I encourage you to do your own research into these incredible beings and make your own mind up as to how close this book comes to presenting the truth on these matters.

GOD The three in one: Also referred to as Yahweh, The Most-High GOD, the Ancient of Days or El. Ruler of Heaven and Earth. The one true GOD. Has no equal in power. Creator of Heaven and Earth and all in them. Appears to men as Jesus his Son and accompanies them as counsellor in the form of the Holy Spirit.

Angel: A malakim who serves in the role of messenger.

Cherubim: A multi winged elohim with four faces, human, lion, ox and eagle. Most often to be found attending GOD's throne.

Councillor: Serving in the Council of the Holy they serve GOD by making decisions regarding the running of New Jerusalem. Three of the councillors are elohim and three are Human. The 7th member of the Council is the Son of God.

Demon: See nephilim

Drone: A soulless genetic creation of the watchers. Short in stature and slender with grey skin and bulging black eyes. Tend to serve as either a host for demons or relatively mindless labour.

Elohim: A collective term for occupants of the supernatural realm. Can be used to refer to Yahweh (El) or any of his Heavenly Host.

Fallen: Also, rebel. A term applied to any being that has turned against God and stands in direct opposition to Him.

Gibborim: Meaning Mighty Ones. Although can also refer to heavenly warriors and in the past, nephilim, is more often used to identify human warriors in service to GOD.

Grigori: Referred to in the Bible as Sons of God or Nachash. Also called watchers. A powerful form of elohim ranking below the archangels, seraphim and cherubim, but above the malakim, possessing the power to transform themselves into various forms but preferring that of a dragon. Assigned to earth to govern nations after the incident at Babel. Many of these fell to temptation in times past and allowed men to worship them as gods using their power to deceive men into abandoning worship of the true GOD. Large numbers of Grigori fled to the stars once GOD began to enact His plan to save mankind and set up empires there. Tall and slender in form with finely scaled skin. There are at least two distinct forms of Grigori, a more muscled variant suited to battle and a less physically powerful variant with an extended cranium suited to administrative functions.

Hatchery: The colloquial term for a structure in New Jerusalem into which redeemed are resurrected into new bodies at the start of the millennium and also during it if they suffer death of their existing body, thus rendering them essentially immortal.

Malakim: A collective term for servants of the Most-High in the roles of warrior or messenger.

Nephilim: The giant progeny of watchers and human possessing no redeemable soul. They tend to range from 9ft tall to 12ft. They possess double rows of teeth and six fingers and toes on each limb. Often, they will grow tusks or horns giving them an ogre-like appearance. They possess an insatiable appetite for carnage and unbridled lust. After death their restless spirits roam the cosmos as demons, sometimes possessing physical beings if permitted to do so.

New Earth: At the beginning of the millennium the Earth is recreated. The oceans, deserts and frozen wastelands disappear, and the mountains are much reduced making the world a far more hospitable place and essentially a paradise. Disease, parasites and famine are eliminated, and the Earth is placed under the rule of Christ who delegates much of His authority to King David who rules Israel from Old Jerusalem.

New Jerusalem: Also, Holy City or Heaven as it is where the glory of GOD resides during the period of the millennium. It is a giant cube 1400 miles long along each side containing 700 levels providing a vast amount of paradisial living space for the redeemed and elohim. It is lit by the glory of GOD which shines throughout it from the temple at its core. It stands in orbit around the Earth and possesses technology which prevents it from exerting a gravitational pull on other celestial bodies. It contains a number of access points for space going vessels but chief among these are the twelve pearl lined gates named after the twelve tribes of Israel.

Ophanim: An elohim possessing an appearance not dissimilar to that of a flying saucer. They are quietly sentient but can also serve as transports for other elohim. From underneath, their contra-rotating propulsion blades look like wheels within wheels.

Redeemed: Also, Christian, Saint. The most commonly used term for human followers of Christ. In the millennium the redeemed possess recreated bodies making them larger, stronger, healthier and more intelligent with a flawless beauty. Through a now perfectly functional cell replacement system they are capable of living for the entire 1000yr millennium if they do not die from trauma at which point, they are resurrected in the Hatchery.

Satan: Also, Lucifer, the Devil. A fallen cherubim who is granted rule over the earth in the time between the fall of man and the millennium.

Seraphim: A multi-winged elohim with a human appearance but encased in fire. Also, an attendant of the throne room. Incredibly powerful.

Shedim: A fallen malakim. Their physical appearance is twisted as a result of their fall. Millennia of service to evil has rendered them numb to the ways of GOD.

Watcher: Powerful Grigori elohim assigned to earth to govern nations after the incident at Babel. Many of these fell to temptation in times past and allowed men to worship them as gods.

Resources

If you liked the contents of this book and wish to find out more then these are some places you might consider looking. Whilst all the below have their own websites, you may benefit more from performing a search for their work on your favourite video streaming platform.

Blue Letter Bible: https://www.blueletterbible.org/
A free online bible and phone app with multiple translations and study resources.

Koinonia House: https://khouse.org/
The online home of Chuck Missler's work which provided me with my introduction to many of the concepts in this book.

Dr Michael Heiser: https://drmsh.com/
Dr Heiser's works are a great source of information on the nature of the Heavenly host.

L.A. Marzulli: https://lamarzulli.net/
Possibly the foremost researcher on the nephilim.

Timothy Alberino: https://timothyalberino.com/
Practically a Christina Indiana Jones. Tim regularly plunges into jungles and other inhospitable places looking for evidence to bolster a biblical worldview.

Jack Hibbs: https://calvarycch.org/
Jack Hibbs as the pastor of Calvary Chapel Chino Hills is fearless in his choice of teaching material and a great teacher.

Michael Pearl: https://thedoor.studio/
Another great teacher who pulls no punches and is extremely well studied.

Daniel Maritz: https://www.dlm-christianlifestyle.com/
Also a favourite teacher of mine whose boldness is inspiring. His videos give good guidance on Christian living.

Mike Winger: https://biblethinker.org/
Mike's 20 questions video series is a fabulous way to find out more about GOD and the bible.

The Fuel Project: https://thefuelproject.org/
A fabulous Christian resource producing numerous practical teachings aimed at helping Christians to navigate a world inhospitable to our beliefs.

Frank Turek: https://www.crossexamined.org/
Christian apologetics at its best.

Discover the Book Ministries: http://www.youtube.com/@DTBM
There are a host of great teachings by John Barnett, the leader of DTBM on YouTube that I'd recommend to bible students.

Living Waters: https://livingwaters.com
The ministry of Ray Comfort and a valuable resource for budding evangelists. There are some great teachings and demonstrations of how to reach people for Christ.

Our church: https://www.ramsbottomcommunity.church/
If you are ever in the Manchester UK area then please visit the church I call home. Our pastor Steve is a phenomenally talented teacher and I'm sure you will be blessed by coming.

Calvary Chapel Otley: https://calvaryotley.com/
Alternately, if you find yourself in Yorkshire, please visit my previous church home where I was first tipped off on the works of Chuck Missler which has led to me being where I am now.

Printed in Poland
by Amazon Fulfillment
Poland Sp. z o.o., Wrocław